I0635590

Artistic Deception

by

CA Humer

Cover Art by *Kristian Norris*

The Wild Rose Press, Inc.
PO Box 708
Adams Basin, NY 14410-0708
Visit us at www.thewildrosepress.com

Publishing History
First Edition, 2024
Trade Paperback ISBN 978-1-5092-5755-3
Digital ISBN 978-1-5092-5756-0

Published in the United States of America

Dedication

For Ruby - Inspiration and love embodied. You are my
Marianne. I miss you every day.

Acknowledgements

Any book is a compendium of personal experiences and research. I'd like to thank the many individuals that encouraged me to follow my dreams, read my many drafts, answered questions and listened to my endless conversations regarding human trafficking and how abuse and manipulation can easily happen. I'd like to thank my sweet husband and biggest fan, Don, for driving up and down McCart St. so I could create the visual I hope you, as readers, enjoyed. All businesses and locations are a creation of my imagination.

I'd like to thank my parents, Bill and Ruby. My Dad built houses so I come by my construction knowledge honestly. In many respects, he is Ray. High expectations, hardworking and deeply loving even though he sometimes didn't know how to show it. My mom? Well, this book is dedicated to her. Marianne's cancer and many aspects of her final months mirror my mom's. I cried writing every word. She also died on April 3rd and I miss her every day.

Finally, no matter how light the reading, there are lessons to take away from every book we read. We all need and want love and approval. Sometimes it can be used to hurt us. I hope we take the time to love and support one another so any attempt at artistic deception doesn't fall on fertile ground.

Chapter 1

Marianne was weak from the flight, so Ray asked for a wheelchair when they disembarked from the plane. He pushed her through the throngs of travelers toward the baggage claim area. His face was weary, his mouth pinched from fatigue and impatience. Couldn't people see he had a sick woman with him? Following the signs, Ray navigated his way toward baggage claim. He clipped the heel of a slower-moving traveler, earning a hard look from the man. Arriving at baggage claim B, Ray struggled to wheel the chair through the glass doors. Sam was picking them up. Ray was scanning the room when Marianne's joyful cry made him turn toward the tall man walking their way.

Sam had been leaning against the gray partition when he saw his folks and Marianne's face brighten. He pushed his six-foot, three-inch frame away from the wall and smiled at her, making double time to her side. His eyes hid the shock and concern he felt seeing her in a wheelchair. The last time Sam had seen his folks was at the weddings. Both Sam and his sister Emily were married in simple ceremonies, with only family and a few close friends as guests. The siblings yearned for a quiet celebration. There had been enough notoriety from Sam busting the Ramirez drug cartel with the help of his best friend, Jake Edwards, Emily's fiancé, now her husband.

Sam remembered how nervous he and Jake had been. Neither had ever expected to find a woman to put up with them, but the love and devotion received and given had blown both away. The two couples wrote their vows and the parish priest performed the weddings in the backyard of Sam's home on a sunny afternoon in September. His folks had stayed four days before heading back to their condo in Cape Coral, Florida. Sam recalled his mom had looked tired and complained of a sore back, but this was a complete change in her condition.

"Sam, oh, Sam." Her smile lit up the room even through the dark shadows circling her eyes. "Ray, look, it's Sam. Oh, honey, I'm so glad to see you." Her hand reached out to him, pulling him close for a hug. Sam bent to his mom, holding her frail body in his arms. All he could think was how thin she'd grown and worried that if he hugged too hard, she'd shatter into a dozen pieces. "How is Kate? Is she with you? And where are Emily and Jake?" Breaking the embrace, Sam stood and curtly nodded to his father.

"Everyone is waiting at our place for you. How was your flight?" he asked, escorting them toward the luggage belt. "Your bags should come out on carousel B." Sam looked for a spot where his mom could wait until the luggage arrived. "Mom, why don't we settle you here and Dad and I can get them? Do you have many?" Sam walked alongside the wheelchair, Marianne holding his hand, a happy stream of conversation bubbling forth the entire time.

Ray steered Marianne to a quiet corner. They stood waiting while Marianne continued to chatter about the flight and the nice airline crew. "The flight attendant was so kind. She gave us an upgrade to business class. Such a sweet girl. Her name was Sarah, wasn't it, Ray?" He grunted in assent. When the strobe light flashed and the conveyor belt started moving, Ray went over to retrieve the luggage. Sam went to stand beside him. He didn't beat around the bush.

"What's with the wheelchair?" The two men had their backs to Marianne. Sam expertly shielded the worry in his eyes, but couldn't do a damn thing about the tension in the set of his shoulders. It matched that of his father.

Ray bent to retrieve the first of the bags as it rounded the curve of the carousel. "She is tired. We'll talk about it when everyone is together."

Sam threw his father a censured look. Ray quickly continued. His six feet one-inch frame was stooped with worry and weariness. Sam noticed the haggard lines bracketing his dad's mouth, the deep creases between his brows. "Your mom would want it that way, son. Don't push it."

Sam felt his back bowing. He hated when his dad called him "son". It was disdaining. One has to be a dad to have a son. Ray had abdicated that role back in 2005 when he had lost his temper and lashed out at Marianne. Sam had beaten the crap out of him before walking out and never returning. Sam bit back an angry retort as Ray reached for the second bag. He walked away, swallowing words of irritation.

While Ray waited for a third bag, Sam found a luggage dolly. They loaded up the suitcases and Sam suggested he go get the car and meet them at the exit. Ray grunted again. He was a man of few words. Sam brushed his mom's cheek with a quick kiss, telling her the plan, then ran out to the parking garage for his jeep. Thinking of his mom's frail condition, Sam wished he had borrowed his sister's sedan.

When they'd stowed the luggage and settled Marianne in the back seat, Sam pulled away from the curb. Since it was still early in the day, traffic would be light and the drive take less than thirty minutes. He texted Kate, letting her know their ETA. Ray stared out the passenger window, silent and brooding. His eyes had dark shadows circling them. Marianne snuggled into her sweater. The weather this Thanksgiving was cool. Sam cast worried glances at her through the rear-view mirror. Her eyes closed as the hum of the motor and the gentle rocking of the jeep lulled her to sleep. He'd wait until everyone was present like Ray had asked, but his mind was racing with all the fears aroused when looking at his mom.

Turning the corner of his street, Sam watched Jake step out the side door to help with the luggage. Emily and Kate trailed behind him, smiling in welcome, ready to welcome his parents. Pulling to a stop, Sam turned around and touched his mom lightly on her knee. "We're here, mom." Ray had already jumped out and was opening the door, helping Marianne with her seat belt. Sam stood, ready to help. Ray ignored him.

"Here you go, sweetheart. Let me help you." Ray was gentle, letting Marianne lean on him as she climbed out of the jeep. He placed his arm around her waist, walking arm in arm. Sam noticed Ray carried most of her weight. Jake and Sam followed with the three bags. After exchanging meaningful looks, they put them in the guest bedroom and returned to stand with their wives. Sam noticed the alarm on Emily's face and listened as his dad tried to set her mind at ease.

"She's just worn out from the flight. We had to get up pretty early to get to the airport. You still got that comfy recliner in the family room, Kate? You'd like to sit there, wouldn't you, Marianne?" Ray walked Marianne to the chair, settling her in. Reaching for the afghan on the back of the sofa, he adoringly tucked it around her legs.

"Thank you, honey." Marianne touched Ray's cheek. He put his hand over hers. She fixed her gaze on his eyes, love visibly present in the exchange. Ray turned her palm to his lips and kissed it before returning it to her lap. "Ray, would you get me a glass of water? It's time for my pill." Ray hustled off to oblige while Kate and Emily looked on, worry lines furrowing their brows.

Within seconds, Ray returned, pulled a chair over next to the recliner, and helped Marianne with her medication. He gave her a supportive look and simply held her hand while she waved at the four young people. "Oh, sit down, please. I feel like I'm on exhibition at the museum with you all staring at me like that." Sam felt his mom's eyes on him as he pulled over the rocking chair Kate always favored. He placed it closer to the coffee table, then stood ramrod straight, like his dad always did.

Jake led Emily to the sofa next to her mom. They sat. Jake kept his arm around Emily's shoulders, his hand holding hers. Kate made Sam sit in the rocker, then perched on the arm of the sofa, her hand on his shoulder. Its gentle weight holding him steady.

"Well, this wasn't how I envisioned everything. I never expected to be so tired." Marianne reached out, patting Ray's hand, then gazed at the waiting, worried faces of her precious children. "I had hoped we could visit and have a few normal days before we had to talk about the elephant in the room. I guess that isn't in the plans. Oh, my dear sweet children. How much I love you." Marianne turned to Ray. He gave her an encouraging nod and a sad smile. "Well, no sense sugar coating it. You can all see there is a problem."

Emily leaned back into Jake, seeking comfort and support. Sam placed his hand over the one Kate rested on his shoulder. No one spoke, waiting to hear what they could only expect would be bad news.

Marianne drew in a shaky breath. She ran her tongue over dry lips and took a sip of water. Then, she smoothed down the afghan on her lap; visibly searching for the courage to deliver heartbreaking news. "The doctors have diagnosed me with lung cancer. It's quite advanced." She huffed a sardonic laugh. "Funny, that nagging cough and the back pain I had in September? Turns out those were the first physical symptoms. The doctors think I will enjoy one last Christmas with my family. I'd like to do that more than anything else."

Sam, Kate, Emily, and Jake sat in stunned silence, searching for the words to say. With his head lowered, Ray held his mouth to Marianne's hand, clasped as if in prayer. No one could see the sheen of tears in his eyes and didn't know he was crying until a single drop fell on their joined hands. Marianne stroked Ray's hair and closed her eyes. The telling had exhausted her.

Emily made a small sound, swallowing hard. Jake increased his hold on her shoulders, lending her all his strength. Jake and Kate looked at Sam. His gaze hadn't wavered from his mother's face. He nodded, gave

Kate's hand a gentle squeeze, and stood. Sam stepped over to the recliner and knelt at his mother's side. He took her free hand and then reached for Emily's, a living tether holding them all together. "Mom, this is sad news. We are so sorry. We have a million questions, and I know you will give us all the answers you can. Do you need to rest first?"

Marianne's eyes fluttered open, and Ray gazed at his son. Sam saw the look of appreciation for understanding on his dad's face. "Maybe for a little while." She turned trusting eyes to Ray. Sam stood and watched his father scoop Marianne up in his arms and carry her into the bedroom. The door closed quietly behind them.

Emily, shocked like the rest of them, stood slowly. She hugged Sam tightly, then turned into Jake's arms, burying her face in his chest. Her sobs were muffled by his shirt. Sam could see Jake's heart breaking as he struggled for a way to take away Emily's pain. Jake didn't know how. Kate crossed to Sam, her arms winding around his waist, resting her head on his shoulder. "I'm so sorry, Sam. We'll do everything we can to help." Sam tightened his hold on Kate and gazed over her head into the garden, seeing only darkness.

Jake and Kate moved into the kitchen, leaving Sam and Emily to talk. Orphaned at eight, Jake was at a total loss on how to comfort Emily. Kate had lost her parents when she was fifteen in an automobile accident. It was both sudden and unexpected. Prolonged illness and death were something with which everyone was foreign. Thankfully, Kate instinctively knew someone needed to hold everything and everyone together. Even though she didn't know if anyone would have an appetite, Kate prepared a light supper of soup and sandwiches. Everyone could eat when and however much they wished.

Sam and Emily had gone into the home office so their talking wouldn't disturb their mom. Jake was putzing in the garage, escaping from a situation he didn't know how to handle. Kate was escaping in her own way, providing comfort by preparing a meal. She put the food and plates on the kitchen island, placing napkins and condiments on a tray.

Ray stepped out of the bedroom. He gave her a wan smile and crossed the room, picking up a carrot to dip into the humus Kate had set out. Perching wearily on one of the bar stools, he lowered his head into his hands. His shoulders shook with the quiet sobs he tried to hold back. Kate circled around the island and put her arms around him. Ray turned his face to her shoulder and cried his heart out. Regaining control, he pulled away.

"I'm sorry. I don't usually break down, but it's been so hard. Marianne is everything to me. What will I do without her? My life will be empty, my heart a hollow husk, dried and withered, blowing away in the hot wind. Emily has a wonderful life here with Jake. They're happy. She won't want an old man crowding her life. Sam has you. And he doesn't want me." Kate read the pain Ray felt from the dissension with his son. She tried to interrupt, but Ray raised his hand to shush her.

"No, no. I ruined any chance I might have had with him when he was a kid. Sam must hate me. I don't know why I was so hard on him. Maybe I wanted him to be better than I was, or ever could be. And he is. Sam is exactly what I'd hoped he'd become. And I'm going to be alone. Marianne will die and I'll be alone. Maybe this is what I earned, what I deserve."

It was heart-wrenching, listening to him. Seating herself on the stool next to him, Kate patted and rubbed his hand, trying to comfort him. "Ray, Marianne is still very much alive and we have precious memories to make while she is. Don't let an anticipation of grief cloud the joy. And don't sell your kids short. You have two very loving children. You have time to get to know the adults they have become and learn to be their friend and father again. It won't be easy, but if you truly wish it, it will be." Placing a single kiss on his cheek, Kate stood.

"Do you feel up to talking with us about what is going on? The diagnosis, prognosis, and your plans?" Ray used a work-roughened hand to rub an old-fashioned handkerchief across his dripping nose. She saw how much older he appeared than his sixty-two years. Ray nodded and let Kate lead him to the rocker, placing a glass of water at his side. "I'll get everyone together."

Kate gathered Sam, Emily, and Jake. The four sat holding hands, facing Ray, waiting for him to collect his thoughts and begin the tale. It took a little less than thirty minutes for him to relate the story. Ray went from despairing to angry to weeping. He talked about how Marianne became so out of breath just walking to the mailbox. Her growing weakness. Their trip to the ER.

"They thought it was her heart. The ER doctor ordered an EKG and lung X-rays. Her left lung was half filled with fluid. They used a needle from hell to drain it. She sat there so damn calm. It must have hurt like hell, but she just kept smiling. Then she thanked the nurse who did the procedure. Jesus God! She thanked the nurse that caused her all that pain." Ray wiped his nose, and shook his head in wonder. "They came in later and gave us the news. Stage four lung cancer. Just like that. Stage four. I asked the doctors what the hell happened to stages one through three? It steamed me, but you know your mom. She patted my hand, told me to take a breath. They gave us the name of an oncologist. He was a nice guy. Started your mom on a drug that's supposed to shrink the tumor. It's called Tarceva. That's the medication she took earlier." Ray paused and closed his eyes. Tears seeped out of the corners and ran freely down his cheeks. The four sat in silence, watching droplets fall onto his clenched fists.

Sam was the first to move, to breathe. He cleared his throat and asked the hardest question. "Dad, Mom said something about time. How much time?" His mom's voice answered from the bedroom doorway.

"Christmas. The oncologist said maybe the New Year." The kids stood as she crossed the room, hugging each one. Ray jumped up and gave the rocker to Marianne. He pulled a chair over to sit next to her. "Ray, quit fussing. I'm fine. I'm rested. The rest of you sit down. It's my turn now. I have some things to say." Everyone exchanged looks and, except Kate, reluctantly took their seats.

Kate's natural nurturing kicked in. "Mom, can I get you a glass of water or a cup of tea?" Marianne smiled gratefully.

"Oh, that would be lovely, Kate. Thank you. Do you have the chai tea you served when we were here last time?" Marianne sat quietly, gazing at her precious children, while Kate fixed her the tea. Marianne looked around at the peaceful comfort Kate had created. It was a loving home without being fussy. It would be a good place to spend her last days. When everyone was settled and everything was done, Marianne serenely smiled. She spoke softly, but her words were full of strength and purpose.

"I am dying, but not yet. There is time to enjoy being with you. I'm sure you have a million questions. Let me tell you what we know and we'll see if that answers some of them."

"First off, the doctors don't know why I have lung cancer. When I was a young woman, I smoked. They don't think it was long enough or heavy enough to have caused it."

Shaking her head dolefully, she continued. "Yes, it was a surprise, but we learned that my primary care doctor actually found a spot last spring. He never followed up and, well, here we are at Stage Four."

Marianne didn't miss the quick intake of breath, feeling their outrage as keenly as she had felt her own, when she'd learned of the old fart's incompetence. But life was too short to hold on to anger.

"I know what you're all thinking. And, no." She shook her finger at each, clearly communicating her thoughts.

"I have to admit, though, it certainly crossed Ray's and my mind, too." She reached out and patted Ray's arm affectionately. "I don't want to sue him for malpractice. It would achieve nothing as he retired at the end of October. Ray spoke with him and dropped a few suggestive phrases and some legal jargon regarding our thoughts on his oversight. Conveniently, his insurance carrier made a generous donation to our church. Much less than a lawsuit would have cost them, but generous none the less."

Ray snorted a sarcastic laugh, muttering under his breath, "Damn quack!" The corners of Marianne's mouth turned up slightly before continuing.

"Dr. Akpom, the oncologist, gave us an idea of what to expect. This could all change if the medication proves effective. As time goes on, I will lose my appetite and lose weight. I will grow increasingly tired. In the end, I will require full-time care. But I will not lose my cognitive capabilities. I will live to the end of my life with my full faculties until one day I will simply go to sleep and wake on the other shore. It is a journey I am at peace making when the time is right and God calls me. Dr. Akpom gave us the name of a Texas doctor. He forwarded my records and requested an order for hospice. Dr. Elyse Chandler will care for me here. I understand she is very good at what she does. We have an appointment to see her on Tuesday. We'll know more after that."

Everyone sat, heads bowed, processing. Sam stoic, strong, and silent as ever; his sorrow and anger tamped down, remained controlled. He thought of how this would devastate Emily. She wore all her emotions on her sleeve, feeling everyone's pain and suffering. Thankfully, he and Emily had a loving mate to support them in their grief. Sam's gaze moved to his father. Ray had no one.

Marianne gave them time, then burst out with forced cheerfulness, "Until we learn more, let's focus on how happy I am to be here with you. What are you preparing for Thanksgiving dinner? This may be the first time I have had an excuse not to cook. I plan on taking full advantage of that."

Emily burst into tears and knelt, burying her face in Marianne's lap. The older woman stroked Emily's head. "Don't cry, sweet baby girl. We all die. It's how we lived, what we have accomplished, that matters. I had three wonderful children." Marianne raised Emily's face and reached out for Sam's hand. "Although I lost one too soon, I am blessed to see the other two happily married." She included Jake and Kate in her gaze and tenderly smiled. "Now, enough gloom and doom. Kate, I think I smell minestrone. Could I have a bowl and maybe some toast?"

****

That was how Marianne did it. Gave them the basics and moved on. Sam marveled at the strength and resilience she showed in the face of this personal tragedy. Out of respect, everyone stepped back from their shock and grief, resolved to take one day at a time as Marianne wished. Their private conversations with her throughout her illness helped them all to accept and understand her wishes.

Although there was sadness during this time, there was also much joy and laughter. Marianne found the silver lining in everything. After a cool Thanksgiving, December turned out to be blessedly warm, so Sam and Marianne spent time together in the garden. He trimmed the trees, mulched beds, and under her direction, planted pansies and other seasonal flowers in the porch pots. Even in winter, the garden had a bleak beauty because of all the textures and colors. She played pinochle with a vengeance and tromped her

13

children at Trivial Pursuit. She worked in the kitchen with Kate, teaching her all the family favorite recipes. When Marianne had the strength, spa visits and lunch out were extra special because she spent them with Emily and Kate. Marianne grew to love Kate as her own daughter. It was clear how much she and Sam loved each other. Marianne watched, impressed, as Jake fashioned the odd piece of wood needed for a historic home he was rehabbing. She helped Emily select paint colors, wallpapers, and lighting fixtures. She was happy her children had found love.

During quiet times, Marianne would watch the two couples. It seemed like ages since their weddings in September. There was no diagnosis of cancer hanging over their heads then. No darkness on the horizon. Only joy and hope for the future. Marianne smiled as happy memories flooded her mind. How she'd laughed when Sam and Jake used humor to ease their nervousness.

The night before the ceremony, Sam had confided in Marianne that he never expected to find a woman to put up with him. Nor did he ever feel he would deserve a woman like his Kate. Her love and devotion had taken his breath away. Sam had shared the challenges Kate faced following her abduction by Ramirez.

"Kate is so like you, Mom. Strong and gentle. I loved her from the first moment I looked into her eyes, but Ramirez was so damn smooth and debonair. God, I hated him for that. I was so afraid of failing her that I wouldn't let myself love her. Emily and Jake saw it. They knew how deeply I felt, both the love and the fear. But until I could get the evidence to prove Ramirez was smuggling weapons into the States, I couldn't say anything to Kate. I had to sit and watch as he wined and dined her, sweeping her off her feet. When I killed his brother, he went crazy with revenge. Ramirez wanted Kate and when he couldn't have her, he took her. Ramirez planned on raping and torturing her. Then he would kill her while I sat helplessly and watched. He wanted me to live, so I'd always blame myself for failing her. Thank God he was the one that failed."

Marianne had held and stroked Sam's head that night. He was once again her little boy, seeking the comfort and reassurance only a mother's love could give. Her son, who felt the weight of failure throughout his life, had fought against his demons and won. Listening to Sam unburden his heart that night, Marianne saw the dark shadows banished from his life. She knew Sam's love had saved Kate as much as her love saved Sam. Marianne was thankful that Sam could be Kate's strength and light in the darkness.

There was a painting in Sam's bedroom Marianne had seen and admired. It was of Kate in a field of wildflowers with a windmill in the background. Sam told Marianne about the life-giving water the windmills provided to the early settlers. She saw that Sam unconsciously recognized that Kate was his life-giving water. Her love could quench his thirst and fill his soul. He could forgive himself.

On the day of the wedding, Sam only had eyes for Kate. Dressed in a classic cream silk that hugged her willowy figure, she seemed to float as she moved down the steps into the backyard and into his arms.

And what mother didn't dream of her baby girl wearing flowers in her hair and marrying her knight in shining armor? Jake had ridden into Emily's life on a white steed in the form of a Harley-Davidson motorcycle. He was rough, unpolished, and the perfect mate for her daughter. They say that daughters marry men similar to their fathers. Jake and Ray had many attributes in common. Emily glowed with her love for Jake and him for her. Jake's work-roughened hands shook when he placed the ring on Emily's finger. And when they were pronounced man and wife, there was such tenderness in their kiss that Marianne was assured that Emily would be loved and cherished until the end of time.

It was what Marianne had enjoyed for almost forty years with Ray and more than she could have wished for both her children.

Marianne took time to paint. She had been an exceptional artist when she met and married Ray. It was a talent Marianne gladly set aside when they had children. As a gift to Sam and Emily, Marianne wanted to paint a special picture. Something that spoke from her heart to theirs. She sought the perfect subject for each.

At night, she sat reading, holding Ray's hand. But it was the one-on-one conversation she had with her children that brought her the greatest joy and helped them accept their eventual loss.

When Christmas Day arrived, the family was holding their collective breath. Marianne was rallying. They prayed the Tarceva was working. Unwrapping their gifts, Emily and Sam turned questioning eyes at their mom. Each held an empty frame.

"I haven't finished the paintings yet." Waving a hand in the air, she laughed. "You know you can't rush art." And although she didn't say it, she intended the paintings as her parting gift to them. The new year came and went. Marianne was holding her own. There was hope.

****

January was rainy and cold. February brought a week of snow and bitter winds. As usual, Texas shut down with icy roads, but the family still gathered and enjoyed their time together. The men were watching football while the ladies played Scrabble. Marianne was good at the game, but Emily and Kate were worthy opponents. Marianne and Kate were busy fiddling with their tiles, looking for their next word. Jake wandered into the kitchen to refill the bowl of pretzels and glanced over at the board. Disguising the twinkle in his eye, Jake leaned in and put his arm around Emily's shoulders.

"Honey, I think you misspelled the word 'pregnant'."

Four eyes darted to the board, then to Emily's and Jake's smiling faces. Marianne was the first to respond.

"Oh, honey! Is it true? Are you pregnant? Are you sure?" Clasping Emily's hands, Marianne's eyes filled with tears of joy to match those of her daughter.

Emily nodded, giving a shaky laugh. "As sure as two weeks of morning sickness and the little blue lines promise. We'll know more after my appointment with the doctor tomorrow. I was going to wait till after that to tell you, but, oh, Mom. I just couldn't contain myself. You know I've never been good at keeping secrets."

By this time, Ray and Sam had clued into the excitement and came over to where the women were seated. Catching the end of the exchange with Marianne, Sam looked at Jake with raised eyebrows.

"Well, how the hell did this happen?"

Jake puffed out his chest. "The usual way, Sam. I'll give you lessons if you need them."

That was another memorable day and one that Marianne relived regularly. It gave her the incentive to keep fighting, to see her first grandchild.

****

Sam was elbow-deep in potting soil when Marianne sat back and swiped at her forehead, whisking away small beads of moisture. It was a warm afternoon in early March. Sam had set up a workstation where Marianne potted snap-dragons, dianthus, and sweet William. "Sam, I've been thinking about how I'd like things managed when I'm gone." He grunted, ignoring her. Marianne had seen the same response in Ray. She reached out her hand, laying it gently on Sam's forearm. He paused, then covered her hand with his.

"I guess we should talk about it." Brushing the dirt from his hands, Sam rose and helped Marianne to the Adirondack chair. The sun was shining, lending a pleasant warmth to the little sitting area. The walls surrounding the garden protected them from any breeze. Sam settled her in and sat in the chair next to her. "What things and how? Your wish is my command."

Marianne chuckled. Sam had always been one to disguise his feelings behind a joke. "Ah, if it was only that easy." Marianne's smile faded. She stared at the paper whites and daffodils waving in the breeze, the lilies bursting forth, ready to bloom for Easter. She was looking at the flowers and seeing so much more. "Your dad, he won't know what to do. I've written everything down. It's in a notebook. I'll give it to you later. When

I die, hospice knows to call the funeral home. I've spoken with Father John. He knows the readings and the psalm. I've selected the hymns. I'd like Kate to read the psalm and you to do the second reading. It's from the Book of Revelation of John, chapter 21, verses 2–7. I've always taken comfort from verses 3-4, the part where John writes, '*and God himself will be with them; he will wipe away every tear from their eyes, and death shall be no more, neither shall there be mourning nor crying nor pain any more, for the former things have passed away'*. But that's the simple part, Sam. It's what follows that I need you to promise me you'll take care of." Marianne turned her green eyes, so much like Emily's, to her son. She looked into his heart and spoke from hers. "Sam, your dad isn't strong like you. He'll mourn, he'll flounder, and he'll need you. I know you have an uneasy peace with him because of my illness and our being here. I need that peace to become permanent." Marianne looked at Sam and thought of Ray. How alike the two men were. If they could only see and appreciate it. It was one thing Marianne hoped to accomplish before time ran out. She sighed. So much to do. So little time.

"All the years, the expectations your dad burdened you with? It was his way of making you into a man who could carry the weight he wasn't able to. You need to forgive him. Your dad loves you. He just doesn't know how to say it."

Sam stood. She watched him pace from one side of the flagstone patio to the other. His jaw tight, nostrils flared with anger. Marianne watched as he struggled to tamp down the years of pent-up anger. Sam turned back to her, shoving his balled fists into his pockets.

"Mom, that happened a long time ago. There is nothing to forgive." Sam closed his eyes.

Marianne knew he was remembering the bad times, the times his dad yelled at him, berated him for not protecting his siblings. Sam ran his hand over his chin in frustration. Marianne gave him her 'mom,' look. She could read his mind.

Sam shook his head. "I don't know, Mom. I don't know. It was so long ago. He always expected so much. Remember when Paul fell out of the tree and broke his arm? Dad took his belt to me because I didn't stop Paul from falling. I was eleven, for Christ's sake. I was up in the same tree. How was I to know Paul would fall? Or stop him from climbing it? When Paul died in Afghanistan, I felt Dad giving me the same look. Like I had failed again. Like I was supposed to keep him from dying over there. It was all bullshit."

"Your dad doesn't blame you, Sam. He blames himself. He has always felt his failure, felt he fell short of the mark. Your dad wanted to teach you to be better than he was. It's always been that way. As outlandish as it sounds, your dad blames himself for everything. Things way beyond his control; every scrape when you fell off your bikes, every fall you kids took, Paul's death, my miscarriage, and now, my cancer. Your dad has never been good at expressing affection, but he loves you more than you realize.

"When we packed up to move to Florida, I found a box on the top shelf of his closet. It contained every letter you wrote to us, every newspaper clipping from your time in college or the service. Yes, Sam, all of what happened was a long time ago, but there is still a lot to forgive."

Sam turned back to her. There was a shadow of uncertainty and trepidation in his eyes.

"Your father is so proud of you and the man you've become. And he regrets how his actions pushed you away. Your dad wants to be a family and when I'm gone, he will need a family. Please, for me, Sam, look in your heart, find forgiveness for him, and help him find forgiveness for himself."

Marianne prayed Sam would read the plea in her eyes. He lowered his head, and stared at his hands, rubbing the dirt from his palms. She watched him work hard to swallow, to consider her words. All she could do was ask Sam to think about what she had said; to understand that his dad blamed himself for everything that went wrong. Sam needed to realize he did that, too. Marianne often wondered if that was a learned behavior, and if Sam was aware he was more like his dad than either wanted to admit?

Pressing his lips together and drawing in a long, shuddering breath, Sam blew it out and turned back to her. "I can't promise forgiveness, Mom, but I can promise I'll try. I'll try."

She cupped his cheek with her warm hand, and her heart shone in gratitude.

Marianne died on April 3rd.

Chapter 2

Sam brushed the dirt from his hand. Somehow, it had become a tradition for him since Afghanistan. A fistful of dust, Genesis 2:7. *And God formed dust from the earth into a man and he blew into his face a breath of life, and the man became a living soul.* Dust to dust. Walking to Kate, he gathered her into his arms and rested his cheek on the top of her head, gaining strength from their love. Marianne Renee Slater, his mother, was dead. She'd left a grieving husband, Emily, and himself behind to pick up the pieces of a shattered family and heal. Sam drew in a shaky breath and looked back at the forlorn row of chairs sitting on the faux turf under the green canvas canopy. It was a warm sunny day, just like his mom liked, but it was a cold, dark day for Sam's dad.

Ray sat alone. He hadn't been a man to show love and now there was no one left that loved him. Sam regretted the distance that had grown between him and his dad. He struggled with how to reach across the chasm, knowing that if he didn't, he wouldn't be able to forgive himself. It was time to pick up the pieces of a shattered relationship and begin to heal. Brushing a kiss to Kate's temple, Sam turned and walked to his father.

"Dad, come on. We planned a small reception at the house." He gently squeezed Ray's shoulder. "Emily and Jake are waiting at the car. Let's go home."

Sam watched his father slowly stand and step to the grave. He touched the burnished walnut finish of the casket, running his fingers lovingly over its satin smoothness. Bowing his head, Ray said a silent goodbye. A single tear fell onto the petals of a white rose on the floral spray, then ran onto the cold, hard metal of the casket. It held his whole heart, his entire world. Sam listened as his father whispered verses from the Song of Solomon, feeling the pain as deeply as if it were his own. *"Arise, my love, my fair one, and come away; Set me as a seal upon your heart, as a seal upon your arm; for love is strong as death. Many waters cannot quench love, neither can floods drown it."* His voice choked as he repeated, *"for love is strong as death."*

All those years Sam had resented his father for demanding he protect everyone, to keep them safe. It had pushed the two men apart. After what his mom had told him, Sam could clearly see that the demand was no less than his father expected of himself. And now his mom was dead. The cancer had done its painful and hideous work. His father felt the failure of not having protected her from its ravages. It was poignant, and Sam understood. He wasn't ready yet to tell his dad about Ramirez. How he'd suffered a loss and fear that had kept him from opening to his feelings for Kate, but meeting and loving her had healed him. The horrors of her abduction and the subsequent killing of the evil criminal, Carlos Ramirez, had melded them into a stronger, more resilient couple than they might have been otherwise. He had been her light in the darkness and she, his life-giving water. Sam listened to his father's words and realized he had heard similar ones in his heart when Kate had come back to him from her darkness. As a result, Sam could now extend his hand and try to fill the void left in his dad by his mother's death. Sam put his arm around Ray's shoulders and the two men walked to the waiting limo.

Back at the house, Aalem, the caterer, and his staff set up a simple repast of light hors d'oeuvres, finger sandwiches, coffee and tea. Aalem had been Sam's translator in Afghanistan. He had immigrated to the States and worked with his brother in the catering business. Aalem also did undercover work for Homeland Security as part of Sam's team. The mourners gathered to support the family, then faded away at the end of the afternoon, leaving them to grieve alone. Father John spoke one last prayer for the family, for their peace and comfort and the repose of Marianne's soul before he left.

The family sat in the quiet house, each alone with their thoughts and memories. Ray brought two small packages out of the bedroom, handing one to each of his precious children.

"Marianne asked me to give these to you when…" He faltered, then collected himself. "…after the funeral. It's her last gift to you."

Emily and Sam exchanged looks. Marianne had tucked an envelope under the ribbon of each package. She'd written their names in her neat cursive. Emily opened hers first. She couldn't read it for the tears in her eyes and passed it to Jake. Clearing his voice to speak past the lump in his throat, Jake read the simple missive.

'*Emily, my dearest and most tender child. Your heart is so generous. You always see the best in everyone. I am glad you have a loving partner in Jake. He keeps you grounded and will always shield you from any hurt or adversity. When I watched you two together, I saw how he made your world as beautiful and precious as you envisioned it. His hands are gentle and he will always hold your heart as you hold mine.'*

Jake held Emily's hand, placing a gentle kiss on her forehead.

Sam took a deep breath and opened his letter. With his arm around Kate's shoulders, he used the back of his sleeve to wipe the tears from his eyes and read the words his mom wrote.

'Sam, your strength has always been your ability to love and sacrifice. You willingly carry the burden of other's grief and suffer any hardship for those you love. Never doubt your capacity to love or to protect. You proved it with a little kitten and have lived it with your perfect choice of a mate and wife.'

They carefully unwrapped the small parcels. Emily let out an audible sob as she gazed at a study of Jake's hands carving their initials into a heart on the headboard of the baby's cradle he'd made. Marianne had captured the strength and love showing just Jake's hands working with a chisel and hammer. She'd painted bits of sawdust dusting his hands. It was so realistic you wanted to reach out and brush it off.

"It's perfect, isn't it?" She turned it for everyone to see, getting nods of approval and agreement.

Sam was in awe of how Marianne had captured the essence of the love Emily and Jake shared. He couldn't imagine how his mom could put paint on canvas to reflect the message in his letter. Sam felt Kate's lips brush his cheek.

"Go ahead, Sam. Unwrap it. Let's see how well Mom knew you, too."

Pulling the wrapping off, Sam turned the canvas toward himself. Seeing the soft stroke of her brush and the subject she'd portrayed; he could only think how well she knew him. Marianne had brought two images to life in his painting. One of Kate, napping in the garden with a book at her side and Ophelia, the rescued cat, lying on her lap. The fountain splashed in the background and the flowers waved gayly. Marianne knew Sam had to save the kitten to prove to himself he could save Kate and was worthy of her love.

Turning it for everyone to see, Sam could only nod, too choked up for words. He looked over at his dad and knew rebuilding a relationship was not only attainable, but after all these years, he wanted it.

Emily and Jake left soon after. The pregnancy and her emotions were taking their toll. She was tired. Emily hugged Ray. "I'll see you tomorrow, Dad, okay? Try to rest, please." He nodded absent-mindedly and wandered out to the garden while Sam and Kate walked Em and Jake to their car. "Sam, I'm so worried about him. Dad seems lost without her. What will he do?"

Sam stroked Emily's arm and pulled her in for a long embrace. "He'll do what he must and what he can. We can be there for him, but it's a journey he must make on his own. Grief is a lonely emotion." Pulling back, Sam tweaked Emily on the nose. "Now speaking about trying to rest." Sam handed her off to Jake, but not before giving his best friend a bro hug.

"She'll rest if I have to tie her down," Jake mumbled under his breath. This was his first child, and he was a nervous daddy-to-be. Sam shook his head and hoped Jake had a son. Sam figured if Jake had a girl, he would build a moat around their house with ten-foot alligators to keep the boys away.

Kate snuggled under Sam's arm, waving goodbye as Emily and Jake drove off. She wrapped her arms around his waist and leaned back to look at him, brushing hair off his forehead. He'd let it grow long for this latest case. Kate claimed to like the look, but hated the reason behind it. Sam didn't talk about his work, but he knew Kate saw and heard enough to know it involved some evil men abducting children and young women. They'd use them in brothels, sex clubs, and pornography. When their usefulness was over, they'd abandon them in the desert where they would perish. A rancher in Kingman had found the bodies of two young girls huddled together. The desert was cold at night. The coroner surmised the adolescents had curled up with each other for warmth, but it wasn't enough. He believed they died from hypothermia. When Kate learned about it, she did the usual online search. It wasn't an easy way to go, and death was so final.

Sam read the concern in her eyes. He knew she was aware of his case and was doing research into abuse and pornography. It worried him she might put herself in jeopardy, but she had proven herself to be damn good at research. She had uncovered information that helped solve the case against Ramirez.

Sam and Kate had survived Ramirez's attempt to kill them, but not without scars. Kate's abduction left her shaken, struggling with nightmares. Sam had been so afraid he'd lose her, but they had found strength in each other. He took a leave from Homeland Security, married Kate, and they settled into his bungalow in the

Fairmont neighborhood of Fort Worth. Sam took time to reevaluate his commitment to Homeland Security or any type of law enforcement. It was dangerous work. He had more to lose now that Kate was his wife, but his sense of honor and duty won out. Homeland Security has the authority to conduct criminal investigations into the illegal cross-border movement of people and other items throughout the US. The Transnational Criminal Organizations, or TCOs, often worked hand in hand with organized crime families here in the states.

His current assignment was as distasteful to him as they came. Sam was looking at young women and children being kidnapped or smuggled into the country for sex trades. Although he'd taken a supervisory position with Homeland Security, focusing on the legal aspects, he never knew when he'd have to go undercover.

Sam and Kate walked back into the house, arms entwined around each other. "I'm going to check on Dad. Take him a beer and see if he wants to talk." Sam kissed her. "I love you, Kate Slater."

She framed his face with her delicate hands, her long fingers playing along his strong jawline, her thumb finding its way to, and caressing, the clef in his chin. "Right back at you, Sam Slater!" Smiling, she returned the kiss.

Kate went to help with the clean-up from the reception while Sam grabbed two beers and walked out to the garden, his oasis from all that troubled him. The design was based on the walled gardens he'd seen in Kandahar. There were beds of fragrant and colorful annuals that attracted birds and butterflies. The entire environment was designed to quiet and calm a troubled soul. Toward the end, they carried his mother outside on warm days. Marianne had loved to sit in the sun and listen to the music of the fountain and birds. They all had prayed for remission or more time, but toward the end, the cancer had moved fast. There wasn't enough time. Family and friends had surrounded Ray and Marianne with love and their priest visited often to pray with them during the hard times. But nothing would fill the void until Ray was ready for it to be filled.

"Brought you a beer, Dad. I figure you could use one after today." Sam handed off the bottle and sat next to his father in the matching Adirondack chair. It felt good to be quiet. To not have to respond to the words of sympathy. Sam knew everyone was sincere, but he couldn't absorb their love and support to climb out of his pit of sadness. "How are you holding up?" he asked, kicking back and stretching out his legs, loosening his tie.

Ray took a long pull of the beer, wiping his mouth with the back of his hand and belching softly. "Better than I expected. This is a lovely garden, son. Your mom sure loved sitting here. Marianne loved Kate and Jake, too. She remarked on how blessed she was to see her children so happy. When Emily announced she was expecting, I remember your mom's eyes overflowing with happy tears. Oh, how she wished she could be here to hold her first grandchild, but it wasn't to be. Kate is a strong woman and I don't know if I could have handled everything without her help. Or yours, Sam. Thank you."

Ray paused, clearly struggling with how to continue saying what needed to be said. He cleared his throat. Reaching out a tentative hand, Ray grasped

Sam's arm.

"Son, I can't make up for all the stupid things I've done and said over the years. I treated you unfairly, expected too much, made unreasonable demands. Thank God, you were strong enough to survive, hell, *thrive*. You are an honorable man. I'm not saying all this because your mom would have wanted me to. No, son. I'm saying it because it's true. I'm so damn proud of you. It would be nice to think you became the man you are because of me, but I figure it was in spite of me. I want us to be a family again." Ray's grip on Sam's arm tightened. "I want you to be my son again. Please forgive all my foolishness. Aw, hell, Sam. What I'm trying to say is I love you. Give me another chance. Please."

Sam sat, elbows resting on his knees, staring at the flagstone patio under his feet. His beer bottle hung loosely from his fingers between his legs. A trail of ants had found a few crumbs from earlier and were busy at work carrying them back to their nest. He pressed his forehead into his hands, blowing air out of slack lips. Sam couldn't remember ever hearing his dad say so many words in one setting. And certainly not what he'd just heard. Remembering his mom's wish and how much he wanted to bridge the gap between him and his dad, Sam was ready to forgive and to love. Thankfully, Kate had taught him how to do that.

"Dad, we have a lot of unpleasant history, but we have one faultless connection. It's mom's love. Neither of us is perfect and if Mom could love us individually, I think we can love each other. I'd like to try, Dad. I really would." They clinked beer bottles and took a sip. It was a good first step. They sat in silence, while the sun dropped below the roofline, casting the garden into shadows, enjoying the quiet of the evening.

Ray stood, stretched, and gave an enormous yawn. "I think I'll take your sister's suggestion to heart and try to get some rest. See you in the morning, son."

Chapter 3

Kate was up early the next morning. Sam was out running, Ray was in the home office, and she had a quiet house. Ophelia was meowing demandingly while head bumping her legs.

"Okay, okay, my little Feelie. Breakfast is coming. Hold your little furry horses." Kate smiled, enjoying the little chirps the cat made. She was such a loving cat, always wanting to cuddle. With Emily pregnant, Kate was feeling motherly, and the cat was the recipient of her maternal instincts.

She was in the midst of making pancakes when Sam came in from his run. He still did a minimum of three miles, five days a week. Kate joined him a couple of days a week, but was finding yoga a better fit. She'd roll out her mat in the garden and execute three rapid sun salutes followed by warriors one, two and, if she was feeling up to it, three. That was her killer stretch and balance move.

Ophelia wound her body around Kate's legs and liked to plunk down under her when she moved into a down dog. Sometimes Sam would return from running and join her in the last stretches and the final resting pose, savasana. Before Ray and Marianne had moved in, it would usually transition into touching and kissing and end in a steamy shower scene. She smiled. Oh, they still had the steamy shower and everything else that led up to it. It just didn't start in the garden.

"Breakfast in fifteen," she said, pouring Sam his orange juice. "Your dad is in the office checking his email."

Sam snagged a piece of bacon and kissed Kate on her exposed shoulder, nibbling his way to her neck. Turning, she wound her arms around his neck, inviting a deeper show of his affection. "I missed you this morning. What time were you up?" she asked, stealing a bite of Sam's bacon.

"Six. You were down for the count. I thought I'd let you sleep a little longer. Yesterday was a long day. I'm going into the office today to catch up on some work." Sam drank down a tall glass of water, followed by the orange juice. "I'll go shower. See you in ten."

Kate was just setting the platter on the island when both men came into the kitchen from opposite doors. She did a double take. Kate didn't think the two men realized just how much they looked and moved alike. Sam had Ray's coloring, height, and build. If you watched them from behind, they even had the same purposeful stride. Sam had shared the gist of their talk in the garden with her. She was happy they were going to mend those long-ago broken fences. "Perfect timing, gentlemen. Grab a seat, I'll get the coffee." While Kate grabbed the pot, Ray settled at his place and laid down a notepad on which he'd written several addresses. "What's that?" she asked, glancing over.

"Well," he hesitated slightly. "I don't want to intrude forever. You two are practically newlyweds. You need this place for yourselves. I've been looking at some houses in the area. There are some pretty good deals. I'd be close to you and Emily and the church.

Father John hinted at some projects they need done and asked if I'd consider helping. It would keep me off the streets and my mind occupied. Plus, it might be nice to have the quiet and comfort of doing something for a good cause." Ray helped himself to a stack of pancakes, slathering on plenty of butter and syrup.

Kate watched Sam dish up his pancakes and do the same thing. Only instead of butter, he chose peanut butter. Sam also didn't skimp on the syrup. "That sounds wonderful. What houses did you find?" Kate asked as she went to the pantry for another bottle of syrup. *Harrumph. Men and their syrup!*

"There is a little bungalow over close to Emily. It's right on the edge of the improved neighborhood. Still pretty rough area," Ray said around a mouthful of pancakes. "It's a little smaller than this place, but I don't need a lot of space. Two-bedroom, one bath. Good garage, so I could set up a workshop. Another option is just a couple of blocks around the corner from here. It's a little larger, three-one and a half, and has a garage apartment. I'm hoping Jake has some time and can look at them with me. Help me make sure I'm not buying a money pit."

"Oh, you mean like this one was?" Sam asked, laughing. "Seriously, if you can get either of them at the right price, you'll have room to invest in improvements and not overbuild for the neighborhood. I'd like to go with you, but I've got some work to do." Kate noticed the shadow that crossed over Sam's face.

They finished their breakfast and cleaned up. Ray left to confer with Jake on the potential houses. Sam went to his office and Kate settled into her workspace. When she and Sam got married, he had carved out a section of their home office for her to use. They were both quiet workers and Kate loved having Sam nearby. She'd take a break from the computer and feel Sam's gaze watching her work. They'd smile and return to their labors, knowing that when the day ended, they'd share more than loving glances.

Kate booted up her computer and combed through the news articles she'd highlighted having to do with child abuse. Ophelia jumped up on the desk and lay across the keyboard. Shooing her off and away, Kate focused on the articles. It shocked her. The many ways perpetrators exploited children and young people was revolting. Still photography, videos, even physical sexual encounters. Each held its own horrors for the victim. From the interviews she had found with some survivors, they were often confused, taught that to be 'bad' was to be 'good' and rewarded for their efforts. It sickened Kate to learn about the often-used indoctrination process. Adults use 'adult' porn to target children they hope to have sex with. Interviewing a child therapist, she learned of a case at a psychiatric hospital where they had admitted a four-year-old for sexually acting out. The therapist discovered that her step-father had been watching 'adult' porn with her since she was two. The child knew no other way to behave. It saddened her to think he had manipulated this poor child in such a disgusting way.

When she found a study on the proliferation of internet porn and linked it with the long-term effects of watching hard-core porn during puberty or early teen years, she had to get up and walk away from her monitor. That this activity often leads to sex addiction and some viewers even become serious criminals in later life caused her to wonder how parents can protect their children.

Kate settled on her next article. She'd write about internet porn, how they targeted and abused young people. She'd offer it to whatever publication that would print it regardless of payment. Hopefully, one with a large readership. She worked throughout the morning, researching news articles, papers from learned people, and personal interviews with mental health professionals and victims. When the sound of Jake and Ray coming in carried from the back, Kate took a break.

"Geeze Ray. That first house? What a mess. Did you notice the roach poop in the cabinets? And I swear, those were gnawing marks from rodents on the baseboards. No way would I buy that one, no matter how cheap." Jake grabbed two beers from the frig and passed one to Ray as Kate entered from the office. "Oh, hey Kate. Hope we didn't disturb you. Just going over the houses we looked at." Jake tipped his beer in acknowledgement. "Ray, here, has a good eye. We saw a couple of dogs, but one decent option just a couple of blocks from here. It's a small three-one and a half with a nice garage apartment. Good income potential."

Ray was nodding in agreement, then took it one step further. "Actually, I thought that with the baby coming, you and Emily might need something bigger. You could live in the house and I could take the garage apartment. That would put us all in proximity and when Sam and Kate decide to start a family, I'd be close to all the grandkids." Ray reached into the pantry, pulling out the pretzels he liked to snack on. He didn't notice the panic in Jake's eyes, but Kate did. She looked from one man to the other, wondering how that comment would go over. Jake stared at Ray, speechless.

Kate heard a boxful of pins drop and watched the recognition of Ray's faux pas dawn on him. He quickly backpedaled. "No pressure. It was just a thought. I mean, I'll still be splitting my time between here and Florida until the condo sells. It would be convenient to have a place to stay without bunking at one of your places. Well, the house is an excellent investment either way. We can talk about it."

Kate saw the hope in Ray's eyes dim, replaced by hurt. Putting a bright smile on her face, she enthused, "I think it sounds like an interesting idea. Even if Jake and Emily aren't ready to move, you could rent out the house and have the garage apartment for yourself when you spend time in Texas. The tenants would be built-in house-sitters."

Both men relaxed at the nice out Kate's idea had provided. They clinked bottles and went out to the garden to discuss their ideas about the potential property and what needed to be done. Neither was ready to discuss the offer Ray mentioned. Kate called Emily and invited her to dinner, then pulled some chicken out to prep.

****

Sam came home to a houseful of laughter. Dumping his briefcase in the office, he wound his way through the house until he tracked down Kate. She was in the kitchen putting the finishing touches on a fruit trifle. Sam would never tire of watching her. Even dressed simply in a mint green t-shirt and white shorts, she took his breath away. Coming up behind her, he nuzzled her ear and nipped at her neck. Kate turned in his arms and leaned into the kiss. God, he loved her.

"How was your day?" he asked, successfully snatching a finger full of whipped cream from the trifle before Kate slapped his hand away. "I see the gangs all here. What can I do to help?"

"My day was depressing. Child exploitation research. I know you are working on a case involving it. It's just so horrible. I thought I'd write an article to educate the public about its proliferation and how parents can safeguard their children. I'll tell you later what I've learned. Oh, and everything is ready to go. Emily set the table. Jake has the beer iced, and your dad volunteered to grill the chicken. Why don't you get comfortable and meet us in the garden?" She gave Sam a peck.

He grabbed her around the waist, wanting more. Sam's hands roamed over her back and cupped her bottom, pulling her closer. His kiss left her breathless, leaning in for more. Giving her a suggestive smile, he kissed the tip of her nose and patted her bottom, promising more for later, then climbed the stairs two at a time to get changed.

After Jake took a tired Emily home and Ray settled in for the night, Sam led Kate upstairs. He'd felt his desire for her grow all evening. She was everything to him, his perfect mate. Drawing her into their bedroom, Sam closed the door and took her in his arms. He ran his hands up her back and into her hair, trapping her face so he could plunder at will. Kate matched his ardor. Sam conducted a slow and complete seduction of the woman he loved.

Leading her to the bed, he started at the patch of bare skin at her collar. Tugging the neck of her t-shirt down, he nibbled on her creamy shoulder. His hands found their way under her shirt and covered her breasts. Releasing the clasp of her bra, Sam freed them to his mouth and tongue. Kneading each one, he gently pinched her nipples, then bent his head to kiss and suck them. Kate sighed. She drew in an anticipatory breath as Sam worked his way down her abdomen. He released the button on her shorts and peeled them down her long legs, following their path with his mouth. When they lay pooled at the foot of the bed, he resumed his exploration, moving from toes to thighs to breasts and back to her mouth. She arched against him and pulled his shirt off as he removed hers.

When her hand went to his pants, Sam stopped her, smiling devilishly. "Don't move," he whispered in her ear, his breath causing her to shiver with anticipation. It was a line from *Out of Africa*, the movie they'd watched the first time they'd made love. With her lying naked, she was at his mercy and Sam took his time teasing and tasting every inch of her satiny skin. Somehow, he lost his pants. The two were skin to skin when his ministrations drove her to a second orgasm. Sam propped himself on his forearms and watched her face as he slowly glided into her, sheathing himself in her velvety softness. Her eyes grew opaque and the darkest shade of blue with passion. Her breathy mews grew louder. Sam covered her mouth with his to shush her moans of pleasure. Kate was a vocal lover. It drove him crazy with desire, hearing how he pleased her. Driving hard and fast, he brought them both to the threshold, then over as they crossed into joy and fulfillment. When they had their fill, Kate nestled her head on Sam's shoulder and sighed in complete satisfaction.

As much as he hated to break the mood, he needed to ask. Sam shifted enough to see Kate's face. "Do you want to tell me about your research into child abuse and exploitation?" Kate let out another sigh, this time filled with a deep sense of sadness. Sitting up in a cross-legged position on the bed, she tucked the sheet around herself and pushed the hair from her face.

"It's a horrible thing, isn't it, Sam? The evil in the hearts of the abusers. The innocent groomed and used so cruelly. It's almost hard to comprehend. I know you are dealing with a case of human trafficking and exploitation. They are smuggling children and young women over the border, even kidnapping them, aren't they? Will you stop them?"

Sam saw the emotion and entreaty in Kate's eyes. He reached out to caress her cheek, rubbing his thumb over her love-swollen lips. "I'm doing everything I can. We have some very good leads. Kate, are you sure writing this article is a good idea? I can hear the passion in your voice. I know you want to call attention to the crime and help parents protect their children. Just be careful it doesn't call too much attention to you. We often connect the people committing these acts to organized crime. They will kill without compunction." Sam sensed the bowing of Kate's back. The stubborn streak in her he both loved and worried about would make her pursue a story, regardless of her safety. Wrapping his arms around her, Sam pulled Kate back into his embrace, kissing the top of her head as it settled on his shoulder. "I know you, Kate Slater. You just be careful, okay?"

Chapter 4

Kate attacked the subject of internet pornography and child exploitation with a vengeance. As with all her research, she started at the library, digging through newspaper articles. Most of the information she discovered revolved around the capture and conviction of the criminals. Kate sought out psychologists and therapists specializing in trauma. She spent time learning about how the perpetrators target a child and exploit them, often without their parent's knowledge. She negotiated a series of three articles with the Fort Worth paper. It didn't have the volume of readers she wished for, but it was a good start.

Her first article appeared in the Sunday paper. It focused on the proliferation of internet pornography. How its insidiousness warped and desensitized those that were exposed. It ran just below the fold on the Opinion Page and she knew she'd made an impact when the local news station contacted her to request an interview.

Kate quickly became a guest speaker at several PTAs and churches. While this was gratifying, she still didn't feel she was presenting the real meat of the subject. She needed to speak with someone who dealt with the nitty-gritty issues.

The DA's office had a special task force designated to monitor and prosecute obscenity crimes. They worked hand-in-hand with the vice squad of the Fort Worth Police Department. They oversaw everything from printed materials to prostitution to so-called men's clubs. Attorney Janet Winburn had the unfortunate honor to direct this group. She led the investigations, while a team of younger attorneys prosecuted the cases. Reaching out to her, Kate set up an interview.

Arriving fifteen minutes early, Kate introduced herself to the receptionist and took a seat. She made mental notes about the lobby. Kate often used her visual impressions to add color to her articles. She glanced around the reception area, noting the mid-century modern furniture often used to furnish government offices. There was a lot of walnut-colored faux wood, chrome and glass, and vinyl leather-look upholstery. Plastic plants in ceramic pots stood in the corners, pretending to be real. The coffee table in front of the long, narrow couch held a couple of magazines, dog-eared and two months old. A slim young man sat in an adjacent chair, paging through his notes and jotting down additional ones on a legal pad. His suit was light gray, off the rack, and Kate surmised he might be one of the court-appointed defense attorneys. An older gentleman came out, introduced himself, and escorted the younger one into the back. Kate sat patiently with her legs crossed at the ankles and her hands casually clasped in her lap.

At exactly one minute before her appointment time, a woman in her early forties entered the reception area. She wore a cream-colored silk blouse that softened the severe lines of a mannish brown pantsuit. Approaching Kate, Janet Winburn extended her hand in greeting. Shaking her hand, Kate noticed the short, unpainted nails on manicured hands. The wrinkles at the corners of Winburn's eyes showed character rather than age. Her brown eyes exuded warmth and confidence.

"You must be Kate Hunter. Or are you going by Slater now that you are married? I'm Janet Winburn. Please come this way. We'll talk in my office. Would you like something to drink? I can offer you coffee, tea, water, or a soft drink." Janet was all about business and strode purposefully toward a small kitchenette where the drinks were available.

"Water would be fine, thank you," Kate replied, doing her best to keep up with Janet's long strides. When both ladies had their refreshments, Janet led the way down a short hallway to her office. The décor was the same mid-century modern style as the rest of the office space, but Janet had personalized it with artwork in soft pastels and colorful pillows on the chairs. Framed photos of who Kate assumed was Winburn's daughter stood in groupings on the credenza. Janet sat on the chair behind her desk, motioning Kate to the one across from her.

Janet led off the conversation in a no-nonsense manner. "I read your recent articles on internet porn. Your writing clearly communicates your sound sense of right and wrong. You don't lecture or condescend. You write for a thinking public—I like that. The public isn't stupid. Just ignorant about the facts. You can teach people if you learn those facts. How can I help you?"

Janet's welcome thrilled Kate. Winburn was knowledgeable, passionate about the work she was doing, and she seemed willing to share all the gritty details. "Thank you, Ms. Winburn. I really appreciate that. Perhaps the best place to start is the beginning. How does an abuser find his victim?"

"Of course, and please, call me Janet." She waved her hand airily, and settled back in her chair, steepling her fingers. "Well, my agency has solved several cases involving human trafficking and the exploitation of young women. We continue to uncover more. Many of these victims are runaways. These kids end up living on the street, and maybe get hooked on drugs. They sell their bodies to survive. The abusers 'rescue' these young people and become their protectors, providing food and a warm place to stay."

Kate's mind went immediately to pimps and prostitution. Ever mindful that her thoughts might bias the story, Kate put that aside. Get the facts, she reminded herself. Kate had her mini-recorder going, jotting down follow-up questions. "So, some choose prostitution to survive?"

Janet, intent on communicating the ugliness of the situation, replied, "Yes. Prostitution is sometimes the only option, but there are other instances when an abuser grooms his target."

Kate made a note. Tapping her pen against her lips, she asked the next question. "Grooms? How is that done? How do they end up with one person pulling the strings?"

Janet smirked. "Oh, these guys are smart. They know how to manipulate a young person into doing whatever they ask. It's a creative and artistic deception, convincing the victim that what they do is their choice. Sometimes they start by providing a safe haven. Some people reference Maslov's hierarchy of needs. Are you familiar with it? The perpetrators use our basic needs to build trust, starting with the physiological. Shelter, clothing, food. Then they move up the pyramid to security and safety. Follow that with the psychological needs we all have. To have friends or intimate relationships. These kids didn't run from a loving home, so when they find someone who professes to care for them, 'loves them', they're hooked. By this time, the abuser has gained the trust of the victim."

Janet leaned forward, placing her clasped hands on the desk. She was laying out a logical series of steps like she would in a courtroom. With her serious brown eyes focused on Kate, she drove each fact home.

"The next step in a healthy relationship would be to build self-esteem. It's tragic, but in their own twisted way, the abusers do. Only they do this by giving positive reinforcement to the less desirable behaviors of the victim. It starts out innocently enough, maybe posing for photos or wearing revealing clothes, letting others see them unclothed. The positive reinforcement the victim receives from the abuser lowers their guard, builds trust. Pretty soon, the abuser is asking for more. He may begin using the victim for his own pleasure. Or, maybe he'll say, 'Hey, baby, I don't want to share but it would really help us if you'd let Joe Shmo touch you', or 'hey, baby, I love the way guys look at you when you're dressed so sexy. It turns me on and makes me want you even more.' The young woman has grown to 'love' the abuser and will do whatever he asks."

Kate had paused at the mention of Maslov's hierarchy of needs. She remembered studying it in college. She wrote a paper based on the pyramid showing how political parties manipulate their constituency by providing the basic needs, welfare, healthcare, affordable housing. The politicians created a 'dependent' class. These people became enslaved to their new masters, the government. Kate theorized that they never helped the individual reach the top of the pyramid: self-actualization. That was back in Kate's younger and rebellious years. Many academics discount Maslov's theory, but her paper made for an interesting read and lots of debate regarding the control one can, or currently, have over society. Kate made a note to do additional research about brainwashing. It would be an interesting perspective on the subject.

Janet continued building her case. "The abuser will do whatever he needs to do to keep the victim under his thumb, dependent upon him for everything and wanting only to please the abuser. Once they have created this situation, built the trust, they introduce them to the public." She made air quotes when she used the last phrase.

Listening to Janet's description of the process left a sour taste in Kate's mouth. "Is there a particular age, socio-economic group, or personality that is more susceptible to this type of coercion? Education? Any common denominator?" Kate asked, hoping that if they could fix the underlying cause, they could fix the ultimate outcome.

Janet sighed. "Sadly, no. And we've only touched on the runaways. The ones already living at risk. The abusers look for the vulnerable. Perhaps they come from an unstable home. The parents are divorcing or working too much. Some are in foster care, others, poverty." Janet's voice was cool and businesslike. She had worked too many cases concerning young women on the streets, understood how and why things happened. She stood and walked to the window.

Kate followed Janet's gaze as she looked out at the traffic rushing along the freeway. An 18-wheeler lumbered along I-30, spewing noxious fumes and slowing traffic. The wind whipped fast-food wrappers in the bed of a battered pickup into a mini-cyclone of trash that flew up and away. The dirt and grime of a city wasn't limited to the litter on the roadside. Turning, Janet continued.

"Then there are the others, the ones the perpetrators find using social media, the mall, teen hangouts or worse, friends and family connections. These people are patient. Experts at indoctrination. Their initial efforts are to build a relationship to promote a sense of trust. They are very charming. A lonely young girl may yearn for attention or romance, so when an older man shows an interest, she wants to do everything to please him. The abuser is gentle and protective. But keep in mind that the end goal is to convince the young woman that their sexual activities are normal and what she wants. The abuser will start out expressing support and affection. He'll zero in on her dreams and desires. He'll feed her ego. The abuser might push the boundaries of decency, perhaps telling her dirty jokes or reading erotic publications to her. The two might giggle over it and promise it will be their little secret. He moves from sharing smutty little secrets to experimental touching, use of sex toys and eventually copulation. It's a sick game. When he has the young woman properly indoctrinated, his abuse becomes more overt. He'll use his emotional hold over the young woman or even threaten physical harm. The victim will lose all sense of self-esteem. The approval of their abuser is tantamount."

Janet wrapped her hands around her coffee mug, staring into its black depths. She took a small sip of the bitter brew, made a face, and set it down. "I'm sure you recall the recent news about a man who catfished a teenage girl in California? He developed a relationship with the girl, pretending to be someone he wasn't, then drove across the country to meet her. Ended up killing her mother and grandparents."

Kate had read about the case. It made the national news. He was a former police officer. The idea was appalling. She sensed a change in Janet's voice when she described this type of victim. Kate stopped writing and watched the waves of emotion wash over Janet Winburn's face. "This is different for you. You're invested in this victim. May I ask why?"

"I have a teenage daughter. She could easily fall victim to this. Any child could. There are people on social media that seek young vulnerable women. Some of these young women come from dysfunctional families, single parent environments. Perhaps the parents themselves are abusive, so partial programming to expect nothing else has already occurred. Maybe the parents are too involved in their careers and the child feels ignored. Inconsequential." Janet's voice faded to a whisper on the last word, as if she felt great pain thinking about it. She paused and looked down, then ran her fingers over her cheeks and through her hair.

Gathering herself, Janet continued. "Or, perhaps, they didn't get asked to the prom or a popular boy at school won't give them the time of day. Some cute guy suddenly pays attention to them and they think it's love. Fated to be. And let's not ignore the influence of soft porn on our youth. It's ubiquitous. Look at the popular music videos that kids are watching nowadays or the lyrics to an alarming number of songs. They promote sexuality, misogyny and violence. A lot of our young people live in fantasy worlds. They think vampires and werewolves are real for God's sake. Someone just has to find the right button to push to suck them into a fantasy world."

Kate heard the emotional escalation in Janet's voice. Curious, but believing it was wise, she wrapped up the interview. Kate closed her notebook and turned off the mini-recorder, placing both in her bag. "This is a wonderful start, Janet. Could we meet again to explore this subject further?"

"Oh, certainly." Janet checked her calendar. They settled on the next appointment. She walked Kate to the elevator and bid her goodbye.

Driving home, Kate considered Janet Winburn's use of the term *'inconsequential'*. A single word that could hold such power.

Kate swung by the market and picked up salmon filets for dinner. Sam was home, working at his desk. Setting down the groceries, she called from the kitchen. "Hi, babe. You're home early. Is that good or bad?" Not hearing a reply, Kate went into the office and wrapped her arms around him, kissing his cheek. She glanced at his computer monitor, noting the official documents before Sam switched screens.

Doing her best Sargent Schultz impression, she snapped to attention. "I know nothing!" Sam pulled her into his lap.

"Ha! You know plenty." He grinned happily, kissing her soundly. "How did the interview with Janet

Winburn go? Enough to write the article on abuse you have in mind?"

"Oh, my goodness, yes. That and more. I don't think I need to write so much about the end results as the everyday risk to our young people. Janet used the example of the recent catfishing of that California teen. I've only heard of the one, but I bet there are plenty of others that just didn't make the news. I'm going to do some digging and see how many other cases I can track down. This is a very productive angle. I can sell this." Kate's eyes had narrowed, and she was nodding, already thinking about how she would pitch the idea to the editors at Texas Quarterly.

Sam smiled. "I can see your gears turning. You are a determined woman. It's one of the many things I love about you."

Kate snuggled into his lap, planting a kiss on his jawline and tracing his ear with a feathery touch.

"Come to think of it, there are several more things." He nuzzled her neck. "Can dinner wait?" His hand was already toying with the buttons on her blouse, his fingers brushing her breasts and teasing her nipples.

Kate giggled and tugged at the snap on Sam's jeans. "Dinner can, but I think I'd like dessert now." He took the hint, and picking her up, climbed the stairs to their bedroom.

Chapter 5

Janet invited Kate to lunch for their second interview. Selecting a quiet bistro, the two followed the hostess to their table and settled in. It was a charming little place with white tablecloths, mismatched estate sale china, and grandmother's silver. The crowd was small, made up of women out for a girl's lunch or business professionals quietly conferring over a meal. When the waiter approached to take their order, it surprised Kate to hear Janet order a white wine. Assuming she didn't have pressing business at the office, Kate ignored it and ordered iced tea.

When the wine arrived, Janet took a sizable swallow and set it down. Without preamble, she turned to the waiter. "I'll have the chicken salad plate. Kate, what do you want?" Janet sipped her wine again, tapping her fingers on the tablecloth.

"That sounds good. I'll have that too," Kate replied, handing the waiter her menu. She tracked the nervous energy in Janet's hand and the way her gaze swung around the room as if she were looking for someone. Rather than ask, Kate waited, knowing silence is an effective tool when interviewing. Sam would tell her it was effective when interrogating them, too. Nervous people don't like long stretches of silence. She hoped Janet would volunteer what was going on.

Janet was taking a third generous sip of her wine as

the restaurant door opened. When Janet noticed the man enter, she visibly relaxed her hand on the stem of her glass and released a pent-up breath. The hostess smiled in greeting and led the lone gentleman to a table near the window. He was tall and slender. His dark hair, fashionably long. He wore dress slacks and a blazer over a white shirt. With the sun shining through the glass, he was backlit, so it was difficult to see his face. Kate watched as Janet tracked him across the room. She remained silent, waiting to see what would transpire.

"I'm sorry. I must seem distracted to you, but it's been a busy week. My daughter has been a typical teenager. When you have children, you'll understand. She has gone to live with her father for now."

"I'm sure you will miss her." Kate recalled the trio of photos of a young woman that had sat on Janet's credenza. This must be the daughter to which Janet was referring. She wondered at the conversation, however. The two women hardly knew each other, and here was Janet, sharing personal information. Janet took another sip of wine and gave a non-committal shrug. Then she made a complete one-eighty, shocking Kate with her angry tone.

"I'm glad she isn't here! Where is that waiter? The service is usually much better." Janet tracked him down and waved for another glass of wine. Kate sat stunned into silence.

"But tell me, how is your article going?" Janet was back to her usual efficient self.

"It is very kind of you to ask." Kate took her time responding. She never shared details about her work, not even with Sam, and she wasn't about to start now. "It's going well. I'm sure you've seen the latest installment in the Fort Worth paper. Your input has been pivotal in communicating key information to parents."

Janet waved off the compliment. "Oh, thank you. I didn't give you anything you couldn't have gotten off the internet." Janet paused as the waiter served their meals. "I'll have another wine, please." She told him, smiling tightly.

Kate lowered her eyes to her plate, busying herself with her napkin. *That's the third glass. What the heck is going on?* Hoping to get the conversation back on track and have a productive interview, Kate pulled out her mini-recorder and a list of questions.

"Janet, I'm hoping to learn more about human trafficking and exploitation. I understand there is a link between domestic violence and human trafficking. Can you tell me a little about that?"

Janet seemed taken aback by Kate's return to the topic at hand. "I can quote you chapter and verse, statistics from the Department of Justice Human Trafficking Task Force, but you can get all that by researching online. It may surprise you how easy it is to be manipulated into doing something against your normal code of ethics."

"I see." Kate paused, clearing her throat, wondering at Janet's comment. "Um, previously, I inquired if there was a common denominator that the victims share. Can you expand on that?"

Janet set down her fork. "Remember that anyone can be vulnerable to manipulation. The abuser just needs to find the right key to open the lock. Those that are facing challenges at home, perhaps divorce, poverty, or drugs, are easy targets. But those from a family where the parents aren't present in the day-to-day are also at risk. The steps to grooming a victim start with targeting and move to gaining trust, meeting needs, and establishing isolation from others. This leads to exploitation and maintaining control over the victim. The abuser is adept at finding the right person for their needs. Their efforts can be equally successful, whether providing shelter or making a young girl's fantasy of modeling or acting appear to come true. That sort of thing." Kate watched as the waiter delivered another glass of wine for Janet and refilled her tea. When he finished his task, Janet shocked Kate by slyly turning the interview tables.

"I'm sure your husband's work with Homeland Security has been a big help. Isn't he working on human trafficking?"

Kate added sweetener to her tea, stirring it thoughtfully. She wondered what business Janet had asking about Sam's work. She took time gazing steadily at Janet's flushed face. "Janet, I respect the work my husband does and make it a practice to honor the confidentiality of his work. I don't ask him about it and he doesn't share anything with me. I'm sure in your line of work you understand and appreciate this." She smiled sweetly at Janet Winburn and deftly changed the subject, firmly closing the door on any further discussion. "Oh, this was an excellent suggestion. The chicken salad is delicious."

Janet took another large sip of wine and pretended to enjoy her salad.

****

The two women finished an uncomfortable meal, with Janet sharing nothing new for Kate's article.

Walking out together, they parted company at the corner, each going their separate ways; Kate to her car and Janet doubling back to the restaurant.

Janet waited until the man paid his check and exited, meeting her in the parking garage as arranged. Throughout the meal with Kate, Janet had tried to smile and act as if nothing was wrong. She felt the pressure of the man watching, waiting. The chicken salad she always enjoyed tasted like sawdust in her mouth. He was expecting her to ferret out information about Sam Slater's investigation. It was one more favor he'd called in. She feared if she didn't have anything to give him, he'd make good on his promise. She couldn't risk it. Her daughter was too precious.

Chapter 6

Ray closed on the house two blocks over. He and Jake made a good team, working to fix the place up. They remodeled the garage apartment in record time and Ray moved in, giving Sam and Kate their home and their privacy back. All the same, Kate made sure the family continued their weekly dinner and game night. The two couples had started the tradition when Emily originally befriended Kate. It had been Emily's devious plan for getting Kate and Sam together. Then when Jake came to town to help Sam with the remodel of his house, the four just seemed to click and it became a regular entertainment. When Marianne was alive, she had taught Kate to play pinochle. Since Ray enjoyed cards, the family scheduled a weekly date. Kate was new to the game, but everyone soon discovered she had a natural talent for counting trump and a cut-throat approach to bidding.

It was a pleasantly cool evening for Texas. Showers had moved through overnight, washing the air and relieving the humidity. Emily had her shoes off, feet in Jake's lap. He managed to drink his beer in between massaging her swollen ankles. Kate called dibs for his services when he finished with Emily.

Sam was playing bartender and everyone was enjoying their pre-dinner beverage while the coals heated, when Feelie trotted up with a mouse in her mouth. Proudly dropping her trophy, she mewed, bumping her head against Ray's legs.

"Whoa, what have we here?" Ray asked the cat, like he fully expected an answer. Feelie chirruped in response.

Kate rolled her eyes and shivered squeamishly. Tilting her head, she motioned for Sam to remove the little critter.

Ray laughed at Kate's feminine discomfort. "Oh, Kate. For such a strong, determined woman, you are still a sissy."

Kate playfully stuck her tongue out at Ray while Sam removed the offending carcass and whispered in her ear, "Yeah, but you're my sissy," causing her to blush.

"She's a good mouser." Ray considered the cat, who meowed indignantly as Sam placed her prize in the trash can, firmly replacing the lid. "I may have to borrow her for a couple of weeks. There is a serious wildlife issue at my place. I thought cutting down the weeds would solve the problem, but the neighbor isn't helping. I went next door to ask about cutting the lawn and a teenage girl gave me the stink eye. She and her brother live there with their grandmother. I don't think the dad is around and I heard their mom is doing a three-year stay at the greybar hotel for kiting checks, theft over fifteen hundred dollars. I think she also had a couple of brushes with prostitution. Not your upstanding citizen. Mrs. Camarillo is the grandmother. I spoke to her. She seems like a real nice lady. I offered to help clean up their yard. Thought maybe I'd wrangle you and Jake to help me, Sam. Can you spare some time on Saturday? If we do it, I figure they'll owe me and we might build a relationship."

Sam laughed and raised his glass to his dad's plan. "I'm sure Mrs. Camarillo will appreciate your efforts, but I'm not sure about the kids. I can come by Saturday about seven. Start on the big stuff before the heat hits." Jake agreed to help, as well. He and Ray had grown closer, rehabbing the old house Ray had purchased. Sometimes Sam was a little envious of their friendship, but he had a lot more hurdles to get over than Jake ever had. The three men talked about what they hoped to do and what tools they'd need to accomplish it.

****

Sam pulled up at 7 a.m. sharp, his jeep loaded with loppers, a weed eater, rake, and trash bags. Jake was right behind him. Besides a similar collection of hand tools in the back of his truck, Jake had a chipper shredder and chain saw. Grinning at Sam, he flexed his muscles and called out, "Bigger is better. More power."

Ray was laughing at Jake's one-up-man-ship as he walked over, handing each a cup of coffee. He led them next door to survey the project. "Don't look now, but we have an audience." Ray motioned subtly with his cup at a thin boy standing inside the back door. Turning on twinkling eyes and a grandfatherly smile, Ray waved hello and motioned the young boy to join them. A reluctant lad, about ten years old, stepped out the door. His hand remained on the handle as if he might bolt back into the house's air-conditioned sanctuary at any moment.

"Good morning. You must be Vincent. Your grandmother said you and your sister, Angela, are living with her. She said you're a big help around the house. Said you might help us with the back yard clean up."

Vincent looked warily at the three men. Then his eyes roamed over the yard, taking in the tall grass, dead tree, and battered lawn furniture. He shook his head and scooted back into the house.

"Okay, that went well, didn't it?" Sam snorted. Ray shrugged.

"Baby steps," Ray said, laughing. "Baby steps." Ray slapped Jake on the back and the three got to work.

While Jake revved up his chainsaw to take down the tree, Sam and Ray cleaned up the collection of broken bits and pieces of furniture and scrap construction materials. Once they cleared the lawn, Ray mowed while Sam trimmed bushes. They were all acutely aware of the watchful eyes of young Vincent. By mid-morning, things were looking pretty good. Mrs. Camarillo came out with iced tea.

"Oh, Mr. Ray. It looks so much better. Not since my Pete died, has it looked like this. You all sit. Sit. Take a break. I have tea and will bring out sandwiches. Vincent, come out here and meet our neighbor and his friends." A less than enthused Vincent stepped out and stood off to the side. Sam thought he wasn't as much indifferent as afraid. It looked like the boy had trouble trusting 'the man'. Lots of kids from families where their folks have trouble with the police are distrustful of authority figures. Sam thought Ray had his work cut out for him if he hoped to befriend the boy. Sam shot the young man a grin, then pulled Jake to the side to discuss his idea for a small brick pad for the rusty grill and a bird bath fashioned from the dead tree stump.

Ray and Mrs. Camarillo visited as Sam and Jake got to work. They checked out the stack of bricks uncovered when cutting back the weeds.

"Mrs. Camarillo?" Sam called. "Do you have any plans for these bricks?"

"No. I don't know anything about what to do with bricks. My Pete was a mason. He was collecting the left-over bricks from his work and wanted to build a barbeque. He never found the time." She pulled a kleenex from her pocket and wiped her eyes. "We use the weber. It works just fine."

Sam noticed the grief pass over his dad's face, thinking the two older folks had a lot in common.

"There looks to be enough bricks to make a small pad for your weber. Jake and I will see what we can do." The two men joked and laughed as they worked. Sam tossed bricks to Jake, who handily caught them and, at one point, poorly juggled three of them. Vincent watched and slowly crept a little closer. Sam went to get a shovel and the bag of sand from his dad's garage. He returned to see Jake studying the layout, hands in his pockets, whistling between his teeth. A shy Vincent crept closer, trying to peer around him.

"What are you going to do with the bricks?" a quiet voice asked from behind. Jake glanced over his shoulder and shrugged, like it was nothing.

"Thought we'd lay a pad for your grill, maybe cut some of the tree trunk to make stools. And Sam? That's the other guy? He wants to make a bird bath out of the stump."

"You can do that?" Vincent was now next to Jake, leaning forward to get a closer look at the pile of bricks. "How?"

"Well, we'll clear a patch of ground here, see? Then we'll dig a shallow square to create a base for the brick. We'll fill it with sand and level it off." Jake was motioning, pointing and using the toe of his boot to draw lines in the dirt. Vincent focused on the process. "Do you know why we lay sand in the square?" Jake asked.

"Uh-uh." Vincent looked at Jake, shaking his head.

Man and boy squatted down, heads together as Jake explained the reasons for sand, the purpose of leveling, and the need for drainage. Sam looked on, thinking Jake would be a patient father. He stole a look at his own father and wondered how their relationship would have differed had Ray possessed some of the same qualities.

"Looks like you drafted some help, Jake. Hi, Vincent. I'm Sam. Ray, your neighbor, is my dad. I live a couple of blocks over. This here is Jake. He's my brother-in-law and best buddy. We really appreciate your helping us out with this." Jake and Sam extended their hands to shake with Vincent. Sam saw his hesitation until realization dawned on the boy's face. Vincent shyly took each offered hand. The first shake was tentative, but both Jake and Sam offered a firm grip. Vincent would learn, Sam thought.

Jake handed the shovel to Vincent and showed him how to cut the shallow square. He and Vincent went to work. Sam stepped up to the porch for more iced tea. He listened as Mrs. Camarillo explained to Ray about the family situation.

"It is difficult. My husband, Pete, died last year. He would have been such a big help with the children. They haven't seen their father in years. We don't know where the man is. Their mother made some poor decisions. She let men… Well, people have to eat, pay for a roof over their heads. Vincent is a good boy. He needs a good man to mentor him. Angela is fourteen. She is a typical teenage girl, more interested in make-up and clothes. She spends all her time on social media. A young girl has befriended her and they're spending some time together. I worry she might follow in her mother's footsteps. But I think having girlfriends is healthy.

"You have a wonderful family, Ray. I am pleased to have you as a neighbor. You're a good man. Pete would have liked you. I wish he were here." Mrs. Camarillo fussed with the cloth on the table and the pitcher of tea. She had added a plate of empanadas for snacking. "A boy needs a father. Vincent is shy, but I see him watching you. He is smart and curious. See him now? He wants to learn what and why." Her gaze moved to Vincent, working side by side with Jake. They'd both stripped off their shirts. The sun beat down on their sweat-streaked backs. Vincent gave Jake a sloppy grin and turned to get the bag of sand. It was heavy for a boy his size, but Jake left him to haul it over on his own. The effort earned Vincent a pat on the back from Jake and a 'well-done' from Sam. Vincent stood a little taller and grinned proudly.

When they finished the grill pad, they took a break to enjoy the sandwiches Mrs. Camarillo had prepared. Jake and Vincent wolfed theirs down, ready for the next project. Sam saw it was his turn at bat. He finished his lunch and took the time to explain his vision for the project to Vincent. After gathering up the materials and tools they'd need, Sam showed Vincent how to drill a hole in the stump. Keeping a watchful eye on the boy, Sam let him use the power tool. Vincent's brow furrowed in concentration, his tongue steering the bit as it cut into the surface of the wood. Sam rescued a chipped basin from the Camarillo's garage. He set the base into the hole, securing it with a water-proof adhesive. They filled it with water and took a break to enjoy more iced tea, looking proudly at the results of their labors. When the first bird found the clear water, Vincent let out a powerful whoop of delight. The bird flew away, but the look of accomplishment on Vincent's face soared.

Sam returned home about three p.m., dirty, sweaty, and grinning foolishly. Kate met him at the door and immediately straight armed him before he could give her a messy hug. "Oh, no you don't, mister. Shower first." She pushed him toward the stairs. "I'll have a cold beer ready for you, along with a kiss when you're cleaned up." His grin only got bigger as Sam managed a quick peck on his way to the bathroom, leaving a smudge of dirt on Kate's cheek.

Fifteen minutes later, with the water drops still glistening on his hair, his five o'clock shadow stubbling his cheeks, Sam returned to the kitchen. He claimed both the beer and the kiss. Kate melted into his arms. "Mr. Slater, what you do to me," Kate purred in his ear. "Now tell me why your smile is splitting your face in two."

Sam took a long swig from his beer and then pulled on Kate's hand, leading her to the couch in the family room. He plopped down and put his bare feet on the coffee table, relaxing back with a sigh. "You should have been there. Mrs. Camarillo is the next-door neighbor. She's been on her own for a while. Her husband died last year, and she's raising her two grandkids by herself. She's a sweetheart. We started by clearing out the debris, took down a dead tree, and trimmed the bushes. Vincent, that's the ten-year-old grandson. He's a nice kid. Slow to warm up, but boy, once that kid lets his guard down, he'll talk your ear off. I think dad will have a shadow whenever he is outside. The granddaughter is Angela. She never darkened the door. From what Mrs. Camarillo says, she is a typical teenager, more interested in girl stuff and boys than in school. Mrs. Camarillo is concerned for her, worried she will make the same foolish choices as her mother." Sam took another sip of his beer. He put his arm around Kate and pulled her closer.

"Mrs. Camarillo and dad seemed to hit it off. I think their shared grief gives them a lot in common. She's a widow and comfortable talking about her husband. I hope it helps dad talk more freely about mom and his loss." Sam grew pensive, thinking.

Returning to the here and now, he motioned with his bottle, telling Kate about Jake's easy way with the boy, the natural camaraderie between the two. "Geez, when Jake took off his shirt and Vincent saw his scars, well, you can imagine the fascination and questions. Jake told him about some of our missions in Afghanistan. Vincent's eyes were the size of half dollars with Jake's exaggerated tales." Sam snorted. "Talk about hero worship. Oh, and, you should have seen dad. He was…" Sam looked for the right word. "Solid. Showed him how to do stuff—had tons of patience. Ruffled his hair a couple of times." Sam's smile faded. "It made me realize how much I wanted that as a kid." Sam couldn't hide the sadness in his voice. Kate laid a comforting hand on his cheek.

"You can't go back, Sam, but you can move forward and cherish every moment. The bonds you build with your dad now will be different, but no less special, and when we have our own son, you will build them with him." Sam covered Kate's hand with his own, bringing her palm to his lips and kissing it.

"I wonder all the time how lucky I am to have you, Kate Slater. You are my life-giving water."

Kate gave him a gentle kiss and went to fix dinner as Sam continued to share the highlights of the day. When Sam paused in his storytelling, Kate turned.

Tilting her head, she asked. "So, your dad is going to teach him to use the mower. He'll let him borrow it for his grandmother's lawn and then Ray will pay him to use it to mow his lawn. I suppose you will hire him to do ours too? You Slater men are very clever."

Sam blew out a loud guffaw. "Ha, not as clever as Jake. Vincent said he'd mow his for free!"

Chapter 7

Sam felt the first flush of dawn on his face. He rose quietly and went downstairs to start the coffee. Kate woke later to an empty bed. Sam was sitting at his desk reviewing files, tracking new leads, reviewing evidence. He saw her slipping on her robe as she padded down the stairs. He sighed, not wanting to expose Kate to the grimness of his work. Human trafficking across the southern border was taking an emotional toll. He never shared a lot about his work, but it was difficult to hide the shadows in his eyes when he came home from work. Kate stepped behind him, using her nimble fingers to work on the knots in his neck and shoulders that lately never seemed to go away. Sam leaned back, closing his eyes, enjoying her touch.

"Sam, this case seems to weigh heavily on you. I understand the challenges faced by the illegal immigrants. If I were in their situation, I might risk everything for a better life for my family too. But the number of illegal crossings is so great. The border towns can't keep up. The influx of people is overwhelming. The towns lack the resources to deal with it. I don't think the so-called sanctuary cities in the north can fully appreciate the difficulties, and now Texas is busing these poor people to them. I'm conflicted. Part of me hates the idea of busing and part of me supports it. It isn't fair to those citizens living near the border to carry the entire burden created by the flood of humanity all by themselves. But that's not all for you, is it? What is it that worries you so much?"

Sam took Kate's hand and pulled her around to his lap. Snuggling her in, he rested his cheek on her hair, taking comfort in the way her soft curves molded to his body.

"Kate, what I'm working on is vile. You know I've been in contact with the El Paso division of Homeland Security. Well, they're working with the Presidio County Sherriff's Department regarding missing girls. They discovered two more bodies of teenage girls in the desert. There's no proof of a connection to kidnapping or child pornography. But I believe the Coyotes that smuggle Mexican nationals across the border for exorbitant sums of money are convincing families to send their children in the hope for that better life you speak of. The human smugglers promise the parents that they will connect the children with family over here or find a loving family to care for them until mom and dad can afford the fee to come over themselves. What I'm finding is that they use those children for their own nefarious purposes. There has been a significant increase in internet and printed porn featuring Latino children. It's going viral, exploding."

"That's horrible, Sam, but how can you hope to stop it? You can't reach every family in Mexico and warn them. And they wouldn't take you seriously, anyway. They'd say it was a lie perpetrated by the US to slow immigration. There isn't an answer, is there? Nothing you can do?"

"The state department is working their channels to curb the influx of illegals. I need to find the criminals and stop the crime. If I can take the profit out of the operation, they'll slow if not stop. Follow the money, right?" Sam's lips curled in disgust; his nostrils flared in anger. "But I'll never find it all. There will always be those who profit off the misery of others. The number of exploitation and human-trafficking cases we prosecute are only the tip of the iceberg."

Chapter 8

The summer heat made Emily's pregnancy uncomfortable. With Kate's help, the women had been charting the pregnancy milestones. Kate made it her mission to take Em's mind off how big she was getting or how tired she was by planning special relaxing activities. They were inseparable during this time.

"Oh, Kate, you have no idea how special a pedicure is nowadays. I mean, I can't even see my feet, let alone reach them." Emily hoisted herself up into the massage chair, turning it on low. She groaned with pleasure as the warm, swirling waters soothed her tired feet and swollen ankles.

Kate let a similar sound escape as she relaxed into position and let the operator work her magic. "Are you kidding? I can see my feet and still wouldn't want to give this up."

Emily nodded. The women were simpatico. "By the way, I found an article on making homemade baby food. With dad planting a garden, we'll have organic veggies. Speaking about dad. Things have been great since Jake and I accepted his offer to move into the house. I can't believe Dad deeded the property to us. Of course, he attached stipulations, like living in the garage apartment and having first dibs on babysitting. How sweet is that?"

"Sweeter than I could ever imagine." Kate felt the

light tap from the technician and shifted her feet. "How are things at the house? Are you okay being so close to Dad? And how is it living next door to Mrs. Camarillo?"

"Kate, it's actually better than I ever thought. We're in separate houses, so it doesn't feel as close as you'd think. And Dad respects our privacy." Emily paused a moment, sliding a look in Kate's direction, uncertainty in her voice.

"Kate, I know Sam is trying to reconcile with Dad. They seem to be making good progress. Has Sam said anything? I mean, does he feel any better about all the…you know, stuff between them?"

Kate's brow furrowed. She knew Ray loved Sam and was proud of him. She wanted the two men to grow closer, to once again be a father and son, but Sam hid his feelings so well that she wasn't sure where he was on the journey to reconciliation.

"Oh, Emily, you know your brother. Sam internalizes so much. I know he wants to be closer to Ray. I see him watching his dad, measuring every word and action." Kate reached over, taking Emily's hand in hers. "The fact that Jake and Ray get along so well and have such an easy comradery helps. It's almost as if Sam is using Jake to test the waters. He sees Jake, someone he loves and trusts, accepting the hand of friendship and affection from Ray, someone Sam didn't trust for so long."

Kate sighed and leaned back in her chair, closing her eyes in a silent prayer. "I think it will happen without Sam even realizing it. Suddenly, he'll just get it."

Emily nodded. She knew her brother. "I think you

hit that nail on the head."

Kate laughed. "Emily, is that 'carpenterese' you're speaking?"

Emily tossed a puzzled look toward Kate. "What? Oh, 'nail on the head'. Yeah. I guess when you spend so much time with two carpenters, you begin to talk like them. I wonder why my art conversations never rubbed off on Jake."

Kate snorted a laugh. "Oh, Emily. He admitted long before you married him, he'd always be a philistine."

Emily nodded philosophically, then completely changed the subject, launching into a new topic. "Hey, did you know Isabell sews and crochets? She said she'll teach us how to do it. I can just see us. We'll be drinking wine and getting all tangled up in yarn."

"Hmm, doesn't sound very safe. But if you're game, I'll give it a try." Kate smiled at the thought of a crocheting disaster in the making. The only dark cloud over their heads was Angela, Isabell Camarillo's granddaughter. "Emily, how is Angela doing? Has Isabell mentioned anything?"

"I don't see her that often. Isabell says she is always out hanging around with a girlfriend. She has missed curfew a few times. It sounds like typical fourteen-year-old behavior. Is there something in particular you're thinking?"

Kate flashed back to some comments Isabell had made regarding clothes and make-up choices. Perhaps it was typical teenage drama. She wondered how much to share with Emily. The last thing she wanted to do was worry her unnecessarily. Kate hummed non-committedly and changed the subject.

"How's Jake doing? Any nerves? Have you run out of dill pickles yet?"

Emily laughed. "Oh, Kate, he is such a goober. Now he's eating pickled beets. I wonder what he'll do when I start breast feeding. Ouch! But besides that, I can't wait for you to see the nursery. They finally unveiled it. It's so precious." Emily bubbled over with enthusiasm about the work Ray and Jake had done. How they had transformed the smaller bedroom into the nursery, painting it sky blue.

"Jake reached out to an artist from the Art from Darkness show I premiered at the McGill Gallery. He painted a mural of Noah's ark on the wall with a pair of storks flying overhead. It's perfect for us. A baby hangs from the mamma stork's beak and the daddy stork is circling around protectively on a Harley-Davidson motorcycle with wings. There is a moat around the house. I picked up a white fluffy throw rug to warm up the bare oak floor and Dad refinished a rocker and covered the cushions in dark blue corduroy. A changing table and bassinet complete the furnishings. Jake is building me a bookcase to hold all the baby's toys and books." Emily smiled contentedly, rubbing at her growing baby bump. "Oh, the little guy is up and raring to go. Here, feel him kicking?"

Kate placed her hand over the baby bump. The imprint of a tiny foot pushed against her palm. She felt a little envious.

Chapter 9

Now that Ray was done with the house, Father John tapped him for special projects at church and Isabell Camarillo had grown to rely on him for help with minor repairs around her home. Ray enjoyed doing the little things. It wasn't unusual to see him and his apprentice, Vincent, working together on the odd handyman job. Ray had invited the Camarillo's to St. Mark's. The youth group immediately welcomed Vincent. He made a lot of new friends, enrolled in the confirmation class, and Ray stood as his sponsor. There was a touching bond growing between the two. It filled Ray's lonely hours. The only troubling concern was Angela. Now that school was out, she was rarely home, and neglected her chores. She spent her time hanging out at the park with her girlfriends. The family had enjoyed some Sunday afternoon get-togethers. Kate liked Angela, but like her grandmother, was worried about her. Angela was fourteen going on thirty. She spent too much time on her phone.

"Angela," Isabell called, "please take the potato salad to the table." The kitchen was crowded, all the women dishing up fresh vegetables. They were feasting on the bumper crop from Ray's garden. Onions, green peppers, green beans, and corn, all of which under Isabell's tutelage, the women had used to create delicious salads and side dishes to go with the chicken

Ray was grilling.

Isabell walked to the door separating the kitchen from the living room. "Angela! Did you hear me?" A sullen teen walked in, tucking her phone into her back pocket and grabbed the potato salad. "Here, don't forget the spoon." Angela let out a bored sigh, turning back for the spoon Isabell held out to her. She snatched it and huffed out to the dining room.

"Some days, I don't know what to do with that girl." Isabell shook her head. "All she does is stay on that damn phone. When questioned about it, she puts it away and says it's a dance video. I hear all these stories about social media and sexting. It worries me."

Isabell's comment reminded Kate of Janet Winburn's observation about soft porn. Angela was watching music videos, which were too often similar to soft porn. They were suggestive and sexualized. The only lack was that the women wore clothes.

While the women worked in the kitchen, the men congregated around the new weber Ray had gifted the Camarillos, swapping stories. Vincent was fascinated by Sam and Jake's service in the SEALs. Since seeing the battle scars on Jake's back, he was constantly quizzing Jake and Sam about their service in Afghanistan.

"So how hot does it get in Afghanistan? I mean, Texas is hot. I bet you guys were cool with it."

Jake opted to field this question. "Well, Vincent, Sam had it easy, but I'm from Colorado. It's not as hot there. We get snow where I grew up. Why I remember one winter we had over four feet fall in one day."

Sam watched Vincent's eyes narrow with disbelief. He appreciated Jake's attempt to change the subject.

But Vincent was tenacious as a pit bull.

"Yeah, yeah, yeah. And you had to walk to school uphill both ways." Vincent rolled his eyes, bobbing his head from side to side.

Hoping to distract him from the topic, Sam sent him to get a platter for the chicken.

Vincent dodged a good-natured nuggie from Jake and ran, bouncing into the house. "Chicken's ready, grandma. Sam says we need a platter." The distraction didn't last long.

At dinner, Vincent wouldn't let it rest. "But did you kill any bad guys?" Vincent was chomping down on an ear of corn, butter greasing the rim of his glass as he took a swig of ice-cold milk. "You were a sniper, right, Jake?"

Jake passed the ball to Sam, clearly in over his head. While both men down-played their role in the military, Sam spoke about his work in law enforcement, and how his education and law degree were used to fight crime. "But, Vincent, I'm sure the ladies would prefer to talk about something else at the dinner table."

Mollified for the time being, but not pacified, Vincent studied Sam's work with Homeland Security. He dug up the newspaper articles about the Ramirez drug cartel and Sam's role as head of the task force assigned to the case. Vincent worshipped Ray for his skills with a hammer and saw, but with red, white, and blue stars in his eyes, Vincent thought Sam walked on water. He'd pester Sam every chance he got about crime, unsolved cases, and bad guys. Sam tried to sluff it off, but Vincent was persistent. He wanted to learn everything Sam could teach him. In the imagination of a ten-year-old boy, Vincent was sure that Sam could single-handedly save the world. Kate would laugh. Sometimes she thought the same thing.

Sam finally caved to Vincent's persistence. Until school started, he agreed to hold 'spy' training.

"So, you think this will be easygoing? Be at my house tomorrow morning, six a.m. sharp. Wear your running shoes. We'll start with calisthenics and strength training."

Sam stressed the importance of personal responsibility, so following their morning workout, Vincent had an hour for breakfast and chores at home while Sam went for his usual run. While Sam was out, he observed odd items along his route between home and the Camarillos, like a newly pruned shrub or broken porch rail. When he returned from his run, Sam assigned Vincent to find these items throughout the day. Vincent reported to Sam at the end of the workday with his detections. The purpose of this exercise was to improve his skills of observation.

"Don't go thinking this is all physical. Spy craft is a thinking man's game. You won't solve crimes or survive without smarts, both book and street." Sam pointed out the importance of good grades. He figured one should take advantage of every opportunity presented. Sam selected a few books on spy craft. Vincent was to read for one hour every afternoon. Sam taught him the value of strength, good nutrition, and sleep. Funny how kids will do things they'd normally shun when it involves something cool, like spy work. Mrs. Camarillo and Ray assisted with the observation challenges. Sam had a small pottery bluebird that they placed somewhere in one of their homes. It was Vincent's assignment to find it. Sam explained to everyone that this exercise trained Vincent to watch for things out of the ordinary or out of place. They timed his efforts. When he got proficient in that, they traded the bluebird out for a small green shamrock, and the hiding places were less obvious.

Ray was so excited for Vincent that he joined in the fun by taking walks with the young man. They worked on identifying car makes and models and memorizing license plate numbers. This was all really cool, but Vincent's favorite thing to practice was following and surveillance. He worked with Sam on Sunday afternoons, learning how to watch reflections in windows, to cross the street occasionally, how to follow at a distance, and how to hide in plain sight. Sam also taught him the basics of evasion.

Vincent drafted Ray to help him with that. They'd hang out at the mall, choosing a mark and following them. Sometimes it freaked people out when they thought they were being watched. Of course, he and Ray looked so innocent that no one suspected them. Vincent was a good kid. Ray enjoyed working with him. Finally, Vincent was ready for graduation from Spy School.

"Are you ready for your Spy Challenge?" Ray asked as he drove an antsy Vincent to the park. "It's going to be a big challenge. Sam won't make it easy on you, but I think you've got this. You've been doing a lot of work on your spy skills. Good luck, buddy!" Ray dropped Vincent off to meet Sam and he hurried off to play his part in the test.

"Good morning, Vincent!" Sam smiled at Vincent's punctuality and reviewed his recruit. "Ready and right on time. Are you prepared for the final exam for Spy School 101?"

"Un-huh," Vincent replied, looking around, pre-occupied with anticipating what Sam would ask him to do. His head swiveled from side to side. Vincent was trying to see everything, anything, out of place. He was sure that would be part of the test.

Sam used his drill sergeant voice to demand Vincent's attention. "I'm sorry. I didn't hear you, recruit?"

Vincent immediately came to attention. "I mean, sir, yes, sir. Ready to begin the exercise, sir!"

"Very good. Here is your assignment." Sam outlined the steps to be taken. It wasn't a recording like Mission Impossible, but the expectation was clear. And so, it begun.

Vincent knew the location of the dead drop. He and Sam had used it in previous exercises. When he got there, Vincent found a typed coded message. He was required to decipher the code and follow the instructions. It was quickly done.

'*Your mission is to find the man in the yellow shirt. Surveil and follow the subject. He will place a dead drop. Retrieve the package and follow the instructions.*'

Vincent looked up. There were two men in yellow shirts. One was older and carried about fifty extra pounds around his waist. His pants were khaki-colored dockers and his shoes, well-worn Nikes. He carried a sack of peanuts, dropping them one by one for the squirrels. The second subject was younger. He wore a yellow t-shirt with the logo of a pro football team on the back. He wore running shorts and carried a football. Both men walked off in different directions. Vincent had to make a split-second decision about whom to follow. Vincent chose the older man. The younger man's shirt wasn't entirely yellow. Vincent thought that might be his first test.

Keeping his distance, Vincent crossed the play area, following his mark. He passed a woman with a stroller. She wore a bright blue jacket and a red ball cap. Her earrings didn't match. Stopping to admire the baby, Vincent kept the yellow shirt in his field of vision, letting a few more yards separate them. He walked by the ice cream stand where a vendor offered Blue Logoon sno-cones for 500 cents. Two teenage girls wearing matching pink sun dresses waited in line. One wore tennis shoes with mismatched shoelaces of red and green.

When a family group walked past him, Vincent followed closely on their heels, giving the impression to anyone watching that he was part of the larger group. He continued with them until the yellow shirt turned toward the Koi Pond. Vincent stopped at the turnoff and waited, reading the signage and looking lost, all the while keeping the yellow shirt in his field of vision. When the yellow shirt took a seat on a park bench, Vincent strolled down the walkway and past the mark. About a hundred feet down the walk, he passed a shrub that encroached on the path. Scooting behind the green screen, Vincent watched as the yellow shirt fed the rest of his peanuts to the squirrels. He stuffed the empty bag in a crevice between the slats on the bench, stood, and walked away.

Vincent waited three minutes. He was sure Sam was watching him. He searched the surrounding area. Vincent couldn't see him anywhere. He shook his head. Man, Sam was good. Vincent hoped he'd be that good someday. Eventually, Vincent wandered back down the path. He took a seat at the vacated park bench to tie his shoe. He sat back and casually laid his hand next to the paper bag. Surreptitiously palming the bag, Vincent put it in his pocket. He sat another two minutes and then moved further along the path, where he pulled it out and read the next phase of his challenge.

'Well done. Phase two. Walk toward the Koi Pond. A woman will approach you. She will give you a coded greeting. -Koi have teeth in their throats.- You will report three things that you saw while following yellow shirt that did not belong.'

Vincent looked around, then back down the path toward where he had followed yellow shirt. He ran through every step of the way in his mind, considering. *What did I notice while following yellow shirt?* When Vincent had it, a grin creased his face. He casually strolled to the pond and waited.

A wizened Asian woman waddled over to stand next to Vincent. "Koi use their teeth to communicate."

Vincent smiled at the woman. "That's interesting. Never knew they even had teeth." He shrugged and walked further along the rail.

It took only a few minutes for a woman wearing a floppy sun hat to approach the rail. He recognized Kate but played along, waiting to see what came next. She squatted down to toss cracker crumbs into the water, laughing as the water boiled with the movement of the fish fighting over the treat. "Koi have teeth in their throats." She offered some crumbs to Vincent, who knelt on one knee next to her and whispered the answers.

"The woman with the stroller had mismatched

earrings, one blue, one green. They spelled the name of the sno-cone wrong. Logoon, not Lagoon, and sold it for five hundred cents. The girl in the pink dress wore shoes with mismatched shoelaces, red and green."

Kate tipped back her floppy brim and smiled brilliantly at Vincent. Sam strolled over from behind some nearby trees. His hand extended. "Well done, Vincent. I'd say you passed this first part of the challenge."

Standing tall, Vincent took Sam's hand, shaking it. His grip was sure and firm. He looked from Sam to Kate with eyes that sparkled with pride.

"One more test, Vincent," Sam said. "Look around. What do you see?"

Vincent turned in a slow circle, taking in everything that seemed ordinary and everything that didn't. He laughed out loud. "Ha. Ray and Jake are posing as park employees. Emily is sitting on that blanket over there. Grandma, you shouldn't nap on park benches and, Angela, don't look so bored."

Everyone bounded up and over, laughing and congratulating Vincent on his success. Even Angela gave him a nudge of approval with a shoulder bump.

"Come on, everyone, ice cream is on me, but no Blue Logoon." Laughing at his 'dad' joke, Sam put one arm around Vincent's shoulders, the other around Kate's.

Vincent's brow creased. He had to ask. "Sam, who was the old Asian lady?"

Sam ruffled Vincent's hair. "Our dry-cleaner. You owe her one lawn mowing for her time." He laughed as Vincent's mouth dropped open in astonishment. It was a good day.

****

While Vincent was earning his espionage epaulettes, Kate took a well-earned break from writing about exploitation. She spent her time tending to the garden, the house, and herself. Nesting was the term she used when she puttered around their home. When she picked up her pen, she wrote about flower shows and the annual competition for the State Fair of Texas 'Big Tex Choice Awards'. It was amazing how creative the entrants were. It still shocked her that fried butter on a stick took the prize one year. Sounded like hardening of the arteries to Kate, but the fair goers would scarf down whatever concoction won. Planning Emily's baby shower filled the rest of her time.

On the day of the big event, Kate was up early, preparing for the shower she and Isabell were giving Emily and Jake. Even though baby showers are traditionally a female ritual, Kate invited couples and many male friends. She drafted Ray and Sam to help with the setup.

"Sam, did you ice down the beer? Oh, and, Ray, can you set up the folding chairs in the family room?" Kate blew hair out of her eyes, elbow deep in fruit salad. "Sammie's is delivering the barbecue at eleven. The paper plates are in the butler's pantry. Would you get those, Sam?" Kate barked out orders and mustered her troops.

Sam carried an armload of supplies in and grabbed Kate around the waist. "I love a woman who knows how to make a man do her bidding!" He nipped at her neck. "Want to try it again later, naked?"

"Sam, shush! Your dad will hear!" Kate felt the heat flow over her face and down her body. "Oh, Sam," she hummed deep in her throat as he nuzzled her neck. "I always want to try a lot of things with you naked!"

He grinned and wiggled his butt, then went to help Ray finish with the chairs.

Isabell and Vincent knocked before letting themselves in. They carefully carried in the three-layer cake Isabell had made, placing it on the table. "Whew! I was afraid it would tip over in the car and we'd have a real mess. Thank you for your help, Vincent. Why don't you go see if Sam and Ray need you?" Freed from having to take part in the conversation about babies and booties, Vincent rushed away, looking for testosterone like a heat-seeking missile.

Kate came up to Isabell and put an arm around the older woman's shoulder. "Oh, Isabell. It's beautiful. Much better than anything we could have ordered from the bakery. I love the blue icing rattles and bottles you piped around the sides. They are absolutely adorable. Just something else you'll have to teach Emily and me to do."

"What are we going to learn now?" Emily asked, coming in the back door behind the two women.

"Cake decorating," Kate said, turning to see Emily carrying a large box. "Emily, put that down, this moment. This is your baby shower. What are you thinking carrying a big box?"

"I'm not an invalid and if you think this box is heavy, try carrying around the two-ton giant in my stomach. I swear, this kid is going to come out ready to play for the TCU Horn Frogs!" Emily waddled over to the stool and plopped down with a sigh. "Can a pregnant woman get a peach tea?"

Kate laughed and hopped to it, pouring one for

herself and Isabell as well.

"Oh, my goodness. He is active today. Feels like a tap dancer in there. Last night, I swear, he was practicing to be a tumbler for Cirque de Soleil. Here, take a feel." Emily opened her arms. "Good Lord. You can see his little feet pushing against my stomach. What a bruiser." Emily shook her finger at Kate's barely suppressed laughter. "Ha. You wait! You'll be here in no time."

Emily was right and Kate hoped it would be sooner rather than later. After a few minutes of visiting and feeling the baby doing River Dance in Emily's tummy, Kate took a last walk through to insure everything was in its place. Satisfied, she gave Sam a radiant smile and a kiss. Sam pulled her into the butler's pantry, taking the kiss deeper, drawing a moan of pleasure from her. Saved by the bell, Kate hurried to answer the door.

The party was going full force with plenty of food, drink, and laughter. Isabell's cake was almost as big a hit as feeling Emily's baby kick in time to the music playing in the background. The women noted Baby Edwards was a contender for a starring role in the next production of 'Cagney, the Musical'. The men tried to hide out as much as allowed in the backyard, risking death from heat prostration rather than brave the air-conditioned house with the chattering women.

When the time came to open gifts, the guys stood awkwardly around the perimeter of the room. The unindoctrinated ones shifted nervously from foot to foot, while the older men smiled knowingly at the younger. The gals sat in a tight circle around Emily, oohing and awing over the cute outfits gifted to the baby. When Emily unwrapped the double electric breast pump, with hands free operation, the men could stand no more. They panicked, quickly retiring to the garden. They drank more beer and teased Jake about things to come. Sam wasn't immune. Beads of sweat broke out on his forehead.

When the last of the guests had departed, Kate insisted Emily sit with her feet propped up and relax.

"Isabell, can I ask you something? Something about babies?" Emily shyly asked.

Kate saw the warmth and love in Isabell's eyes when she looked at Emily. Isabell had grown to be like a mother to both young women.

Taking a seat next to Emily, Isabell patted her hand. "Of course, sweetheart. What do you want to ask?"

"I read an article on breast feeding and when to wean the baby. Some books suggest up to two years. And in olden days, they did it for up to seven years!"

Kate looked over and watched the blood drain from Jake's face. Holding back laughter, she sputtered, "Sam, you better take Jake out back to the garden and give him another beer. He has a pickled beet glaze in his eyes." Sam was pale himself.

****

Emily grew bigger and rounder while Jake grew more anxious. When the big day arrived, Emily calmly walked into the workshop to announce it was time.

Jake had on ear protectors so didn't hear Emily when she entered. Since he was working with power tools, she didn't want to flick the lights to get his attention, as she had done in the past. Shrugging, Emily walked over and unplugged the saw. Jake ripped off his safety goggles, thinking something was wrong with his

85

equipment. He turned with a frustrated harrumph and gazed at a smiling Emily, patting her belly.

"What?" he asked. Then the light dawned and his mouth dropped open. "Oh. Oh! Wait, wait, wait. Hold on. I got this." Patting his pockets, Jake ran through his checklist. "Um, car keys? Cell phone? You okay? Contractions coming fast?" Jake was holding Emily around the waist, walking her to the car. "Let's get you loaded up. We'll call everyone on the way, right?"

"I'm good. Contractions are about eight minutes apart. I think you have time to get the suitcase by the back door." She was laughing softly and smiling widely when she stopped. "Oh, buddy. Here comes another one."

"Breathe baby, breathe. I got you." Jake held on, was a rock all the way to the hospital. Ray, Sam, and Kate arrived just as they were wheeling Emily off to prep her. They walked in to witness Jake sinking down onto the bench, white as a sheet and grinning like a loon. Fifteen minutes later, the nurse directed Sam and Ray to the father's waiting room and escorted Jake and Kate to Emily's room. She was comfortably settled on the birthing chair.

At 2:03 p.m. on August 24th Emily delivered a lusty 8 pounds, 6-ounce boy. He was not shy, loudly proclaiming his entrance into this world. Jake took time to thank his wife for the most precious gift he'd ever received. He used a gentle hand to touch and count each tiny finger and toe. When the nurse brought Ray and Sam to the room, Emily watched Jake carry their infant son to greet his family. There was a visible swagger to his step when the men noted the amount of hair and firm grip of the baby's fingers.

Jake passed the baby around for everyone to hold, ending with Sam's hand off to Kate. Their eyes met over the tiny miracle, making a promise in those silent seconds. Kate smiled and placed a kiss on the baby's forehead before returning him to his mother's breast.

Emily named the bouncing baby boy for Jake, whose given name was John, and MacDougall, for his mother's family. Emily was a beautiful mother, and Jake was a surprisingly gentle father. Ray amazed everyone by stepping into the role of doting grandfather. Sam watched, hopeful for himself.

Friends and family grew closer. Sam worked several cases revolving around the immigration crisis at the southern border. Even in his administrative capacity, Sam traveled more than he or Kate liked, but that was part of the job. Kate wrote a series of articles on Child Protective Services, their function, funding, and the lack of qualified employees to investigate all the cases. It wore her out and left her feeling depressed.

Jake rehabbed another house and decided it was time to expand his business. Forming a partnership with Ray, the two purchased a four-plex, would do the basics to bring it up to code and become landlords. They planned on using this as the jumping off point to build a multi-family housing complex. Emily was busy with the baby, but kept her hand in the art gallery. She worked three days a week helping her artist friends develop their web-sites and promote their work. Much to Jake's relief, she decided that breast feeding would only last until John Mac had his first tooth. Jake denied existence of the electric breast pump. Isabell happily babysat John Mac on the days Emily was at the gallery.

Vincent liked his new school. He found a kindred

spirit in a new buddy named Dale Kilmer. The two spent hours studying and practicing their spy craft. Angela joined the dance club at school. She spent hours watching dance videos and practicing with her friends. Isabell was relieved to see the children settle in and thrive. Summer moved into fall.

Chapter 10

Amateur Night was a huge draw. Everyone was welcome to get up on stage and perform. Sometimes they got real dogs, but other times, there were some hidden gems. Marchetti encouraged Ricco and his guys to recruit college co-eds. They'd get their drinks for free and often egged each other on to be more brazen. Ricco saw the success when he counted the take at the door, but he wanted them younger. They could no longer guarantee the older ones were virgins. Ricco had ambition; had bigger plans than the old man. Amateur Night was small potatoes, but Ricco recognized it as a good starting point.

The coffee shop Ricco chose was across the street from the high school. It was a favorite hangout for the students. They'd come in at breakfast, lunch, and after school to grab a high-priced latte, maybe a snack if their allowance held, and scope out the other students. Ricco thought there would be an opportunity to meet and move on a potential mark.

Ricco, dressed casually in jeans, leather jacket, and expensive shoes, carried a high priced designer backpack. There was an expensive watch on his wrist and a blue star sapphire ring on his pinkie. His young cousin, Tony, was with him, dressed less richly but in stylish, good quality clothes. They looked exactly like the pampered college students they intended to. Picking up their coffees, they selected a table near the windows and waited for the next batch of prospects to cross the street from the high school. A lot of students hung out there and did their homework. Ricco could pass for one, even though he was pushing twenty-seven. The more adventurous girls from the high school liked to hang out with older guys and flirt. They rarely suspected danger.

Ricco had several talent scouts, as he liked to call them. He took this assignment because of his youthful looks. Tony was actually younger, just seventeen, and, currently, his driver and potential apprentice. Once Tony learned the basics, Ricco would teach him how to identify a potential mark and bring them along. The two men settled in to enjoy the view. A short while later, the last bell rang and students poured out of the front doors of the high school like fire ants after having their nest kicked. The two men watched a group of five young women separate themselves from the others. They stood near the steps in the building's shade, hips angled out, attempting to look sexy. Two guys in letter jackets sauntered over to make a move. Four of the five girls blushed and giggled, but one shot them a brazen look and threw her long blond hair over her shoulder provocatively. The taller of the two boys leaned in to whisper in her ear while she pouted her pretty pink lips and played with the top button of her blouse. When he'd had his say, the blonde walked her fingertips up his arm and smiled invitingly. Ricco nodded when, with true 'PT' panache, she flipped her hair back, wagged her finger 'no' in his face, and laughed at him. She motioned for her friends and, blowing kisses to the jocks, swayed her hips suggestively as she and the others crossed the street to the coffee shop. The two jocks watched, drool running down their chins.

Ricco's eyes narrowed behind his dark glasses. He watched the encounter between the blonde and the jock unfold with a smile on his face. "Shit, look at the tits on the little blonde. Oh, I like that one. She's a looker. Knows it too. Those are the easiest ones to sucker. Give me your take on this batch. Any with good potential?"

"Okay, yeah." Tony scrutinized the five girls crossing over to the coffee shop. "The blonde is definitely a keeper. Of the other four, one is okay-looking. She's a little too skinny and has a flat chest. Two are ordinary, and one of those, too fat for what you're looking for. The tall brunette, though, she's good. Thin, but pretty. She has a friendly smile. I gauge their age about fourteen. I'd say the blonde is older."

Ricco smiled approvingly at his apprentice. The two watched as the giggling group of girls entered through the glass doors and huddled at the counter, counting their pennies to order their drinks. Ricco and Tony observed, eavesdropping to pick up bits and pieces of information to use as they laid plans to reel them in.

The girls stood off to the side, waiting for their order. Ricco coached Tony on what to listen for. They overheard names and some personal details. Melanie was the blonde, the tall brunette was called Angela, and the fat one was Susie. Angela, Sandi, and Joanie had auditioned for the dance club. Angela and Sandi made it and Susie was 'sooo excited' for them.

"It's okay, Joanie," Susie spouted supportively. "Dancing is so fun and cool. We'll keep practicing with Angela and try again next time."

Ricco watched, reading their wants and desires as

easily as a large print book. Not that he ever picked a book up.

Melanie rolled her eyes. "Well, you guys can dance all you want. I want to be a model."

Susie just wanted to be liked.

"Two Skinny Vanilla Lattes, two Mochaccinos, and one water," the barista called out.

"I'll get them, Melanie," Susie, the chubby girl, said. She was working hard to earn her place in this little clique of cool girls. "Are we going to the park to hang? I have that hot new dance video on my phone. We can practice the moves."

Ricco smirked as Melanie feigned boredom. She looked around, scoping out the room for some interested guy to flirt with. "I guess. There isn't anything else to do here." Ricco raised his eyebrows and gave her a knowing smile. Her face lit up. "Or maybe you guys should go on and I'll just hang here for a little while."

"Okay, catch you later." The four shrugged and headed out with their drinks while Melanie sauntered over to Ricco's table.

"Hi. I don't think I know you." She smiled transparently. She looked around for a chair. Tony knew the drill.

Jumping up, he grabbed his backpack. "Here, take mine. I gotta go anyway. Catch you later, Ricco." Tony winked broadly and walked out.

Melanie sat. She leaned her elbows on the table, lacing her fingers beneath her chin, and smiled invitingly. "Do you go to Paschal?" One hand dropped to her necklace and her fingers toyed with the small pendant, running it back and forth along the chain flirtatiously. "I don't think I've seen you before."

Ricco read her body language. The toying with the necklace spoke volumes to him. He let the silence lengthen, making Melanie more brazen in her approach. She leaned forward, giving his eyes a clear path down her blouse and along her cleavage. Ricco had so many ways to go with this one, but knowing the modeling angle, chose that path.

"No, I go to TCU. Do you go to Paschal? You look too old for high school," Ricco said, charming her.

Melanie sat back and sipped her latte. Ricco knew he was good-looking and had been sure to plant the TCU story, knowing it was an expensive school. Melanie looked like the kind of girl that wanted flash. Flash took money. Ricco became the guy he imagined Melanie pictured herself dating.

"I thought I saw you with a guy earlier. You don't have a big football player boyfriend who might not like me talking with his girl, do you?"

"Him? He wants to date me, but high school boys are so immature. I'm almost eighteen." Ricco smiled, thinking she lied. "You don't mind younger women, do you?" Melanie dropped her eyes and gazed up at Ricco through her eyelashes, feigning innocence. "What are you studying at TCU?"

"Oh, I'm working on a bachelor's in fine arts. I want to do fashion photography."

"Really? How interesting. I've always been interested in fashion and modeling."

Ricco smiled widely. "This must be fate." He toasted her with his coffee and thought, hook, line, and sinker.

****

Tony wanted to hang around and watch Ricco in action. The guy was really good, and the boss liked his work. Tony wasn't sure about all the details of what Ricco did, but Tony liked the money he was making just hanging and driving Ricco around. He thought he'd wait in the car or maybe he'd walk down to the park.

The small pocket park was located two blocks down. Tony kept his eye out for the other girls who had come into the coffee shop with Melanie. He heard the loud blast of music before he saw them. They were using the concrete pad where a picnic table had once stood as a stage. Angela was watching the screen of her phone intently. Tony could hear the pounding of a music video. She swayed with the music, showing some moves to Sandi while Susie and Joanie stood behind, copying their steps. They were having fun and laughing. When the song ended, Susie plopped down.

"That's a tough one. You do it really well, Angela. Sandi, you're good too. It's no wonder you guys made the dance club. So, what's it like, the club I mean? Are you going to perform or what? I bet you'll have lots of guys wanting to ask you out," she finished, not a little envious.

Angela threw a quick glance at Sandi, then shrugged. She couldn't contain her excitement. Hugging herself, she laughed with delight. It tinkled like little bells. Tony thought it sounded sweet.

"We're learning a routine that we'll perform with the band at half-time of the football games. It's kind of stupid. No cool or sexy moves, you know? But the dance club instructor says we are going to have a competition to see who can choreograph a really jazzy routine that we'll do for the homecoming game. Sandi and I talked and we want to do it that new release "Hot Dancing". It has such a great dance rhythm. I have tons of ideas, and practicing with you guys is really helpful."

Angela laughed again and Tony felt a small smile curve the corner of his mouth. She was cute; he decided. Tony watched and listened, tucking all the information away to be used when the time was right. The dance hook gave him a way to approach the girls. Tony felt the buzz of his cell phone in his pocket. He looked down to see it was a text from Ricco. Punching in a reply, he walked back to the coffee shop.

****

Melanie stopped hanging around with the gang. Angela missed her. When she saw Melanie's number on the caller ID on her cell phone two weeks later, she squealed with excitement and dashed to her bedroom to take the call. "Hey, hi. Where have you been? We miss you."

Melanie gave a bored huff of air. "Oh, yeah, you mean the dud and the wannabes. They are pretty lame. I mean, Sandi is okay, but you are way too cool for Suzie and Joanie. And, I just found something more fun to do. I've been seeing this really cute guy. His name is Ricco. He has a friend and asked if I knew someone. Maybe we could double date. Go to the movies or something. Do you want to meet him?"

Angela paused a second to think about it. She didn't think the other girls were lame, but she didn't want Melanie to think she was lame, too. "Yeah, they are nerdy. I just feel sorry for them so I hang out with them. The movies sound like fun. What's this guy like? Have you seen him? Is he cute too?"

The two buzzed happily on the phone about the

guys, hair, make-up, clothes, and the latest dance steps Angela was learning. Before hanging up, Melanie promised to ask Ricco about the movies and call Angela back. Angela chewed her fingernail, thinking about cute guys and double dating. She glanced at herself in the mirror, pulling her t-shirt tighter against her boobs. She wished she had boobs like Melanie. The guys always looked at and flirted with Melanie. Big boobs were important to guys. Well, she hoped Ricco's friend wasn't a boob guy. She was looking forward to it anyway and bounced her head from side to side, humming a hip-hop song. Then she went back into the kitchen to help with dinner.

"Who was that on the phone? If it was another rehearsal for your dance club, you know it's a school night. You have homework," Isabell said when Angela walked into the kitchen.

"Grandmother, I'm not a baby. It wasn't a rehearsal, just a friend. She asked if I wanted to get together. And I don't have that much homework." Angela slammed the cupboard door in frustration. "Geez, you'd think I was twelve instead of almost fifteen."

Angela tried to ignore Isabell's disapproving tone. "Even fifteen is too young to stay out late and not do one's homework, young lady."

"Okay, okay. It was Melanie. We haven't talked in a couple of weeks. She wants to get together, go to a movie or something." Angela held her hands up, palms out. "Not tonight, just some time."

Isabell held up one finger. "But not on a school night. Your friends should know better than to suggest a movie on a school night." Angela huffed and rolled her eyes.

Chapter 11

When the phone rang, Kate raised her eyes to heaven and thanked God for the interruption. Dropping the tangled yarn into her basket, she reached for the phone.

"Kate, it's Isabell. Do you have some time for a visit? I have something I'd like to talk about with you." It was Mrs. Camarillo, sounding troubled. Twenty minutes later, Isabell knocked and let herself into Kate's kitchen. She wore a simple sweater over a printed cotton housedress and low pumps. A small black handbag swung from her wrist. She was wringing her hands.

Kate could clearly see Isabell was distraught. "Please, sit down, Isabell. How about a cup of tea?" Kate led her friend to the kitchen island and started the kettle to boil. "You look worried. Is everything all right?"

Isabell pulled a tissue from her pocket and dabbed at the tears forming in her eyes. "Oh, Kate. I don't know who to talk to. I'd tell the priest, but he's a man. A priest won't understand how teenage girls can be. It's Angela. She's running around with a group of young girls that…well, one of them is not a good girl."

"I thought you were happy Angela had made friends. Isn't she in the dance club with her friend Sandi? So, what is going on?" Kate set out tea cups, waiting for the water to boil.

"I thought it was good that Angela found friends, but there is this one. Melanie is her name. She is the ringleader. This girl is not a nice girl. She encourages the others to misbehave. I overheard Angela and Melanie talking the other day. She is seeing an older man. Apparently, he buys her gifts and takes her to clubs. Melanie was showing Angela a new outfit her boyfriend bought for her. Later, after she left, I confronted Angela. She denied doing anything wrong. She says all she does is go to movies and hang out at the park with her friends. They talk and practice dancing. I don't know what to believe, so I grounded Angela and told her not to hang out with this Melanie anymore."

Kate placed a cup of tea in front of Isabell and encouraged her to drink some. "Angela is almost fifteen now, isn't she? That's about the age when kids rebel against authority. How did she take being grounded?"

"She yelled at me. Angela told me she wasn't like her mother. She said Melanie was her best friend, that Melanie cared about her. But I see the light of envy in Angela's eyes. This man Melanie knows? I think he must be someone with money. Someone who buys her things. Things a young girl doesn't need. Shouldn't have. Sandi is also wearing some new clothes and has fancy jewelry, too. I'm afraid Angela will want these things and will make bad choices." Isabell raised stricken eyes to Kate. "I don't even know what kind of man this girl is seeing or what he is to her. And I've seen how Melanie dresses, how she encourages the others to dress. I worry about the clothes this man buys her. She gave some to Angela, who hid them in her closet, but I looked. Sheer, short, and low cut, they show off too much skin. They are the clothes a whore would wear." Anger and embarrassment bubbled to the surface and colored Isabell's cheeks.

Kate ran a hand through her hair and pressed her lips together in thought. Isabell clearly felt uncomfortable confessing to snooping on her granddaughter. Reaching over, she placed a calming hand over Isabell's trembling one.

"I don't know what I can do to help. You say Angela is ignoring you, flaunting the rules you set down. Outside of locking her in her room, what else can be done?"

"I don't know, but Sam, he's in law enforcement. Maybe if I learn the man's name, you could ask Sam to look into it? Maybe talk to him, tell him to leave the girls alone? This Melanie is only sixteen. If an older man, an adult, is taking advantage of her, it's illegal, right? Maybe Sam could have him arrested."

Kate's immediate thought was of her initial interview with Janet Winburn. Was this a case of grooming? And would it be possible for a young woman to groom other young women to do the bidding of their abuser? Why not? During her research, Kate learned about the power of social or peer pressure. It wasn't dissimilar to autocratic or authoritarian leadership. Kate sat at the island with her tea, musing.

"Isabell, you said Melanie has influence over the girls? Is she the leader of the clique?"

Isabell pursed her lips in thought. Her hand came up, and she pointed her finger in an 'a-ha' motion. "I think so. Every time I've heard Angela and Sandi talking, they always mention Melanie. What she would do or what she would think. It seems they can't make a decision without her approval."

Kate leaned forward, the gears in her brain turning full tilt. "Isabell, I learned recently about social structure and how cliques work. The leader has full control and responsibility for every aspect of the group's activities and even status. It discourages independence. The members give full trust and control only to the leader. An autocratic leader has the power to enforce member dependence, to bully and mistreat their members."

Isabell had raised her cup to her mouth but now put it down quickly. "There is one girl, Susie. She is very sweet, but she is chubby and not as pretty as the others. Melanie is mean to her and has encouraged the others to do the same. Is this something that happens in these groups?"

"It could be, yes. From what I've read, in the so-called cliques where social pressure is predominant, the members follow strict codes of conduct. There are rules imposed by the leader regarding how they act, dress, and talk amongst themselves or with outsiders. Does that sound about right? The members are loyal to the leader, in this case, Melanie, rather than to each other. It's a circular relationship where the leader is the center. All things flow from the leader."

Isabell sat thinking. Kate could see her eyes tracking back and forth, remembering everything she'd seen and trying to put it into perspective. "I see what you are saying and I agree. Melanie is using her leadership position to exert power and influence over the other girls."

Kate sat back, stunned by how powerful the

hierarchy in the group was. She wondered if Melanie formed a clique that drew in young, lonely teens, those outside of the popular kid circles at school. From what Isabell shared, Melanie could use social pressure to get them to do any number of things. This group of young women would form a strong bond with Melanie and look to her as their guide. Melanie could be the driving force or be a pawn of the older man, using her to get the other young women to do his bidding. The man could use gifts to buy affection. It could be the perfect storm leading to sexual exploitation.

"I think at some level, Melanie is controlling the girls. The question is, is someone controlling Melanie?" Kate saw the hope in Isabell's eyes. "I don't know if Sam can do anything. But this sounds like someone could be exploiting Melanie. I have a contact with a special task force that works with these types of cases. Let me talk to her and ask what she suggests. In the meantime, be patient and watchful. If you can learn names or what they do, where they go? It might be helpful. I don't want to suggest you spy on Angela, but she may throw away a ticket stub or receipt that will give us a lead."

Isabell's eyes lit up. Of course, it was a good idea. She desperately needed to do something. Feeling better about sharing her concerns, Isabell headed home. Kate called Janet Winburn and outlined what Isabell had told her concerning Angela. Janet agreed to meet with her the following day.

****

The next morning, Kate sat in the home office making notes for her appointment with Janet Winburn later that day. She had shared some of Isabell's concern with Sam and her conviction that Melanie could be a victim of exploitation or the exploiter herself. Sam listened attentively, but Kate could tell something else was on his mind when he gave her a metaphorical pat on the head and told her to be careful. With her cup of coffee steaming at her elbow, she watched him shift through his emails and reports. It was difficult to ignore the information he was processing, but Sam wasn't one to share the details of his work. He was protective of her. His concern for her sensibilities and safety was endearing, but sometimes annoying. Kate wasn't a shrinking violet and certainly knew how to take care of herself.

Kate picked up her mug and sipped, thinking about the times she'd tracked and written about crime. Sure, it was white collar crime, but some of those guys were aggressive and could hurt you if you weren't careful. Sam's worry was sometimes over the top. He saw death and destruction in everything criminal. As a journalist, she was driven to find the facts and to report them. Sam seemed to forget she had been doing this type of work for years. Sam had his work, and she had hers. That he was involved in something that might segue into what Isabell was concerned about didn't mean she could involve him or ask about what he was doing. She respected the confidentiality of his work and would never use it for her writing or this situation. When they published her initial work on the proliferation of pornography, she'd achieved celebrity status. After a time, she had her fill of talk show, expert commentator, and rubber chicken guest speaker appearances. Kate had left behind the idea of any further articles on child abuse and exploitation because of how sordid the subject was. There were some things that were too emotionally charged for her to write about objectively. However, now Kate saw an immediate threat to someone she knew.

Kate entered the same government-styled lobby and gave her name to the receptionist. It didn't take long for Janet to come out. She led Kate down the same hall to the same office. They passed the same desks, the same staff. Today, though, there was a kinetic energy in the room that had been missing before. Janet invited Kate to take a seat while circling behind the desk to her chair.

"I'm so sorry your friend has this concern. It's her granddaughter, you said? And you said her mom is in prison in part because of prostitution? That certainly could inform the young woman's attitudes toward sex. Perhaps make her more vulnerable, more de-sensitized. You mentioned the name Melanie as the older teen the grandmother feels is influencing the young woman's behaviors. Do you know Melanie's last name? We could run a background check. It wouldn't be the first time a woman has been involved in abuse. There could be many reasons she would do it. Misery loves company, the control or power she gets turning young women to the prurient lifestyle. Or, it's even possible she is being abused herself and the abuser is coercing her to do this, to groom the other young women for his purposes. This sounds like it could be classic child exploitation." Janet paused at a knock on her door. An older gentleman stuck his head inside. He'd rolled his shirt sleeves to the elbows and his tie was askew. There was a harried expression on his face.

Looking surprised to see Kate sitting in the office,

he paused, looking with raised eyebrows at Janet. After a quick nod from her, he continued. "Sorry to interrupt. We have what we need. Can you spare a moment?" Janet glanced at Kate and excused herself to step out, closing the door firmly behind her. When she returned, the color was high on her cheeks and she was huffing with excitement.

"I'm sorry, Kate. I won't be able to give you as much time as originally planned today. A case we have been working on busted loose last night. We are scrambling to get all the warrants in place." Tilting her head to one side, Janet scrutinized Kate, chewing on her lower lip thoughtfully. "Actually, it matches the situation about which you are concerned. Perhaps you'd like to track the investigation with me, get firsthand experience."

Kate's eyes lit up, and she smiled an affirmative. Sensing she could be totally open with Ms. Winburn, she leaned forward in her chair. "It would be an amazing opportunity to follow you in your investigation. How is it connected with Angela and exploitation?"

"How about teenage girls dancing in a topless bar? Exploitive enough for you?" The disgust was apparent in the curl of Janet's lips and the tone of her voice. "Vice will make the bust tonight. I'll be watching from the command post when they go in."

Kate had read about the dedication the DA's team had to fight obscenity, pornography, and exploitation. She read the passion in Janet Winburn's expression. This probably wasn't the exact information she could use to help Isabell, but that focus faded from her mind. The article she'd placed on the back burner was suddenly front and center in her mind and at full boil. This was something she could sink her teeth into. What could come out of it would be incredible. To have a real-life case would lend extreme credibility to her writing. No more having her articles relegated to the Opinion section. Kate could get front-page by-line notoriety. National publications sprang to mind. She stuck her hand out to shake Janet's. "Where do I sign up?"

Janet's cell phone chirped. She read the text message and a triumphant smile spread across her face. "Judge Abaya just gave Vice the warrant. Dress comfortably and meet me back here at seven tonight. I'll have the forms for you to sign: confidentiality, liability waiver, etc. Welcome on board."

Kate had to hold her speed in check all the way home. She could gather key information to write the article she'd wanted from the start. When she saw Sam's jeep in the driveway, Kate rushed into the house, calling out the news. "Sam, I'm glad you are home."

Sam was at the kitchen counter, fixing himself a snack. He smiled and reached out for a hug, only to have Kate give him a quick kiss on the cheek on her way to the refrigerator, where she grabbed a bottle of fizzy water. Plunking down on the sofa, she curled her legs under herself.

"Sam, you know Isabell is worried about Angela running around with a rough crowd, maybe making some bad choices? Everything she told me made me think about child abuse and exploitation. I called Janet Winburn. I just met with her. She agrees there might be something to it. Apparently, this is very possible and very real. Janet was outlining all the things that support our concern when one of her colleagues interrupted us. She stepped out to speak with him and you won't believe it! They are planning a raid tonight. She asked if I'd like to go with them to witness everything firsthand. Sam, I am going to be in from the beginning on a bust with Janet Winburn's Obscenity Crimes Team. I'm meeting her tonight and will sit next to her in the command post when it all goes down. This is an incredible scoop!" Kate hugged her fisted hands to her chest. She didn't see the flash of anger in Sam's eyes.

"Whoa, what the heck? This goes way beyond writing informative articles or helping Isabell with Angela. Tell me about the case, Kate. What and where is the bust happening?" Kate's excitement made her blind to Sam's tone and his concern.

"I don't have the specifics or the location, but Janet says it is teenage girls dancing at a topless bar. The Vice Squad is going in tonight to arrest the club owners. Judge Abaya issued the warrant while I was talking with Janet. She feels Angela's friend Melanie might be involved in some sort of abusive relationship. I want to teach the public about obscenity crimes. She approves of my writing, so she invited me to join her for an exclusive, inside view. Sam, can you believe it? An inside view of the entire tawdry business and the arrests." Kate bounced up, pacing off her energy. "This is an enormous opportunity. All I kept thinking as Janet talked about it was the potential for a national publication picking up the story. This could take my writing to an entirely new level. This could be more than just local recognition and human-interest articles. I could earn some serious creds with this. I'm going to change and whip up dinner." Kate was already heading for the stairs as she called over her shoulder, "Thought I'd do pasta with homemade pesto. Sound good to you?" She didn't wait for his reply.

****

Sam held his emotions in check. It was one thing to ask for expert advice on a potentially abusive situation to support a friend, but Kate was going out on an actual bust. It could put her in harm's way. He had breathed a sigh of relief when she originally set this project aside. Sam was familiar enough with the entire repugnant business to know the type of people involved. He had worried about Kate drawing attention to herself when she wrote the first articles. The way the news had identified her as an expert in the field and called on her to comment was bad enough. Now she was going into the field. She was touching the coals. Kate could get burned with this level of involvement.

Sam followed Kate's climb up the stairs with worry creasing his brows. He was privy to some cases Vice was working on and thought he knew which one they had finally cracked open. Sam didn't like it one bit that Kate would be that close to the action or even involved with this bust. If it was the club Sam was thinking of, it was part of the Marchetti family business. Old man Marchetti had run gentleman clubs across the southwest for years. He was adept at walking the fine line between legal and illegal. Lately, the clubs had been offering Amateur Night, inviting college girls to strut their stuff. Sam wondered if Marchetti was expanding his business. Could it be tied to the increase in child pornography? Was the old man working with the criminals, moving human contraband across the border? All Sam knew was that Marchetti's activities had been getting increasingly violent. Although they hadn't killed, they beat and maimed. Sam didn't think they would take kindly to interference in their operation.

Sam respected Kate and her work enough to give her the room to pursue the story, but it didn't mean he wouldn't be there in the event something went south.

****

Kate met Janet Winburn and Craig Spencer, the detective in charge of the team doing the takedown. She signed the papers, and the three got into a late model, white Crown Vic, the government issued vehicle used by many police departments. Kate rolled her eyes. Did they really think no one would suspect they were with law enforcement? They drove across town into a neighborhood that grew seedier as they wound through the side streets. Industrial buildings, convenience stores, and pawnshops populated the area. A neon sign flashed in large red and white letters, 'Fantasy Palace'. Under that, 'Girls Topless Girls Topless', continuously scrolled in smaller letters. A canvas sign hung between the sign posts advertising 'Amateur Night'.

They parked a block over at the end of a street lined with small industrial businesses. The trio walked the last part of the way, picking their way along cracked sidewalks strewn with empty beer cans, burrito wrappers, and cigarette butts. The command center was a dilapidated Winnebago parked behind a dumpster in a trash-strewn vacant lot. It's dented and rusted brown over dirty white exterior looked anything but a computer center to monitor radio and CCTV transmissions. Spencer banged on the door. A skinny, scraggly bearded kid dressed in a faded 90s heavy metal rock band t-shirt and jeans opened it. He had headphones hanging around his neck. Spencer introduced him as Officer Welch. He stepped back to make room for the three to enter, then closed the door after them.

"Yo, captain. Everyone is in place. Gutierrez went in first, took his usual seat at the end of the bar. Arndt and Turpin will arrive in fifteen. The floor show starts at eight. Hey, did you bring coffee?" Spencer handed the technician a Styrofoam cup and took a seat at the console, putting on a second set of headphones. Janet squeezed in next to him.

Kate stood at the rear of the camper, looking for a place to sit. She didn't want to get in the way. The skinny guy moved some binders, freeing up a space on the bench. She thanked him, noting that up close, Welch wasn't as young as he first appeared. That or the work had aged him prematurely. Kate perched on the edge, straining to see and hear everything. Welch, the technician, had hacked into the closed-circuit security cameras in the club. He set up split screens on a bank of monitors. Each one showed different camera angles. There were the front and rear doors and three views of the inside. She could see the length of the bar, the main seating area, and the stage. The lights were low, but the stage lights gave off sufficient illumination to make out most details.

Most of the patrons were older, blue-collar workers with a sprinkling of suits. Waitresses wearing short-shorts and revealing mid-riff tops circulated the room, delivering drinks and suffering the pinch and pat of wandering hands. They appeared to be older women. It was sad that women sometimes had no other choice than to exploit their bodies to make a living. Of course, Kate knew several women chose the profession because it was far more lucrative than their education could earn. It certainly paid better than working in the fast-food industry. In fact, it sometimes paid better than teaching.

Arndt and Turpin entered and took a table at the foot of the stage. Dressed in khakis and polo shirts, they looked like work weary mid-management types, blending into the crowd. The waitress took their order. Kate was scribbling notes about her impressions when Detective Spencer swore out loud. Looking up, Kate watched on screen as a black town car pulled up at the door and four large, muscular men in black jeans and dark shirts got out. They all wore dark glasses even though it was nighttime. The driver didn't bother to give his keys to the valet. Apparently, they could park where they wanted.

"Shit. That's Marchetti's goons. What the hell? Did someone tip them off?" Speaking into his headset, he warned the undercover officers. "Guttz, heads up! Goons gone wild. Don't call attention to yourself guys. Just get the 'F' out. Arndt, you and Turpin, stand down. I have to think this through." Spencer ripped the headphones off and threw them down on the console. "This is flippin' three months of planning and surveillance. Okay, Welch. Keep the camera footage rolling. If the girls are still dancing, we'll get it for trial evidence." He got on his radio and told the black and whites to stand down. Spencer blew out a frustrated breath. "Look, I don't want to waste the warrant, but we can't go in with those guys there. There might be more of them we don't know about. We might need more manpower. It's too much of a risk. Okay, you guys, make your way to the camper. We need a pow-wow."

Kate watched the man Spencer had referred to as Guttz finish his beer. He threw a twenty on the bar and was getting up from his stool when one of the large men bumped into him. It was obvious from the camera feed, he and Guttz were exchanging words. Things were getting heated when the bouncer walked over. The bouncer placed his frying pan-sized hands on each man's chest and separated them. He stuck out his arm and pointed to the door, then not so gently shoved Guttz toward it. Guttz maintained his cover and shrugged indifferently. What did he care, Guttz seemed to say and staggered toward the door as if he'd had one-too-many beers. The other two goons had taken a table next to Arndt and Turpin. Just their presence intimidated the surrounding guests. One group got up and moved toward the back of the room, well out of reach of the goons. Arndt and Turpin made to follow suit when one goon stuck his foot out and tripped Turpin. Once again, the bouncer magically appeared. He motioned to both Arndt and Turpin where the door was and visibly suggested they leave and not return. The message was crystal clear. Marchetti knew, and he wasn't having it.

It took twenty minutes for the three men to make their way to the camper and once everyone was inside; it was close and hot. Stuck in a corner while they talked, Kate watched the camera feed from the stage. The dancers followed one after another without a break. Strutting across the stage from the back corner, dressed in feathery, flowy, or sparkly costumes, they did a lot of hip grinding and thrusting. They threw their bottom around or shimmied their barely covered breasts at hands holding out dollar bills. Eventually, they stripped mechanically down to a G-string and pasties, picking up more dollars and enduring a few fingers that copped a feel as they stuffed the bills. None of the dancers looked younger than twenty.

Kate touched Janet on the shoulder. "I don't think these are teenagers dancing."

Janet turned back to the monitor and studied it. Slamming her hand down on the arm of her chair, she swiveled around to face Spencer. "Damn it, Craig. They switched out the girls. They knew we were on to them. We got nothing. What they are doing is disgusting, but not illegal. Close it up." She stood, rubbing her forehead with the heels of her hands and shaking her head. "It's hot and stuffy in here. Kate and I will wait outside until you finish up. Don't take too long." Spencer exchanged pained looks with his team. Janet Winburn pushed open the door to the Winnebago and stepped out. Kate followed but saw Spencer flip Winburn off out of the corner of her eye as the door closed.

The warmth from the tight space in the Winnebago made the fall Texas weather refreshing and welcome. The two women talked quietly until Detective Spencer came out. They walked silently back to the car, only to find that they had a flat tire.

Janet was the first and most vocal to react. "Oh, this is just dandy." Turning to Kate, she said, "Do you want to wait for Craig to change it or call for an Uber?"

It was misting, so Kate pulled her collar up and tucked her hands into her pockets against the damp, staring at the flat. When Janet said Uber, Kate raised her head, surprised. "Call an Uber? Can we do that?

We're in the middle of a criminal investigation. That's just weird. How do we explain why we are here in this neighborhood?"

"Just kidding, Kate. Although Uber doesn't hire rocket scientists. The driver probably wouldn't think a thing about it." Janet stuffed her phone back into her purse and paced impatiently while Craig shot daggers from his eyes in her direction. He mumbled obscenities under his breath and skinned his knuckles, struggling with the spare tire.

No one noticed the man in the shadows listening in to their conversation, snapping photos of the two women. No one saw him make a call, then melt away into the darkness.

****

Sam watched in disgust as the scene unfolded. His wife and the inept Task Force were standing in plain sight after failing to complete a bust on one of Marchetti's joints. He wanted to read Janet Winburn the riot act for putting Kate in a dangerous situation. Judas' priest, they were just standing there in this neighborhood in the dark. In the GD freakin' dark! Sam was angry enough to spit. Sweeping the surrounding area with his eyes, he didn't see any immediate threat. He kept his vigil until Spencer had changed the tire. Finally done, the detective wiped his hands on a towel, tossing it into the trunk. Everyone climbed into the Crown Vic, and Spencer pulled away from the curb, heading back to the precinct. Sam engaged his engine and was preparing to follow when a maroon coup slid out of the alley after Spencer's car passed. It kept its lights off until the Crown Vic was two blocks ahead. Sam held back a beat, then followed, keeping enough distance between him and the coup to avoid detection. Spencer was clueless. He didn't notice either tail.

Using his key code, Spencer pulled into the secure precinct parking lot. The coup continued down the block, then turned right. Sam swore in frustration. He hadn't been able to get close enough to get a complete license plate. The partial would have to do. He'd run it when he got home. For now, though, Sam waited for Kate's Honda to exit the lot and followed her home.

Sam was right behind Kate when she pulled into the driveway. Climbing out of the car, she smiled her surprise at seeing him. Walking toward him, she beamed a greeting and leaned in for a kiss as he climbed out of his jeep. "Hi, babe. You didn't mention you were going out tonight. Something unexpected come up?"

Sam took a breath and dialed back his barely suppressed fury. He felt the warm glow of her love. It filled him, calmed him, made him whole. Sam didn't know what he'd do if he lost her.

"I'm glad you're home. It was a trying night." Sam returned Kate's kiss absent-mindedly. Taking her arm, he hustled her to the door and shielded her with his body as he opened it and guided her in, locking it behind them.

Kate cyed him suspiciously. "What's going on? You're acting weird. Is everything all right?" She stood with her feet firmly planted, hands on hips.

Sam didn't respond as he moved to the office and stood in the dark, watching out the window for any suspicious cars or movement. Satisfied, he closed the blinds and turned on the lights. Kate stood in the doorway, waiting for Sam to release his pent-up breath.

"Okay, what is going on? What are you looking for?" The timber of her voice had risen in concern. He saw the shadows of worry building in her eyes like storm clouds.

Sam went to Kate, taking her in his arms. "Nothing now, but we need to talk about what happened tonight."

Kate drew back and looked at Sam. "Okay. I'll make coffee." She led the way into the kitchen and set about the task. Sam watched Kate's quick and efficient motions. He knew doing homey chores calmed her nerves, and it gave him time to consider how to tell her she was off the story.

Kate poured two mugs. Adding cream and sugar to hers, she opened the conversation by explaining how her evening had gone; the covert ops, the hacking into the CCTV, the Marchetti henchmen, and Janet's asinine suggestion they call an Uber. "I'm no expert, but the entire operation lacked organization. It felt like the owners of the club knew what was going to happen. It appeared Detective Spencer was angry at Janet Winburn. Although Spencer was supposed to be the one in charge, Janet pushed for control. She was quick to point out his failure with the operation. Didn't sugarcoat any of her comments either, which surprised me. I thought lawyers measured their words more carefully. I think it embarrassed the men." Sam waited patiently until Kate had shared her experience before he added his own observations.

Sam set down his coffee and rose to pace. His fingers tapped on his thigh; his jaw clenched. Rubbing his hands over his face, he returned to his stool at the kitchen island. Sam took Kate's hands in his.

"Kate, I watched everything from when you

entered the Winnebago to when you exited. I tracked you back to the car and watched Spencer fumble with changing the tire while you and Janet stood backlit by the streetlight. You two were perfect targets for anyone wishing to do you harm." He pressed his lips together, drawing in a calming breath before continuing. "Do you think it was safe to just stand around while Spencer changed the flat? Where was the backup? Why couldn't they have called a black and white to get you, to take you to your cars?"

Sam gave up the pretense of calm. He stood, stuffing his hands in his pockets to keep from shaking some sense into her. "For God's sake, Kate. You'd just witnessed the bust going south, saw Marchetti's goons make the cops and subtly threaten them. This was an incredibly stupid and poorly executed operation. I don't know if Winburn or Spencer ultimately do the planning, but it's a wonder they can find their ass with both hands."

Sam couldn't be still any longer. He stalked to the French doors, gazed out at the garden specifically designed to soothe, then turned back to Kate, fury still sparking in his eyes. "And Winburn? Does the woman have a death wish? Jesus Christ, Kate! Marchetti's goons could have killed the two of you where you stood. They could have swooped in, taken out Spencer before the man even thought about pulling his weapon. Then they could have taken you, driven you to a deserted location, and killed you. Before they killed you, they could have done much worse." Sam threw himself into a chair, placed his elbows on his knees, and rubbed his forehead. A monster of a headache was building behind his eyes. He blew out a breath and collected himself.

Kate sat on the stool at the kitchen island, turning her coffee mug in her hands. The ice maker dumped its load and refilled, breaking the silence that hung like a lead weight between them. "I'm sorry. I seem to have put you in the middle, Sam. But you forget, I was doing investigative work long before we met. You might give me a little credit here. My work requires some risk, but I don't put myself in danger deliberately. I attempt to follow all your instructions regarding safety. I am always aware of my surroundings. Vincent isn't the only one you've put through Spy School 101. I didn't perceive any threat and thought it was prudent to stay with Spencer rather than go off on my own. I always carry a panic button and pepper spray in my purse. You know full well, I wasn't totally without resources."

"Oh, and I'm sure those resources would have stopped a bullet." Unable to hide his sarcasm, Sam threw up his hands. He saw the fire ignite in Kate's eyes too late; recognized her stubborn tone and stance. "Look, I know you are an intelligent and capable woman with incredible instincts. But you are *my* woman and I don't like you being put in danger by someone else's incompetence. I don't know how, but, Kate, someone leaked their operation. Marchetti knew it was going down. They were watching. They followed Spencer when he drove you back to your car."

Sam resumed his pacing, rubbing his hands through his hair. "Kate, you were in on a bust at a club owned by the Marchetti syndicate. If Marchetti made Winburn's operation and he takes an interest in you, it could be dangerous. Look, I am beyond angry at Winburn. You know that. I really don't want you involved with her or her operation. I don't want you involved with anything having to do with the Marchetti Syndicate. You need to fly under the radar for a while. Stick close to the house."

Sam's voice had taken on a proprietary tone. Kate slowly slid off the stool and brought herself up to her full height. Her spine stiffened. She looked him dead in the eye.

"I seem to recall we had this problem once before. Or perhaps I should say, *you* had this problem with my work. I do not heedlessly put myself in danger. I pursue a lead, a story. Much like you do with your Homeland Security investigations. I am on the trail of a story that could translate into national exposure." Sam sensed Kate's veneer of control was slipping. She had her fists squeezed tightly. She clamped her mouth shut. "I think I should walk away before I say something we'll both regret."

"That's not what I meant and you know it, Kate." Sam tried to reel in his comments to de-escalate the conversation before it became a full-blown argument. "Tonight's little escapade put you in the spotlight. What if that happened when I wasn't around? For Christ's sake, Marchetti's men followed you back to the station." Sam felt the volume of his voice rise in tandem with his anger at Kate's blindness.

"And so? What if they did? I made it home safely, didn't I?" Kate was pacing angrily now. Her arms waving wildly. The cat took refuge under the table, warily watching her diatribe. "I was with a police detective. Do you think you're the only one that can keep me safe? Oh, of course you do! After all, I'm *your* 'woman'. Jesus, what a crock!" Kate's pacing had brought her face to face with Sam. With fists balled at her sides, she emphasized her words, shooting them out like bullets. "I am my *own* woman and don't you damn forget it!" She spun on her heel and stomped up the stairs. The house shook with the slamming of their bedroom door.

He gave himself a metal dope-slap. *So much for reeling it in. Shit.* Sam sank onto the couch and rubbed his face furiously with his palms. Resting his elbows on his knees, Sam rubbed at his temples, soothing the ache building in his head. He couldn't have anger between them. He wouldn't win this argument. Sam replayed everything he'd said and knew if he pushed too much, Kate would simply ignore him and all his warnings. Might even go off on her own without letting him know her plans. That would be unacceptable. Blowing out an exasperated breath, he reminded himself how to spell 'compromise'.

Sam knocked softly on the bedroom door Kate had so soundly slammed before. Going to bed angry was never the answer, but how did he make it right when her safety was all he could think of? Sam didn't hear anything. He quietly opened the door. Kate was curled up on her side of the bed, her back to him. He could see the shaking of her shoulders, hear her tears.

"Kate, honey. Can I come in?" Sam slowly approached, sitting on the end of the bed, wanting to touch her. "You mean everything to me. I couldn't bear it if something happened to you. Please, I don't want us to fight."

Kate sat up, leaning against the headboard. She took a tissue from her pocket and noisily blew her nose. Sam smiled. It was so damn romantic. So normal. So,

Kate.

"Oh, Sam." She practically wailed. "I don't want to fight either. I'm so embarrassed. My stupid little tantrum was juvenile. But it felt so good to slam that damn door." She sniffled again, wiping her nose with her sleeve. "This is the first actual fight we've had. The first time we exchanged angry words or raised our voices. I hate that. I hate having you mad at me."

Throwing herself face first on the bed, she muffled her sobs in her pillow. Sam wondered if they were tears of anger or hurt. Either way, he hated how he felt and wanted to take her in his arms. To comfort her. Sam reached out a tentative hand, gently touching her shoulder.

Kate turned and threw herself into his arms. "Oh, Sam. I'm so sorry. Please forgive me."

Her words wrapped around Sam's apologies. Neither one heard the other speaking, only feeling the depth of their shared despair over hurting each other. Sam shushed Kate with a kiss, ending with eyes closed, their foreheads pressed together. The mist that had been falling earlier turned into a soft drizzle, lending its special music to the air.

Sam stroked Kate's arms and back, hearing his name on a sigh as his mouth traced her face with kisses, ending at her soft and inviting lips. Pulling back far enough to gaze into her deep blue eyes, he tenderly cupped her cheek with his hand, running his thumb along her jaw.

"Oh, Kate, my love, my fair one," he whispered in her hair. Letting his breath fan across her cheek, he placed a simple kiss on each cheek, ending at her trembling mouth. His fingers stroked her hair, her shoulders, her back. When Sam felt her shivers of anticipation, he laid her back on the bed. His hands moved to her shirt, undoing each button one by one to expose her warm flesh to his mouth. Nibbling and kissing, he lingered, then moved on to the next button, prolonging their pleasure. Sam traced a path down her abdomen and undid the button to her slacks, sliding them down her long, lean legs. Then he followed the path back up with his mouth, pausing at the soft warmth between her thighs. Sliding his fingers under the lace of her panties, he found her moist and ready. Sam pleasured her while he slipped her panties off. Making quick work of her bra, he had her naked under him. Kate moaned and ran her hands through his hair. Using his mouth, he moved to her breasts and took a taut nipple in his mouth, laving it with his tongue. His fingers worked magic. Kate cried out. She reached for him, wanting him.

"Please, Sam," Kate said, shaking her head back and forth, rising to the precipice. "I want you. I need you inside."

"And I want to give you more, Kate. Let go, my love. Let go." Her breath grew ragged with the rise of desire. She arched her back, straining against his hand as he kneaded and cupped her sex, until, with a cry, she crested and soared over the summit. Sam felt her nails dig into his shoulders as her muscles rippled and tightened. He watched her eyes widen in release and pleasure.

Stripping his clothes off, Sam watched as she began her slow slide down the other side. He entered her. Gently at first, letting the heat build, the flames re-ignite. When he felt her quicken to him, he deepened the power of his thrust. Their sweat slick bodies slid against each other. The slap of their hips as the rhythm increased. Sam clasped Kate's wrists above her head and ravaged her neck and face, ending with her mouth, stifling the cry of her climax as he felt himself spill his seed. Slowly floating downward toward rest, they surrendered to sleep. Make-up sex was so good.

Sam was lying in bed with his hand clasped under his head, watching the sky lighten from gray to the first flush of pink as the sun rose on a new day. Snuggled in his arms was the love of his life. He gazed from Kate to the painting of her in the field of wildflowers, the windmill in the background. Sam recalled the day Jake and Emily had given him the painting and he asked Kate to marry him. He smiled into her hair and was about to wake her for a repeat of the night before when his cell phone buzzed. Not wanting to wake her, Sam rose quietly, taking his phone downstairs to his office.

"Slater", Sam answered quietly. He heard John, his second in command's East Texas drawl.

"Morning, Sam. I'm sorry to bother you so early but the El Paso office got a call from local law enforcement."

Sam pulled out a pen and flipped to a clean sheet of his legal pad. Making rapid notes, he simultaneously checked flight schedules. Hanging up the phone, he sat back in his chair, worried that the timing couldn't be any worse.

Sheriff Domingues with the Presidio County Sheriff's Department had called the El Paso office of Homeland Security. He was good at working with both federal and local agencies in that part of the state, having formed a Border Operations Security Task

Force. Domingues was seeking support. The El Paso office would give it to him. Sam wanted to be involved in the meeting to see if his investigation into the Marchetti Syndicate was justified. That meant Sam would have to take a trip down there to review the evidence. This part of Texas was sparsely populated. Presidio County covers over 3,800 square miles. The small towns lack the infrastructure to handle major crime. They had found bodies in the Chihuahuan desert, some that appeared to be connected with the crossing of illegal immigrants. It overwhelmed the local sheriff's office. El Paso had a good team. They'd back up the Sheriff's department and Sam would have access to what he needed for his investigation.

He heard Kate making coffee and went into the kitchen. She had tossed on his shirt and it hung just below her very inviting tush. The moons of her bottom peeked out just below the tail. He slipped his hands under it and ran them up and over her hips, pulling her back against his growing erection. "God, I love you." Turning her, he drew her into his arms and his kiss.

Kate moved into his embrace. When they came up for air, she took his hand, turning his palm to her mouth, kissing it and sucking each fingertip. Then she led them up the stairs, where they made love again. This time Kate took the lead, bringing Sam to the brink more than once before she straddled him and rode him to heights known and often enjoyed.

Sam closed his eyes, enjoying the feel of Kate's slender fingers playing across his chest and down his belly. There would be a second performance if she kept it up.

"Sam, I've been thinking, and you're right. It was

foolish and an unnecessary risk last night. I won't involve myself in the child exploitation work anymore."

Sam relaxed, knowing this was one less thing on his plate to worry about. "Kate, I got a call this morning. John and I need to make a trip down to the El Paso office." Kate sighed in resignation. She knew he sometimes had to travel for his work.

****

Sam watched Kate place a saucer covered in tiny blue flowers on the floor. She absently put the cover on the cat food can and put it in the refrigerator. Her movements were stiff and mechanical. Feelie pounced on the soft food, purring loudly. Two minutes later, having licked up every morsel, the cat sat washing her face, occasionally meowing and casting longing looks at the empty dish. Sam tried to lighten the mood. Putting his arm around Kate's shoulders, he spoke to the cat. "Are you sure you're done? You haven't licked the pattern off the plate yet." Sam felt the weight of Kate's gaze. It didn't work.

She and Feelie followed him upstairs and watched silently as he packed his carry-on. Kate's expression was anxious and troubled. She held the cat to her chest like a lifeline. Her nervous fingers tugged at a loose thread on the bedspread.

Sam used the tip of his finger to tilt her chin up. "Kate, I can't leave without your smile sending me on my way."

"I wish you didn't have to go," she murmured against his neck when he took her in his arms.

Noticing the tension in her body, Sam pulled back enough to tuck her hair behind her ears and place a calming kiss on her forehead. He told her his plans.

Sam hoped knowing as much as he could tell her would ease some of her fears.

"It's just a trip to observe, and gather some additional information for my case. John is coming to pick me up at ten. Our flight leaves Love Field at noon. We'll fly to El Paso and drive 194 flat and boring miles to Marfa. I should be home by Friday night at about seven. I called Dad to let him know I'd be out of town." Sam watched Kate stare at his suitcase, stroking the cat. He didn't think it was to prevent Feelie from jumping in. "Hey, are you okay? You look worried. Dad said he could come stay here if you are uncomfortable being alone."

Kate looked up. She shook her head. "I'm sorry, Sam. It isn't easy. Every time you go away, I am reminded." Kate pasted a tremulous smile on her face. "I'll be fine. I have Ophelia, the ferocious guard cat. She'll keep me safe." Kate turned the little black and white face to her and bumped foreheads with their fur baby. "Won't you, Feelie, you mighty huntress and attack cat." Ophelia was none too thrilled with this mushy attention and pushed away. She jumped down and crawled under the bed. "First-rate protector you are, you little fur ball." Kate laughed derisively.

Sam hugged Kate, resting his cheek on her hair. He held her tightly and gazed out the window. The sun was peeking through the leaves of the trees, twinkling as it danced merrily across the room. "Jesus, Kate, I don't know what I'd do if anything happened to you. Maybe it's a good thing Dad is so close. You won't be alone while I'm away."

He felt Kate share a sigh of relief, but she was trembling. Sam leaned back and read her sudden raw fear of being alone. The horrible visions of Carlos hurting her came roiling back to him.

Kate buried her face in Sam's shoulder, swallowing hard. "Oh, Sam. I am so sorry." Kate turned her face to him. Her blue eyes drowning with unshed tears.

Sam hated himself for failing to protect her.

"Promise me, Sam. Not again. Please, not again." She shuddered with the memory of that not-too-distant time when she'd been alone and they'd almost lost each other.

Sam ran his hand over her hair and brought his hand under her chin, raising her face to his. "Shush, my love. Never. Never again."

Checking his weapon, Sam placed it into his gun case, then into his suitcase. He zipped the bag closed and went to Kate, taking her once again in his arms. "I'm sorry, Kate. I wish I never had to leave you. Let Dad come stay. He's happy to do it. Says he eats better over here than at home. You'll sleep better and so will I." Sam nuzzled Kate's ear and let his kisses trace a path along her jawline to her mouth. He covered it with his, letting their tongues entwine. The kiss grew more passionate and drew a moan of pleasure from them both. "God, I'll miss you. Touching you, loving you." He let his hands roam down her back and cup her bottom, drawing her into him. Bringing his mouth back down on hers, Sam savored the soft, sweet taste of her. He'd pulled back and pressed his cheek to hers, wanting desperately to stay, when he heard John beep his horn. Sam picked up his suitcase, and they walked hand in hand to the car.

Kate watched as Sam drove off, waving until he

turned the corner. Then she went back inside, locking the door behind her. The man in the maroon coupe parked two houses down flicked his cigarette out the window. He started the engine and pulled away from the curb.

****

Kate took Sam's concern to heart. She called Ray. He'd be over later that evening. Busying herself with the laundry and cleaning the house, her mind kept going back to the reason for Sam's trip to south Texas. Human trafficking was a terrible crime, but when one considered child exploitation, it went from bad to worse. It was horrific. She wondered how anyone could hurt an innocent, let alone look at a child sexually. How sick did someone need to be to do that? Kate knew in her heart it was a story that needed to be written, but reluctantly put all thoughts of it aside. It still troubled her, though. She didn't have any answers for Isabell and the concern over Angela's actions. Kate knew that there were too many young people being drawn to that darkness and their lives ruined. Whether it was sex, drugs, or violence, parents were often ignorant or uncaring, sometimes both. Society turned a blind eye, and the vultures were circling, looking for their next meal. She hadn't witnessed teenage girls dancing topless at the club. But, after seeing the sign for 'Amateur Night', Kate knew there still existed the potential for problems for young innocent women.

Putting the final touches on dinner and popping it into the oven, Kate wiped her hands on the kitchen towel. Ray would be over soon. They planned on an early dinner, followed by binge-watching Jack Ryan. Pulling the salad from the refrigerator, she was humming the theme song to herself and smiling at the prospect when the phone rang.

Thinking it might be Sam checking in after landing, Kate practically sang into the mouthpiece. "Hello." She heard a familiar voice speaking in hushed tones, as if the caller didn't want anyone to overhear the conversation. It was Janet Winburn. She was calling from a private telephone number and breathing hard, like she'd just run up a flight of stairs.

A puzzled look crossed Kate's face. "Janet? Is that you?" Kate had emailed Janet after Sam left, explaining that she was no longer pursuing the topic. She didn't mention the failed operation as the reason. The call struck her as extremely odd. Kate never expected Janet Winburn to contact her again, especially after she'd closed the file. With caution, she continued. "Janet, what is going on? Is everything all right?"

Blowing out a frustrated breath, Janet's words rushed out. "Kate, you must continue writing about exploitation. I mean, I know the operation didn't go well, and you said you wanted to back off, but we have new information. We feel sure it will be a successful operation this time."

Kate pulled the phone from her ear and looked at it in disbelief. *What the heck?* "Janet, I still believe in the article's importance; however, circumstances have changed. Someone else will have to do it." Kate listened to Janet's ragged breathing on the other end of the line. There was a man's muffled voice in the background. Janet covered the phone and mumbled a reply to the anonymous voice. Feeling that there was other business Janet needed to address, Kate tried to be gracious and conclude the conversation.

"Janet, there are many talented reporters out there. Find someone else to write the article. It sounds like someone needs to speak with you. You should go."

"No, no. I just really want you involved, Kate. Your husband is working on an exploitation case as well, I understand. I'm sure that gives you a unique perspective. Perhaps you can share some of what he has learned, so I know what additional information to share so you can write the article. And I promise, the next operation will be a success." There was a tension in Janet's voice that Kate hadn't heard before. An insistence. "Really, we should talk and you must come, Kate. You'll get so much for an article." Janet's tone was demanding. Kate didn't recognize this Janet Winburn.

"Janet, you need to do what you feel is best. As do I. Circumstances have changed. I am not writing the article. I cannot share anything about my husband's work and I will not accompany you now or any other time." Kate thought she heard the voice in the background grow angry. It made Kate uncomfortable. "Goodbye, Janet."

Kate hit the end button and sat staring at the phone, thinking that the entire conversation had been weird. First, Janet wanted Kate to be there for the arrest, then she mentioned Sam and his work. Thanking her lucky stars that she had other things to do with her time, Kate put the conversation from her mind.

****

Janet hung the phone up slowly, searching for a way to satisfy Ricco, even though she'd failed to get him what he wanted. She wiped her sweaty palms on her slacks, ran a nervous tongue around dry lips. Ricco was leaning against the wall, watching her, his arms crossed casually across his chest. He had an irritating, all-knowing smirk on his face.

"She didn't give you what you need and now you can't give me what I want." Ricco pushed off the wall and came around behind her, brushing his hand over her hair. "Your daughter's hair is this same shade of brown, but she has added highlights. I like the highlights. You should try it."

Janet shuddered in revulsion and fear. She desperately wanted to think Amy was safe. For Christ's sake, the girl was across the country, living with her dad, Janet's ex-husband, under his name. But Amy had added the highlights just last month. Did Ricco know where her daughter was? Janet pushed up from the chair, ignoring his veiled threat. Walking to the other side of the room, she tried redirecting his attention back to Kate and Sam.

"You are right, Ricco. But, Kate told me again that she doesn't know anything about her husband's work. She said she won't write any more articles. Isn't that what you want? I'll keep Spencer and his crew chasing their tails. They keep focusing on Marchetti and the gentlemen's clubs. Your other business ventures are not on Spencer's radar. You are not on his radar."

Ricco sat down in the chair Janet had just vacated, leaning back comfortably, hands resting lightly on the arms. "So, what exactly did she tell you, Janet?"

Chapter 12

Vincent stayed late at school, searching the library shelves for more books on the FBI and CIA. He was in a serious conversation with Dale Kilmer, his best buddy, about a new book he'd purchased. It was called *How to Become a Spy: A Guide to Developing Spy Skills and Joining the Elite Underworld of Secret Agents and Spy Operatives* by Maxwell Knight.

"You know, Dale, being a covert operative isn't just babes and booze, like in the movies. This book will help me hone my spy skills." Vincent wanted to be an investigator, like Sam. He thought a little extra research wouldn't hurt in his quest. Interrogation and observation were two important things Sam said. Even though Vincent had passed his Spy School 101 exam at the park, he and Sam still continued to practice. Sam challenged Vincent's skills of observation, surveillance, and research. He'd put something in the room that was out of place, and Vincent had to figure out what it was. He'd do the same and see how long it took Sam to find it. Sam was really good. He could find anything within seconds. Vincent wanted to be just like him. Turning to his buddy, Dale, Vincent regaled him with more tales of Sam and spy-craft. Barely containing his excitement, the two turned toward the exit.

"No, really. It's a brilliant book. Talks about what a spy has to do, you know? My friend Sam is kind of like a spy. He's training me. I'm keeping a journal of all my reports. I use code names, so no one but me knows who I'm spying on." Dale snorted in disbelief. He was a chubby boy who wore his jeans rolled up because his mom bought them too long and a Western-style plaid shirt with faux pearl buttons. Dale was beyond nerdy, but he had the same passion for espionage as Vincent. The two spent hours poring over anything and everything spy-related.

"Code names? Do I have one?" Dale asked.

Vincent gave him a friendly nudge with his shoulder. "That's easy. I call you Kil-cuffs."

Dale smiled. "Kil-Cuffs. I like it. Sounds way cool. Tough, ya know?" Dale puffed out his chest and wiggled his shoulders a little, swelling with pride. "Kil-cuffs", he repeated with a fierce tone in his voice. "Do you have a code name?"

Vincent had the good sense to blush. "Yeah. I like Cam-Man." Dale gave Vincent a high five, nodding. "Way cool, dude!" The two swaggered out the door.

Vincent noticed his sister across the way. She was standing in the bus stop shelter, talking with a couple of girls. He recognized Sandi, the high school dance club girl. He wasn't sure who the other one was. She was smoking. She offered it to Angela. Vincent watched his sister shake her head. That was good. Smoking was bad for you. He was glad she was smart enough to say no. Thinking about it, Vincent figured the blonde girl was Melanie. The one Angela wasn't supposed to be hanging out with. Boy, Grandma was going to be mad about that if it was. Probably earn Angela another grounding.

"Hey, there's my sister. I have to go. I'll see you

tomorrow." Giving Kil-Cuffs their secret handshake in parting, Vincent crossed the street, calling to Angela.

"Yo, Angela. What are you doing? Want to walk home together?" His backpack bumped on his hip as he jogged across the street. He'd grown three inches over the summer, and his gangly legs seemed to outdistance the jeans his grandma bought him every other month. Vincent continued his strength training like Sam had taught him. He spent several minutes every morning after his shower admiring the muscles developing in his upper arms. Vincent didn't miss the rolling of her eyes or the 'it's my stupid brother' comment as he approached her. "Who's your friends?" Vincent asked, all innocent.

Angela didn't hide her embarrassment or disgust at having her little brother bother her. "Go away, you little pest. I'll go home when I want to. I'm hanging with my friends now." She flipped her hair and turned her back, giggling at something the cigarette girl whispered. They walked off, swaying their hips like the movie stars Vincent had watched with his grandma on the academy awards red carpet.

Vincent looked at his watch. They were supposed to be home by 5:30 for dinner. He bet she'd be late. Shrugging, he turned to head home. On impulse, he cut across the park and was just emerging from the other side when he saw the three girls again. Sandi and Melanie had taken off their jackets. They were wearing see-through blouses cut way low. Vincent could see the swell of their breasts and Melanie was wearing a red bra. It matched the red of her lipstick. They reminded him of his mom. Vincent ducked behind the shrubs, wanting to see what Angela was up to. He hated she might do something bad. His mom had done this kind of stuff and look where it got her. She did drugs and drank. Sometimes she hit him and Angela. Now his mom was in jail. Vincent was worked up enough to march right over to Angela and yell at her to stop when a car pulled up. He stepped further back into the screen of the trees to observe, just like Sam had taught him.

Vincent watched a guy get out of the car and climb into the back seat. Melanie joined him and they started making out. The guy had his hand down her blouse and they were kissing with lots of tongue. He leaned his head back against the seat and Melanie sunk below the window line. All Vincent could see was the top of her head. Vincent didn't know what she was doing, but the guy seemed to like it. He rested his hand on her head.

The driver had gotten out when Melanie got in. He walked over to Angela and Sandi. The trio walked over to a picnic table perching on the top, talking. It was pretty lame and boring. Then the driver guy was laughing at something Angela said. He clucked her under the chin. The driver guy had a Bluetooth wireless speaker, found some music on his phone, and turned it on. Giving her an encouraging nudge with his shoulder, Angela stood and motioned to Sandi. They moved to the center of the concrete pad and executed some dance moves. The driver guy had cued up "Hot Dancing" and Angela and Sandi showed off their routine.

Vincent recognized it. Heck, Angela practiced the dumb thing almost every night. He teased her about how stupid it was and she only thought she looked sexy. Vincent figured that's what brothers were supposed to do, tease their sisters about goofy stuff.

When the song finished, the driver guy applauded.

He waved his hand as if he'd touched something hot. Angela blushed. He gave her a caramel candy, Angela's favorite. Then Sandi did her own dance. She added a lot of hip action and butt wiggling. Vincent thought Angela was way better.

Sandi sashayed up to the driver guy, rubbing against him and giving him a peck on the cheek. She turned and bragged to Angela, mostly about boring girl stuff, hairstyles, and clothes. No one seemed interested in what Sandi had to say, which seemed to make her mad. Sandi flicked her hair back and made a perturbed smile. Vincent heard her say she had to go home. She picked up her backpack, leaving Angela alone with the driver guy.

The driver guy actually looked okay. He was more Angela's age, Vincent thought. After Sandi left, Angela and the guy talked about movies, music, and school. Vincent heard him say he worked for his cousin Ricco. He was driving him around and doing odd jobs. The driver guy was going to study business at the community college. That was only until he could move up in the company. They were laughing and joking. Vincent thought the driver guy might like Angela. She sure acted like she liked him. At least he wasn't putting his hands on her or giving her tongue. During the conversation, the driver guy kept Angela facing away from the car.

Vincent worked his way around to get closer to hear more of what they were saying. From his new vantage point, he could see the car. Melanie's blonde head bobbed up and down. Vincent forgot to look at his watch, but thought it wasn't too long before she got out of the back seat of the car, followed by the backseat guy. He was tucking his shirt back into his pants. The backseat guy reached out and pinched her boob, then slapped her on the butt and said something to the driver guy. Vincent watched the driver guy kiss Angela on the cheek. The two men got in the car and drove off.

Vincent moved closer to the girls. They were too busy watching the car drive away to notice him. He was close enough to hear their conversation. It confused him.

"Oh, did Sandi have to go home? I wanted her to see this, too. You see, Angela? Just a little touching, and Ricco gave me this tennis bracelet. It's gold, and I bet these are genuine diamonds. It's easy, and he gives me lots of nice things. Ricco says I'm his special girl." Melanie was holding her wrist out, turning it so the light glinted off the jewelry, showing off.

Angela was looking like she wanted a bracelet, too. "All you did was let him touch your boobs? Does Ricco always give you something when he does that?"

"Oh, yes. At first, all we did was hug and kiss. Little things, you know? I'd do something nice for him and he'd give me things. Movie tickets or gift cards. Then one day, Ricco asked if he could see my boobs. He was real polite. Then he asked if he could touch them and kiss them. I let him and you know, it felt kind of nice. And did I tell you? Ricco is a photographer. His studio is called Virgin Photography. Like the record company, you know? We've done some fashion shoots. Ricco has these fancy clothes he borrows for me to wear. He says the pictures are good but ordinary. As a professional photographer, he knows what the modeling agencies are looking for. Ricco bought me some bubble bath. Said he wanted to get some shots of me in a bath with bubbles all around. He says pictures of me in a bubble bath would be really cool. I could get paid to pose. Be an actual model, you know? We went to a hotel. It had one of those big, round tubs. Ricco set it all up, bubbles and everything. I posed. It was really professional. He paid me fifty dollars and gave me a bottle of perfume."

Angela looked impressed. "An actual model? Sometimes when you and Ricco are together, me and Tony hold hands. He's very nice and brings me caramels. He always kisses me on the cheek when we say goodbye. I like him. Do you think he'd give me things if I let him see my boobs?"

"I don't know. Why don't you ask him if he wants to see them?" Melanie, or 'the backseat girl,' as she would be in Vincent's report, wiggled her wrist in front of Angela again. "You might get something nice, too."

Vincent stood watching with his mouth hanging open, listening to the backseat girl brag about what she'd done. He felt sick. It was just like their mom. Turning as quietly as a spy should, he ran home. As his feet ate up the pavement, Vincent didn't feel the tears running down his cheeks; the snot clogging his nose.

When dinner time rolled around, Vincent said he didn't feel well and stayed in his room.

****

The next day, Ray found Vincent in the backyard throwing stones at a row of tin cans he'd set up on a plank.

"You paint a face on that can and they would consider it murder one." Ray had been watching long enough to recognize the anger and hurt welling up from the boy. He didn't want to pry but wanted to give the boy a chance to talk about what was bothering him. "You need to talk about something or just kill the cans?" Ray reached out a tentative hand, placing it on Vincent's shoulder, turning the boy so he could see his face. "Come on, son. Let's have it. What has upset you so much? Anything I can do to help?"

Vincent dropped the fistful of stones he had been tightly clenching. Plopping down on the porch steps, Vincent looked over his shoulder to make sure his grandmother wasn't within earshot. His hands hung limply between his knees, and he bowed his head. Ray sat next to him and waited until Vincent was ready to open up. It didn't take long. It started with a shuddered breath and a quick hand swipe at his running nose.

"I hate my mom. I hate what my mom did." Vincent all but whispered it, tears streaming down his face. Ray put his arm around thin, shaking shoulders and held on.

"What did your mom do, Vincent? And why do you hate her?" Ray knew some things. Isabell had shared enough for him to know that these kids had seen and experienced things no kid should.

"She let men do things to her." He squinched his eyes tightly shut as though trying to block out hurtful memories. "She didn't have to do them. She wanted to. And I'm afraid Angela will want to do it too."

Ray felt a stab of fear. Young people sometimes made bad choices. Isabell was worried about just such a thing with Angela. She worried about the friends Angela was hanging around with. Hoping to not make a big deal out of it, Ray nudged Vincent in the ribs. "Everybody does dumb stuff every so often. Do you know something specific that Angela is doing we should be worried about?"

Ray saw Vincent's eyes shutter as the boy shook his head. Something was up, but Vincent wouldn't rat out his sister. Ray sighed inwardly and continued. "Angela has you to look after her. Help her not be stupid. That's what brothers are for. Sam was always there for Emily when they were your age. You are there for Angela, right? You've got her back. And your grandmother and I have yours."

"Yeah, sure. It will be okay." Vincent didn't look convinced nor sound it. "Well, I have some homework to do. See you later, Ray." He didn't make eye contact as he slunk away into the house. Ray watched with a worried expression on his face, determined to talk with Isabell at the first opportunity.

Chapter 13

"What did he say?" Angela was in her room, cupping the phone to her mouth, speaking as quietly as her eagerness would let her.

"Yes, yes, yes. Ricco says we can go Monday morning," Melanie gushed back, as excited as Angela. This was way cooler than anything she had ever done. "Angela, the bubble bath pictures worked. Ricco says his contacts think I'm pretty enough to be a model. I didn't tell you before, but I did some other pictures too. Ricco posed me like a picture of some old actress, Farrah, something. She was wearing a bathing suit in her picture." Melanie giggled. "I wasn't in mine. Ricco says it was perfect. And as a photographer, he should know. Ricco wants to take some more pictures of me to show to an agent. He says he thinks I could get an offer. Maybe be a magazine swimsuit model. Ricco would be the photographer. It could be the start of his dream studio, Virgin Photography."

Angela was happy for her best friend. With Melanie's long blond hair and curvaceous figure, of course, she could be a model. Angela frowned at her own reflection in the mirror, turning her face side to side. She had thick brown hair and eyes, but she felt her nose was too wide, her eyebrows too thick. She was much thinner than Melanie, with long legs. Angela looked at her almost size B boobs and thought she didn't have the figure to be a model but she had always dreamed of being a dancer. Angela practiced the moves she watched in the music videos at the park with her friends. And she danced them for Tony when they hung out. She wanted to dance and wondered what other talent the agent represented. Angela bit her thumbnail, wanting to ask more. Tony had told her she was good. "Melanie, do you think this agent represents dancers, too?"

"I don't know. Hey, do you want to come with me? Tony will be there. You'll have to skip school. Can you do that? It would be fun to have you there. Ricco says he set it up at some sort of dance club. He says the lighting will be good for taking pictures. There are costumes I can borrow for the photo shoot. Maybe you can borrow some and practice dancing on an actual stage? That would be so cool. I'll ask Ricco if you can come and if it's okay if you practice dancing."

Angela thought about how she'd get out of school. "I don't know. It's easier for you to skip. Your mom is so busy dating that new guy, she doesn't pay a lot of attention to what you do. I've never skipped school. What if my grandma finds out?"

"Oh, come on. You are such a chicken. She's not your mom, she's only your grandma. You'll never be a professional dancer if you don't have experience. You want to be a dancer, don't you? Come on, Angela. It will be so much fun."

That was all it took. Angela was in. She didn't know how she'd work it, but she'd be there.

****

Come Monday morning, Angela left for school like always. She had packed her dance gear in her backpack.

Melanie told her they'd meet at the park. When the dark gray Chevy pulled up, Angela climbed into the passenger seat. Tony smiled at her and gave her a caramel. They took the expressway south and exited toward a Love's truck stop. Just beyond it, they turned into a potholed parking lot with a metal building at the back. A small strip shopping center with a package store and some place called Crystal's Videos fronted the lot and faced the expressway.

Tony leaned over, an apologetic expression on his face. "I'm sorry it isn't fancier, but Ricco says we can use the lights and stage and sound system. There is a room he can use for his photography." Tony unlocked the door and flipped the switch for the lights. The stage bloomed with bright-colored lights, circling round a seductive silver disco ball. They reflected off the mirrors and other shiny surfaces, sending sparkles flashing around the room.

Angela sucked in a breath. This was what she imagined a Vegas dance show would look like. When Tony showed her the costumes with the feathers and sequins, she knew for sure this was Vegas style. She turned bright eyes to Tony.

"It's the most amazing place. And look at these costumes. Are you sure I can try them on and dance in them? No one will get mad at you?" Angela had pulled a purple satin and silver sequin dress from the rack. She held it up in front of her, swaying back and forth, admiring the movement of the material. She looked at Tony's reflection in the mirror, her fingers wrapped tightly around the hanger. He smiled and held out a pair of silver glitter dance shoes to match the dress.

"Ricco said you could try on anything you wanted.

Pick one out and I'll go cue up some music. Hip-Hop okay with you?" Angela twirled around in a circle, laughing.

"Oh, yes. That would be perfect. Thank you, Tony. You are the best friend a girl could have."

She shooed him toward the door, but before it closed, he called out, "We can order pizza for lunch. It's okay if you have pizza, right? You're not on a diet or anything?" He laughed. Tony always laughed when Angela smiled at him.

"Sure, whatever." Angela wasn't listening to anything he said. She was too busy flipping through the dance costumes. Some were sequined and others were satin and lame. Some were very sheer. Many had cutouts where they should have covered the boobs. Angela wasn't sure how one would wear something like that. They must use a body suit under it, she thought. Her gaze returned to the purple and silver dress. It was tight, but the spandex had enough give for her to pull it up and over her bra. But then, there were no sleeves. She didn't want Tony to see her bra straps. That would be lame. She took off her bra. The dress looked killer and Angela thought she looked sexy.

She opened the door a crack and peeked out. The sound of Beyonce's "Single Ladies" was pumping out of the speakers. The bass rocked the room. She heard the music, it called her. Its beat matched the pulse of her blood. Angela moved sinuously to the center of the stage. Tony turned out the lights and hit Angela with the spotlight. He restarted the song from the top and Angela became everything she ever dreamed of being. Tony increased the volume and the bass. He flipped the lights on full and Angela watched her reflection in the mirror, hypnotized. She swayed and gyrated, she strutted her stuff. Tony used his cell phone camera to capture everything.

When the song ended, he ran up on stage, grabbing Angela around the waist, rocking her side to side, and finally picking her up to spin her round in a joyous hug. "That was fabulous. You rocked it!"

Angela had to catch her breath when he finally set her down. "Was it good? Really, Tony?" She was shaking with excitement. Everything was so cool. How could she not want to dance professionally? Angela hoped the agent handling Melanie's modeling career handled dancers, too.

Angela sat with Tony, watching the video he'd taken with his cell; their heads bent together in concentration. His hand stroked up and down her back. Excitement about her dancing made her oblivious to his touch. Angela was so engrossed in watching the video, she didn't notice his eyes darken with worry.

"This is so cool. You do a great job with the lights and music. You'd think you did it all the time. Can I dance to another one?" she asked, her eyes bright.

"Absolutely. Why don't you pick out a different costume?" He ran his fingers along her bare shoulder and down her arm. "One a little sexier. I want to see the moves you make to "Hot Dancing". That video is all yours, ya know? It makes me think of you. It's got heat just like you do. Hey, I think there is a red dress and all the other stuff in the dressing room that your favorite singer wears in her video. Go check it out while I cue up the song." His voice had gone a little softer. He ran his hand up her arm and used his index finger to tilt her head up. Angela felt heat in places she didn't know she could when he touched his lips to hers.

"Okay," she stammered. Tony turned her toward the dressing room.

Angela looked for the red dress Tony said was there, finding it at the end of the rack. The stockings and garter belt were with it, the shoes there too. She held the dress up in front of her and studied herself in the full-length mirror. Feeling bolder and knowing the song, she stripped off the purple sequined and pulled on the red satin dress. She resisted the urge to look in the mirror until fully outfitted. Turning, Angela gasped and her hands flew to her mouth. She looked like a dance star. She ran a brush through her hair and used red lipstick for the finishing touch.

Angela stepped out of the dressing room and walked onto the stage. Tony shook his head in disbelief. "You look fabulous. Let's see your moves." He walked over to the soundboard and hit the play button.

The song started slowly, the volume low and seductive. Angela swayed just like she learned from watching the video. She'd seen it a zillion times, and knew every move. Angela used her hands to lift her long hair off her neck. She ran her hands over her body, then back up, pulling the hem of the dress up, exposing the garter belt and stocking tops. She rolled her head and her long hair swung invitingly. It mesmerized Tony.

Ricco had already turned Sandi. She'd be dancing in the club this Friday. Today Ricco had told Tony he needed to convince Angela she should pursue her dance career. Ricco said it was easy and it would advance Tony's position from being just an errand boy and driver to a more responsible position. It was just Amateur Night, Ricco assured him.

Chapter 14

Sam arrived home at about 5:45. He was looking forward to surprising Kate with a long weekend at the Keipersol Winery Bed & Breakfast for their anniversary. It was one of their favorite get-aways. They'd spend the day walking hand in hand through the vineyards and then enjoy a candlelit dinner. After which, they'd retire for some very special alone time. The house was redolent with garlic and curry. Kate was in the kitchen, chopping vegetables, talking with Emily. The baby was snoozing in the playpen they kept set up in the family room. Sam gave Kate a lingering hello kiss, said hi to Emily, and leaned over John Mac, running a gentle hand over the fuzz on his head. Feelie wound in and out between Sam's legs, looking for a head rub. "Hey, guys. Smell's great. Jake with you?" he inquired, taking a soda from the fridge.

Emily sniffed. "He and Dad are at the house. Poor John Mac couldn't nap with all the saws and hammering. They are building custom bookshelves for the family room. I swear those two are becoming thick as thieves. They said they'd be here by six." Emily heard a faint rustling and soft cooing from the playpen. "That child has a built-in clock. Never misses a meal. I'll be in the guest room or, as I might start calling it, the milking room." Sam swallowed his soda before he spit it out of his nose.

"Hey, just because you were as big as a cow when you were pregnant doesn't count." He narrowly avoided Emily's punch in response to his wry observation.

"I'll get you for that, Slater!" she said. "And just you wait. Your time is coming. You two can't keep your hands off each other. Jake and I have a pool going on when you'll be in the family way!"

After Emily went to nurse John Mac, Sam nuzzled Kate's neck. "Practice makes perfect, I always say."

****

The boisterous bookshelf builders arrived a little after six. The gentlemen took their beers to the garden to make manly conversation until dinner was ready. Kate delayed serving to let the men have their bonding time.

Following dinner, everyone chipped in to clean up while Jake rocked the baby, singing "Let me Call you Sweetheart" softly under his breath. It was how Jake expressed his love. Emily smiled at the two men in her life. She leaned her head on Kate's shoulder, sighing. "It's all so perfect. Sometimes I have to pinch myself to make sure it's real."

Kate looked at Jake and John Mac with envy as Emily bumped their hips together. "I can't wait for you and Sam to start your family. If you succeed by Christmas, I'll win the bet and split the pot with you."

"Really? How much is in the pot? And who wins if it's after Christmas?" Kate asked, with a twinkle in her eye. Emily's mouth formed a big 'O' and Kate had to shush her before she let the cat out of the bag.

Whispering excitedly, Emily pulled Kate into the guest room. "Are you? Are you pregnant?"

"I don't know. We haven't been officially trying,

but I'm late. When did you know, Emily?" Kate asked, trusting Emily to keep things quiet until it was certain.

"Oh, Kate, honey. You'll know. Your body will feel full, like love overflowing. Have you taken a test yet?"

Shushing Emily again as her voice squealed in excitement and rose in volume, Kate shook her head. "I bought one to have on hand just in case, but it's still too early to take it. I think I'm just hoping, you know?"

Emily hugged her and danced her around in circles. "Oh, Kate, when you are, you'll know and it will be such a happy day. I can't wait. Of course, Christmas is almost three months away. I still might win the pot. And with Sam whisking you away to the Winery for a romantic anniversary weekend? Heck, even if you're not pregnant *now*, my chances of winning just increased exponentially." Emily pulled Kate down to sit on the bed. "You know, with John Mac, Jake and I will stay in town, but Dad and Isabell have volunteered to take him for the evening. I have to tell you, my six weeks postpartum period are up and…" Emily paused, blushing furiously.

Kate's eyes danced merrily. "Emily Edwards. You little slut!" The two women giggled. "That's why you asked about the Velvet Box."

Emily slapped Kate's shoulder playfully. "You shush, Kate. I asked that in confidence. Besides, I wasn't the only one looking at the website. Did you decide on red or black?"

Kate smiled coquettishly. "Neither. I got the emerald green lace one."

Chapter 15

Sam pulled Kate from the car and into his arms. Just like he'd done on their wedding day, one year before, he picked her up and carried her across the threshold into the tiny cottage. The fairy tale image created by the flower laden vines climbing over the entryway and lattice windows made a perfect romantic picture. The winery had set out the wine and charcuterie as ordered. Fragrance from a dozen long-stem red roses filled the air. The staff had turned down the bed and sprinkled a few petals on the crisp white sheets. Sam set Kate down and ran his hands through her hair. Capturing her face, he brought his lips softly to her mouth, teasing and tasting her. Kate moaned in pleasure.

"Sam, we'll miss the wine tasting."

"I'm tasting everything I am thirsty for right now." His voice grew husky as he pushed the straps of her sundress down over her shoulders, following with his mouth. Sam turned Kate in his arms, holding her against his growing erection. He kissed and nuzzled her neck, whispering his intensions into her ear, causing shivers of excitement to skittle in Kate's belly and below.

He sucked her earlobes, first one, then the other. His hands found the tiny buttons on the bodice and slowly undid them, one by one. Kate leaned back into

Sam, reveling in his loving. When he'd freed her breasts, he gently squeezed each one, rolling and elongating her nipples.

Sam turned Kate in his arms to face him. He watched her delicate hands undo the buttons of his shirt and push it from his shoulders. He felt the fire fan as she feathered her fingers over the hair on his chest, traveling downward to his rising erection.

Framing her face with his hands, Sam kissed her. Softly at first. As their tongues teased and tempted, the kiss grew more demanding. Kate pressed against Sam, grasping his shoulders, and pulling him closer. He felt her hands loosen his belt and he let her push his pants down. Sam broke the kiss and stepped out of his pants, standing naked before her. He slipped Kate's sundress and panties down over her hips. Standing back, he let his gaze wander over her nakedness. Kate's breath caught and Sam heard the quick pants of her arousal. His look grew bold, possessive. Kate moaned and moved her hips, pressing against Sam's erection. Her tongue darted out, licking her lips, her eyes locked with Sam's, inviting him to touch, to taste.

Kate grew more aroused. Sam held her hands captive over her head. He used his knee to nudge her legs apart. Then stood back again and let his gaze wander from her slim feet to her blue eyes. She was writhing, begging him to take her. Sam smiled wickedly. Keeping her wrists braceleted with one hand, he moved the other to her breasts. Their fullness begged for his mouth as much as her mews of pleasure did.

Sam brought her hands down, pinning them behind her back. He dropped to his knees and buried his face in her breasts, kissing and laving each taut nipple.

Replacing his mouth with his hand, he moved downward. Sam found her hot and moist, ready for him. He tortured her with his tongue, darting and sucking at her sex until her legs quivered with weakness. Sam placed Kate's hands on his shoulders and his hands under her bottom to hold her up while he continued to lick and suck. When he heard her breath grow ragged and felt her knees weaken, he grew more aggressive. Ever attuned to her body's response, Sam knew when she was at the brink. Rising quickly, he drove into her, sheathing himself in her velvety softness and covered her climatic cry with his mouth.

Sam stood still, fully encased in Kate's tight warmth. He watched and waited for her to float back down. He lifted Kate's legs, wrapping them around his waist. Once again, he ensnared her hands and held them above her head. He kissed her, running his tongue over her lips. He moved his mouth to her throat, sucking at her pulse point, and slowly, oh so seductively slowly resumed his slide in and out. Kate held Sam's gaze and matched him thrust for thrust. When he saw her eyes darken with desire and felt her vaginal muscles tighten, he slowed, lifted her, and, still inside her, walked to the bed. Lying Kate down, he steadily increased the rhythm of their loving. When Kate rushed for the precipice once more, he leapt with her, calling out her name as he came.

The three p.m. tasting was forgotten. Dinner reservations delayed.

****

Feelie greeted Sam and Kate at the door when they returned home on Sunday afternoon. It had been a glorious weekend. Kate walked in wearing a Mona Lisa smile. She was relaxed and well-loved. But coming back to reality meant chores needed doing. There was a lonely cat looking for attention, mail to check, emails to respond to, a garden to water, and preparing one's own meal instead of eating like royalty at a five-star restaurant.

Monday saw the two of them back to normal. Work, work, work. Sam came home, hiding the frustration he felt, in not making headway with the Marchetti case. He put it aside and spent a quiet evening with Kate, watching the ballgame, while she read.

It didn't take long for the family entourage to intrude, issuing an invitation for Thursday dinner and a game night. Emily had taken over the hosting duties. It was easier with the baby to do it at Casa Edwards. Nothing to haul over to Sam and Kate's place.

Sam greeted Emily with a hug, tossed baby John Mac into the air, eliciting a happy gurgle, and gave each man bro hugs as he accepted a beer from Jake. Kate hugged Ray and Jake, snatched a smiling baby from Sam and turned to give Emily a one-armed hug.

Emily was grinning from ear to ear like a cat lapping up a saucer of cream. She and Jake may not have had the romantic weekend get-a-way Kate had enjoyed with Sam, but it was clear Emily and Jake had made the most of the release from their six-week waiting period. The two women exchanged knowing looks. Emily's held a question. Kate smiled enigmatically.

Following a simple meal and a rousing game of Trivia Pursuit, the party wound down and everyone headed home.

****

Sam watched the ten o'clock news and closed up the house before heading to bed. Kate had gone up earlier. Stepping into the bedroom, he saw Kate sitting on the side of the bed, idly brushing her hair. Her loosely belted silk robe covered a matching nightie in soft shades of blue that picked up and enhanced the color of her eyes. Sam watched her from the doorway, his heart beating a rhythm to the love he held for her. Even after a weekend filled with passion, he still couldn't get enough of her.

Kate hummed softly, a dreamy expression on her face. Crossing to her, Sam took the brush from her hand, and using long sinuous strokes, began a slow seduction. She purred as the sensation of the brush tugging gently on her hair sent shivers of anticipation to her core. When Sam put down the brush, Kate leaned back into his arms. Sam knew that with Emily delivering in August, Kate had been thinking about family. They had talked about it and, although they didn't have an exact plan or timeline, each agreed Kate would stop taking the pill.

Sam ran his hands up under the simple silk sleep shirt, finding her breasts full and heavy in his hands, the nipples already taut. He let his lips roam over her neck and across her shoulders as his hand moved lower on her abdomen. His fingers grazed her soft and inviting folds. He felt the wetness of welcome as he let his fingers probe and tease. Kate arched back against him, reaching up, encircling his neck with her arms. Sam released her breast long enough to run his hand up the satiny inside of her arm, using it to turn her to face him. Sam lay her back against the pillows. He watched Kate surrender as he continued to arouse her with his fingers. He held her gaze as he took her over the top. She moaned out loud, then sighed his name.

Kate smiled seductively at a grinning and smug-faced Sam when her focus returned. He peeled away her sleep shirt, then stripped off his clothes until they were skin- to-skin. He ran his hands up and over every inch of her, tantalizing her with his feathery caresses until she was crying out for release once more. Entering her slowly, Sam watched her eyes lose focus again, her tongue darting out to wet dry lips. Her panting grew rapid and shallow. When she was at the edge, he drove into her hard, taking her over the edge. He lifted her hips to meet his urgent demands. Kate wrapped her legs around his waist and opened to receive all of him, matching him thrust for thrust. The two soared over the mountains, plunged into the valley, and came to rest on the peaceful shores of satiation.

Catching her breath, Kate snuggled under Sam's arm, resting her head on his shoulder.

"Sam?" Kate ran her fingertips across his chest, tickling his hair and sending electric shocks to his loins.

"Mmm hmm?" he murmured. Sam was thinking he'd be ready for round two in no time if she kept that up.

"If you could have anything in the entire world, what would you want?"

Sam wasn't paying a lot of attention to her words. His focus was on her hands; what they were doing and where they were heading. "Hmmm. Is this a trick question? I have you. That is everything I could ever want."

"Good answer but, would you want anything else?"

Kate snuggled in a little more.

"Are you angling for a special gift? Giving me hints?" He made lazy circles on her back and ran his hand down her hip. "I can give you a special gift now." Cupping her bottom and pulling her in for a nip on her lips, he rolled her onto her back.

She melted into his arms and let his mouth wander over her face, neck, and body, arching as he took her breast in his hand and ran his tongue around her nipple. She had trouble putting her thoughts into words. "Ahhh. Yes, I'd like a special gift. I'm thinking I'd like a boy."

Sam's mouth froze on its way from her breast, down her abdomen. "Have we already wrapped this gift?"

"Oh yes, Sam. With a big blue bow. Of course, it might be a pink bow. It's too early to know for sure." She was smiling at Sam as he looked at her with an incredibly jubilant and satisfied expression, grinning from ear to ear.

Laughing in joy, Sam hugged Kate, kissing her mouth, her cheeks, everywhere. He pulled back and gazed into her beautiful blue eyes. "Oh, Kate. Are you sure?"

She nodded, eyes dancing in delight. "Yes, Sam. I'm sure. I took the test this morning."

"Our child…" Sam shook his head in wonder. His hand moved with reverence, his fingers splaying over her stomach. "Oh, Kate, I'm thrilled. You make me so happy. A baby. Our baby." He smiled widely, hugging and kissing her again, this time more gently.

Kate drew him deeper into the kiss, telling him with her mouth and mews of pleasure that she wanted the other special gift he had promised earlier, now.

****

Sam and Kate invited Ray, Emily, and Jake over for dinner the next evening and shared the news. Emily jumped up and hugged Kate, then Sam. The men hugged Kate and shook Sam's hand, slapping him on the back proudly. Jake mentioned Sam wouldn't have known how to take care of things had he not forged the way.

"I knew, I knew it, I knew it! That's why you opted for water with lemon last night with dinner. I'm so happy for you. Have you called your doctor? Will you use my doctor? Oh, I have a million questions." Emily went on and on about how their babies would grow up together and there would be hand-me-downs to share. She teased Kate that it wouldn't be long before she was big as a house, too, remembering her swollen belly toward the end. Then she crowed in triumph.

"Ha, ha. Pay up, Dad, Edwards!" Emily had won the baby pool.

At the end of the evening, Jake guided an excited and still talkative Emily out the door, citing that Kate probably needed her rest now that she was in the family way. Kate went up to bed and Ray had a moment to visit with Sam.

"I'm so happy for you, Sam. It's a big step in a marriage. I remember when your mom and I learned she was pregnant. We had just celebrated our third month anniversary. Your mom was such a romantic. I didn't mind at all. Brought her flowers. She loved flowers, remember? She cooked my favorite meal, candles, and the whole shooting match. When she told me, I thought my heart would burst with happiness. I'm sure you're feeling something similar right now."

"I've never been so happy, Dad. Kate is everything to me, the world. But a child? How can I hope to live up to the responsibility?" Sam ran nervous hands through his hair and took a big swallow of the scotch he and his dad were enjoying. "I've been swinging from happiness to God's awful fear of failing."

"Damn right you are!" Ray stood, jubilant for his son and appreciating Sam's apprehension. "And you will be until the day they put you in the grave. Do you think parental worry stops when your child moves out?" He paced the floor, his comments growing soft and sorrowful with memories. "When your mom first told me she was carrying our child, I was blind with the joy. I missed the signs, but instinctively, your mom knew something was wrong. She tried to tell me. But no. I was in denial."

Sinking down on the sofa, Ray hung his head in shame. "When your mom lost the baby, I totally screwed up. It was my fault. I should have seen how tired she was. I should have saved the baby. When I failed, I turned away in my grief, forgetting that your mom felt the loss, too. The guilt ate at me every day. I questioned God, hated him. I thought he'd forsaken us."

Sam didn't know how to respond to this. He'd always assumed the unplanned pregnancy had trapped his mom into marrying his dad. She gave up her promising art career for him. To learn that he had been wrong all these years shocked him, made him wonder how many other things he had assumed were untrue.

"I never was one for church, but that was when your mom started going. The priest was a good man. He'd lost his wife and knew grief when he saw it. He counseled Marianne. She found peace. I struggled for so long. Then God gave us you, Sam."

Ray put his hand on Sam's shoulder, squeezing it affectionately. "I think I rode you so hard because I was trying to make up for failing with our first child. It was difficult to trust God. I wondered what I'd done wrong to deserve to lose a child. My fear was that he would take you from us, too. I couldn't fail you or your mother again."

Sam understood some of what had driven his dad. After all, he had his own fear of failure and still battled his demons. "Dad, I think I get it. I think I've lived it." A small crack formed in the hard heart Sam had held for so many years.

Chapter 16

Since he'd overheard the bracelet conversation, Vincent made it his primary mission to follow Angela whenever she left the house. Ray was right. He'd keep watch over Angela and make sure she didn't do anything stupid. She never saw him and if she would have, he'd just shove the book in her face and tell her he was practicing his spy skills. She didn't do much of interest. Stupid girl stuff, shopping, and coffee shops. Vincent didn't see the backseat girl hanging with Angela or her other friend, Sandi. He hoped maybe they had a fight and weren't friends anymore. Vincent made up a lot of explanations that were better than what he imagined was the truth about that. He was afraid they'd run away and Angela would run away, too. Vincent had to know, had to ask. Planning his approach, Vincent timed it, so he ran into her on the way home from school.

"Hey, Angela. Fancy meeting you here." It was something Ray always said. Old people's talk was corny. "Are you heading home? Want to walk together?" He fell in with her longer strides, ignoring the daggers she shot toward him.

Vincent reached for something generic to talk about. "Did you hear Ray got a cat? He rescued it from the shelter. It's older but real sweet. Remember when we wanted to get a cat and Mom said no? Ray said we could come over and play with it." Vincent was rambling, trying to work up the courage to ask about the backseat girl. His spy book didn't have a lot of information on how to interrogate suspects. They fell into an uneasy silence. Vincent thought Angela looked nervous, like she was afraid someone would see her with him. Unsure how to ask, he just blurted it out.

"Hey, what happened to your friends? I don't see Sandi or Melanie hanging around anymore. Did you guys have a fight or something?"

Angela stopped and stared at Vincent; squinting at him suspiciously. "No, we didn't have a fight. Why are you asking? Did Grandma put you up to it? Did she ask you to spy on me?" Angela shoved Vincent with each question until he tripped over his feet and fell on his bottom. "It's none of your business what I do or who my friends are." Angela stalked away, leaving Vincent to pick himself up. He brushed his pants off and hefted his backpack over his shoulder. He waited until Angela turned the corner, then followed at a distance, keeping her in sight until she arrived safely home.

Vincent grew bored following Angela. She didn't do anything now that Melanie wasn't around. The driver guy he'd seen her with didn't come around anymore, either. It had been a while since she'd pushed him down. Man, she'd been pissed at him. After blowing off following Angela, Vincent practiced his spy skills on Donnie Little. He was a bully, and Vincent hoped to catch him in the act. He could report it and be a hero. Vincent figured everything was fine with his sister until that changed.

Chapter 17

Angela hated her life. Her grandma was so old-fashioned. She had set a curfew and bedtime. Angela toed off her shoes, kicking them toward the closet. Her socks came next. She almost hit the hamper when she threw them. Pulling off her jeans and t-shirt, she tossed them carelessly on the chair and yanked her sleep shirt over her head. Angela was mad at Vincent. Sometimes he was a little tattletale. He better not be telling Grandma what she did, or she'd clobber him.

She sat on the side of her bed, thinking about Sandi and Melanie, and Vincent's question. They didn't have a fight. Her two friends had just stopped coming to school. The last thing Melanie had said was that she was leaving with Ricco. She was going to be a model. Angela was happy for her, but confused, too. Sandi just disappeared. And Tony? He hadn't been by for a couple of weeks. She missed him. He had been funny and kind. Tony brought caramels, and they'd talk about music and dancing while Melanie and Ricco visited in the car. Angela never had the chance to ask him if he'd like to see her boobs. Punching her pillow she lay down, turned off the light, then stared at the shadows on the ceiling until she finally nodded off.

****

Ordering a latte, Angela was digging through her purse for the money when she heard a familiar voice tell the barista, "Just add her latte to my order." Angela turned to see a smiling Ricco standing behind her.

"Ricco. How are you? Is Tony with you? Where have you been lately? How is Melanie? Did she get that modeling job?" She felt heat suffuse her face, thinking that was rude, asking him where they'd been. It was none of her business, really, but she wondered about Melanie and had missed Tony.

Ricco laughed. "Tony is out in the car. I was getting our coffees to go, but we can come in." Ricco's smile turned into a smirk. "Oh, and Melanie has been busy. She said to tell you hi."

Ricco texted, and the next thing Angela knew, Tony was walking through the door. He had a radiant smile on his face. He pressed a caramel in her hand and kissed her cheek. Ricco stepped away, sitting at a different table, letting the two talk privately.

Tony took their coffees and steered Angela to a table in the shop's rear. "Hi. I missed you. Ricco has been keeping me busy. Tell me, how have you been?"

The loneliness Angela had felt when Tony was gone melted away. They talked and laughed. Tony touched her hand and smiled into her eyes. Angela was in love.

Tony told her about Ricco working as a talent scout, looking for dancers.

"He's been assigned to find dance talent for a club in Houston. It means he has to travel and I have to go with him, like his assistant. I rent cars and get hotel rooms. Stuff like that. Ricco organizes auditions for the dancers. You should see the costumes the girls that are dancing wear. An agent from Las Vegas came to the Houston club and offered a job to one dancer. Ricco says she's a big deal in a Vegas show now. Ricco sent one of our local girls down to Houston to replace her. But now he has to find someone to take her place at the Fort Worth club. He says we'll have to travel again unless he can find talent locally." Tony sighed, sounding exasperated. "I'm glad you aren't mad at me for going away. I don't want to leave again."

Angela remembered how Tony had said how well she could dance. Maybe someone would discover her. Shyly broaching the subject, she touched his arm. "Tony, do you think I might be good enough to audition? If I am, you wouldn't have to travel. I could be the replacement dancer."

Angela watched Tony sip his latte thoughtfully. He looked at Ricco. If she could have read minds, she'd know he was following the instructions Ricco had given him. She would have heard the scripted presentation leading her along until she would willingly follow Ricco's plan.

"I'll ask Ricco. He is pretty particular." Tony glanced over his shoulder. Ricco was idly checking his phone. "Hey, I should go. Do you want to meet up at the park? I'll text you when I can, okay?" Tony planted a sweet kiss on Angela's cheek and motioned to Ricco. Giving Angela one last smile, the two men left. Angela sighed. She was in love and might audition for a real dance job.

****

Ricco climbed into the passenger seat. He noticed how Tony glanced back at the coffee shop and gave a little wave. Ricco had enjoyed watching the bright light of excitement build in Angela's eyes as she and Tony chatted over coffee. The kid was following his instructions well. But Ricco remembered how something changed in Tony after they'd all gone to the club that day so Angela could dress up and dance for fun. Ricco wasn't sure what was going on or where the kid's head was at. He would make sure not to include Tony in any of the other activities the girls did until he knew more.

Putting his phone away, Ricco scrutinized Tony. The kid had potential, but he was going soft on Angela. Ricco needed to turn her. He slapped Tony on the shoulder and gave him a pep talk. "Look, this is a straightforward job. Just because she is cute, don't get all lovey-dovey with her. There are plenty of cute girls out there. Your job is to meet them, charm them, and then leave them to me. I'll introduce them to their future employment."

Tony blushed. Ricco saw this as a problem, but didn't say so. "You did a good job getting to know Sandi. She is an excellent dancer. The agents liked her. She moved on in her career. I'm proud of you, Tony."

Ricco settled back into the seat, letting his mind wander while Tony drove them back to the club. He remembered turning Sandi. She really got off on Amateur Night and ended up being one of the more popular dancers in the club, even though she wasn't the prettiest. Ricco would never understand, but in his experience, the less pretty girls were easier to manipulate. Somehow, they felt they had to try harder. He'd placed Sandi in the Sexy Slippers dance club with three teenagers found by other talent scouts. She was the best one of them all. Her tiny titties appealed to the more prurient of patrons; the ones that liked little girls. When Sandi wasn't dancing, Ricco had her posing, dressed in mini skirted school uniforms. She'd asked once about going home, but the black eye Ricco gave her changed her mind.

Ricco wanted to build the business. It had been his idea to set up a sex shop in the little frame house. He had partitioned the house into six small rooms. The girls were available to entertain guests for the right price. The business was efficient and knocked down about two grand a week. When they weren't servicing the in-person clientele, the house manager kept them locked in a dormitory-style setup. Their only clothes were thongs and filmy nighties. Ricco had installed hidden cameras to capture footage of the girls going about their day. The organization had a lot of online subscribers. When you added in the subscriptions to the live feed of the girls parading around in little or nothing, you could double the weekly take. Ricco recalled when Sandi started causing problems. He'd given her a few more bruises to think about and moved her from dancing to this division of the business.

Since opening the house, Ricco learned some girls enjoyed being on camera. They strutted their stuff. Others had to be persuaded. Fists or drugs worked for those that were reluctant to take part. Melanie had been the star of the videos. He kept feeding her the 'starlet' story. When she wasn't acting in the private porn videos he shot of her, Ricco enjoyed her company in the little frame house. She liked him and was a willing student, embracing his kinky sex styles. As long as he took pictures and talked about the talent agents who wanted her to model and act, she did anything he wanted. But then she bitched about having to let some fat old man do her, even though Ricco lied and told her the guy was a Hollywood director. It got old fast. She and her friend Sandi were getting mouthy and demanding. It wasn't good for business. Ricco shipped them south to let the coyotes take care of the inconvenience.

The house on the corner of Gambrel and McCart was ideal for Ricco's business. The loft over the three-car garage gave him the space he needed for the dormitory. There were already bars over the windows, but Ricco nailed plywood up, just in case one of the girls got smart and tried to wave for help. He'd painted the plywood black. To a passing motorist, it resembled solar screens. There was an efficiency apartment on the first level for the house manager. She prepared meals, cleaned, did the laundry for the girls, such as there was. Her sister managed the business end with the clients, taking the money and bringing the selected girl from the loft to the house. Marc was there for muscle.

Ricco thought about the many perks of having his little side business with the house. He could enjoy the freebies with any of the girls whenever he wanted. There was a dark-haired seventeen-year-old Ricco was currently favoring with his attention. She had massive jugs and full red lips. He smiled, recalling how compliant she was. After one enjoyable session, Ricco had slapped her on the ass and sent her to the door for Marc to take back to the garage. Before she left, he pulled a Ziplock bag from his pocket and removed one of the rhinestone tennis bracelets. He clasped it around her wrist. "Here you go, baby. You're my special girl." She'd earned it.

Bringing himself back to the matter at hand, Ricco considered what to do about Tony and Angela. He'd watched her dance. The girl had moves. He wanted Angela in the club. She obviously had a crush on Tony. Now all Ricco had to do was figure out how to get Tony to see the advantages of turning the girl. Then Tony could have Angela any time he wanted and Ricco could make money off her talents.

"Come on, Tony. I think Angela might be an even better dancer than Sandi. We need to replace the girl that the Vegas agent stole. I'm counting on you."

Tony didn't take his eyes off the road. His hands tightened on the wheel. He nodded, but didn't look happy.

****

During the next two weeks, Tony met Angela at the park almost every day after school. Their conversations centered on her dancing, movies, and family. He liked to imagine Angela having dinner with her grandmother and brother. It sounded better than the fast food and pizza Ricco usually brought home. Tony wanted to be invited to share the family time. The only family he had was Ricco.

Following Ricco's instructions, Tony gave Angela little gifts. He thought about her wanting to audition to be the replacement dancer. She had asked about it more than once. Tony always put her off.

"That is an interesting idea, Angela. Let me think about it." Ricco wanted him to tell her yes, but he didn't feel right about having Angela make those moves on the stage, to have men whistle at her, ogling her. Tony learned that the girls who danced eventually stripped and sometimes they disappeared. He wondered what Ricco would do if he just said no. Tony remembered Mike had told Ricco no, and now he wasn't around anymore. Ricco said they fired him. Tony really needed this job to pay for college. He reluctantly agreed to bring Angela to the club on Friday night.

Tony was waiting at the park when Angela rushed up. "Tony, Tony, Tony!!!" She was bouncing around, dancing in circles around him. "My dance arrangement for the Homecoming was the winner. I will teach all the girls how to do it and we'll perform at halftime." Angela grabbed his hands and leaned in to kiss him. "It wouldn't have been as good if you didn't let me practice for you all the time. Will you come watch it?" He saw her excitement, how she watched him with hopeful eyes.

Giving her a big hug, Tony let his happiness for her shine past his worry. That might have been why she didn't see the dark, dirty side of what he was going to offer her. "You bet I'll come. I wouldn't miss it. But Angela, I have good news too. Ricco says they are holding auditions. He said I should bring you."

Tony watched Angela's eyes grow wide with surprise and excitement. "Oh, Tony. A real audition, real dancing. Yes. When? When is it?"

Tony explained everything. When he was done, Tony showed her the blue sequined dress like Ricco told him to.

Angela clapped her hands. He watched as she carefully rolled the dress and stuffed it into her backpack. "I'll have to sneak it into the house. My grandmother already found the clothes Melanie gave me. Hey, by the way. Have you heard from Melanie? She told me she was going out of town for a photo shoot. She must have gotten the job because Ricco said she was busy and to tell me hi. I thought she'd be back by now."

Tony looked up from the backpack where Angela had stuffed the dress. His eyes narrowed. Something wasn't right. That wasn't the story Ricco had told him. Tony knew he'd have to ask about it. For now, he didn't want to worry Angela.

"I don't know. Ricco hasn't said anything to me about it. I'll ask him. But you're going to audition!" Tony talked about the important men who would watch her dance as he held her hand. He feathered his fingertips over her forearms, watching goosebumps form and feeling her little shivers. She was innocent and probably didn't understand what she was feeling, but he could tell she liked it.

Leaning her head on his shoulder, she sighed. "Tony, I want to be a dancer more than anything in the world. Thank you for helping me make this dream come true. You are the sweetest guy I know."

Angela's eyes closed as she leaned in for a kiss. Tony hesitated. Ricco had said the men who watched her dance might want to touch her. He placed a caramel in Angela's hand and kissed her goodnight. "You head on home, try on the dress. I'll see you Friday night, usual time. Okay?"

"Sure. See you then."

Tony watched Angela in his rear-view mirror as he drove off. He was walking a damn fine line, trying to make both Ricco and Angela happy. She wanted to dance, to audition. Maybe there was a way.

****

Returning home, Angela quietly went to her room, closing and locking the door. She carefully laid the dress across her bed and ran her hands over the satiny softness, smoothing it out. Stripping down to her underwear, she pulled it on. She had to shimmy to slip the dress over her hips and boobs. It was low cut and short with a slit up each leg almost to her hips. Angela knew enough about costumes to know the dress was to be worn with a thong, so the material would lie flat and sparkle during her dancing. She pulled down her panties, kicking them under the bed. Turning, Angela looked at herself in the mirror. A small gasp of surprise escaped her lips. She was beautiful, sexy, just like Tony said she'd look. She twirled. The blue sparkles bounced around the room, reflecting off the light from her bedside lamp. Angela clasped her hands over her mouth and giggled.

Chapter 18

Sam sat at his desk, reading through the reports from the Presidio County Sheriff's office. He was no closer than when first assigned the case. It had dragged on for weeks and now they uncovered two more bodies of young girls in the desert. The autopsy put their age around sixteen. The only identification on either was a cheap tennis bracelet tucked into the lining of the shorts one girl wore. Sam's team was getting closer, but still lacked the definitive evidence to tie in the Marchetti family. Setting aside the photos of the dead girls, he took a break. His gaze settled on Kate. She was curled up in his leather chair with a book. Sam loved to watch her and took breaks more often than he should to do it. It was an unusually warm day for fall, so she wore loose capris and a t-shirt. Her legs were tan and her feet bare. The book she was reading was about brainwashing. How she came up with her story ideas always surprised him. It was as if she were prescient, choosing topics that were ahead of whatever was an upcoming trend or crisis for her articles. She absently tucked a lock of hair behind her ear and jotted down something in her journal. It was a compendium of thoughts, ideas, witticisms, and profound discoveries.

Sam's eyes settled on Kate's stomach. It was still too early in Kate's pregnancy for her to show. That didn't stop him from wanting to touch her tummy. He loved to lie next to her at night and rub oils into her tight belly. Sam remembered feeling John Mac move in Emily's womb. How incredible it would be when he felt his own child move for the first time. As if feeling his eyes on her, Kate looked up, smiling.

"Time for a break? How about some iced tea?" She uncurled from the chair and walked barefoot to the passageway through the butler's pantry toward the kitchen. "Eeww. Feelie, please don't bring your trophies into the house. Sam, would you take it out to the trash? Yuck!" Kate took a wide step over the dead mouse as Sam came up behind her.

"Good job, Feelie! Mighty huntress." He patted her on the head, giving her a quick ear rub, and followed Kate into the kitchen for a paper towel and plastic bag.

"Don't encourage her! Next thing, she'll be bringing them into our bed." Kate shuddered at the thought.

Sam did the dirty work, wiping up the floor and taking the dead mouse out to the trash. He knew to keep quiet. The phone was ringing when he returned. Kate let the answering machine pick up.

"Kate, it's Janet Winburn. I know you have put your article aside, but I wanted to reach out to you once more. There is so much to discuss. You need to know the specifics about child exploitation. I have an opening in my schedule on Tuesday at ten. Would you like to meet? Call me." Kate walked over to the machine and deleted the message. Sam saw the abrupt way she pushed the button and the tightening of her jaw. This wasn't Kate's usual response. This wasn't hormones, this was anger.

"You're upset with that call. What's up?" Sam

came around the island and took Kate in his arms. He ran his hands up and down her back, feeling the tension in her shoulders. She was trembling.

Kate wrapped her arms around Sam's waist and held on tight. Easing her back, he raised her face to look at her, searching her troubled eyes. "That was Janet Winburn. You told her you were no longer interested and now she is pestering you again. Do you want to talk about it?" Sam led her to a stool, perching her on it but still holding her, stroking her hair.

"She called when you were out of town and said the teenage girls were dancing, this time at a different topless bar. She asked me to accompany them on the arrest again, insisting I go. Then she asked me questions about your work. I swear she was pumping me for information. There was a man speaking to her in the background. I couldn't make out what he was saying, but she seemed to listen to him and then try another tack to convince me to go on the stakeout. It all felt off, you know what I mean?" Kate sighed and rested her head on Sam's shoulder, letting him carry her weight. "I'll just ignore her and hope she gets the hint."

Sam considered the information Kate had shared. It was unusual for a DA's task force director to be so insistent a civilian be present at an operation. It was too dangerous. He also didn't like her questioning Kate about his work. His team suspected the Marchetti's had someone on the inside feeding them information. Sam hoped it wasn't Janet Winburn. It would be messy. Giving Kate a squeeze, he changed the subject. "Hey, weren't you getting us some tea?"

On Tuesday, Sam met with John Shoemaker, his second in command. They were going over the intel gathered to date. It looked like they'd have to make a trip down to the valley. Sam wanted to sit in on the interview with the deputy who had found the bodies of the two teenagers and review their case. Sam shared what Kate had told him about Janet Winburn. Both men agreed that digging a little deeper into Winburn wouldn't do any harm. They assigned a man to sit on her.

Chapter 19

Janet took a rare break for lunch. She was working on several cases of child obscenity and steering Spencer and his team away from Marchetti's clubs. It was stressful. Lately, she was drinking her dinners. Today she was going to change that, determined to enjoy a quiet, healthy meal. The weather was pleasant, and she needed to walk off the tension tying the muscles around her neck into small painful knots. Janet chose a favorite of hers, a little family deli called Alma's. The casual atmosphere of the little café let her relax, breathe, and enjoy the light-hearted romance novel she was reading.

The owner waited tables and helped in the kitchen. She knew what Janet preferred and seated her at a window in the back corner. The view of the tiny garden was soothing. Janet breathed in deeply through her nose, and released a long slow breath, letting her mind go blank, pushing all the morning's headaches away. She gazed out the window, enjoying the twittering birds splashing in the birdbath, and the musical tones from the wind chimes. Alma delivered a mango tea and inquired if Janet wanted her usual California club on wheat.

"That would be wonderful, Alma. By the way, how are your grandbabies?" Janet inquired solicitously. She'd been coming here for several months and had even met the tiny tots.

"They are frisky as can be. You'll soon have your own and you'll learn. Wears a woman out." She laughed. "I'll put in your order. Enjoy your quiet time."

Alma crossed the room to the kitchen to put in the order while Janet watched a dark cloud blow over the bright sunshine of her day. Yes, she'd know because she'd rescued her daughter from the clutches of Marchetti and sent her to live with her father on the east coast. It broke her heart to be separated from her only child, and it turned her stomach to think she now had to answer to Marchetti. Do his bidding. His insistence that she pump Kate Slater for information on her husband's investigation was fruitless. Janet had tried to explain that repeatedly to Marchetti's man, but he just didn't get it. His standard operating procedure was to muscle information from people any way he could. Janet felt the start of a migraine behind her eyes and was reaching into her purse when that same young man joined her at the table.

"Good afternoon, Ms. Winburn. Mr. Marchetti sends his greetings." Ricco smiled and sat at her tiny table.

Janet's frightened gaze darted from the young man to the front door to the kitchen, gauging her escape. Her voice remained calm while her color drained. "I'm sorry, sir. This is a table for one."

He smiled. "Why yes, it is, especially since your daughter went away. Do you really think we don't know where she is? That she is beyond our reach?"

Janet felt a stab of panic. How could they know about Amy's current location with her dad? Amy had changed her name to her dad's when she went to live with him. Janet used her maiden name since the divorce.

Janet tightened the hold on her mango tea and brought the glass slowly to her lips, buying time to think. How could they know? Surely this is a bluff. "Since you know where my daughter is, what is it you want?" Janet was smart enough to play along with them, feed them tidbits and hope for the chance to take the syndicate down, even if she fell with it.

Ricco idly reached for a breadstick from the basket and sat back in his chair, munching contentedly. "Oh, these are very good. I must try the menu. What would you suggest? Something with red meat. Is it fresh? I do like my meat fresh." His snide expression and tone made Janet's blood boil. The bastard was playing with her. He had been the one to seduce Amy, to draw her away. The pictures they had sent to Janet were disgusting. The scum had captured Amy in several compromising positions, being touched and touching both men and women. They had a video of her servicing two men at once. When Marchetti's man reached out to Janet with the offer, Janet couldn't say no. She got her baby back, traumatized and humiliated. Janet got Amy the best therapy money could buy and entered into a deal with the devil. Swallowing the sick in her mouth, Janet was planning how to respond to his coarse comment when Alma arrived with Janet's sandwich.

"Oh, I apologize. I didn't realize you were meeting a colleague." Alma fussed, arranging a place setting in front of Ricco. "What can I get you to drink, sir?"

Ricco smiled charmingly at Alma. "Ah, I regret I cannot stay for lunch. I was just delivering a message to Ms. Winburn. Her daughter and I have mutual friends.

We've spent some fun times together. Perhaps I will return to enjoy your restaurant another time." He stood and extended a hand to Janet. "Ms. Winburn, we look forward to hearing from you with an update on our project." Ricco pulled two twenties from his wallet. "Please allow me to buy your lunch to make up for so rudely interrupting it." He put the money on the table.

"Oh, sir. That is too much. You could buy two lunches for that amount!" Alma protested while she eyed the money.

"Your kindness and graciousness are worth every penny." Ricco smiled once again at Alma and walked out the door.

Alma dimpled at his compliment, brushing her hand over her graying hair. "Oh, such a good looking, charming man. Looks very successful. Is he dating your daughter? If not, I have a niece about his age. I could introduce him."

Janet turned horrified eyes to Alma. She grabbed her forearm, squeezing too hard, and whispered fiercely. "Don't! Don't even think that. Don't talk to him, don't introduce him to anyone you love. Stay away from him!"

Alma stepped back in shock, giving room for Janet to rush out. "Wait, you didn't eat. I'll give you a to-go box." But Janet was out the door, walking rapidly back to her office. Alma cleared the table, thinking that Janet must really want her daughter to hook up with the young man. She obviously didn't want anyone else horning in. Well fine. Alma knew other nice young men for her niece.

****

Kate used her foot to close the door behind her.

She was flipping through the envelopes. "Bills and more bills." She tossed those onto her desk. The rest she was going to throw out when she noticed one envelope was different. There was something in it. Tossing all the other miscellaneous advertisements and credit card solicitations away, Kate examined the mysterious package closer. It lacked a stamp, so it wasn't mailed. Someone had stuffed it into the mailbox. There was no return address. Simple block letters written in black sharpie formed her name. Careful of any evidence there might be on the packaging, she took out her letter opener and slit open the envelope. Someone had folded a single blank sheet of paper around a flash drive.

Kate sat at her computer. Even though Sam had installed the latest anti-virus on their computers, loading a flash drive from an unknown source was like playing Russian roulette with viruses. Sam was out of town again, so she couldn't ask him. Kate needed to think about it. She set the flash drive aside and called Emily.

"Em, do you still have that old lap top? The one you were going to wipe and donate to Goodwill?" Kate thought it would be a safer way to see the information on the flash drive with minimal risk of downloading a virus onto their own computers.

Kate heard Emily coo to John Mac. "Come here little man," followed by an audible grunt and the rustling of a baby being picked up. "Golly, this little bruiser is getting heavier every day. So, yes, I have the old boat anchor somewhere. What do you need it for?"

Kate responded to the cheerful babbling in the background. John Mac was a precocious child and his parents and grandfather indulged him. Of course, his aunt and uncle were also guilty as charged.

"Is that my little man I hear?" Kate couldn't resist asking. "If it's convenient, I could come over, and see my handsome nephew. While I'm there, well, I have a flash drive and I don't know if it's clean. I thought if it wasn't, your old laptop wouldn't be a major loss if it imploded."

Emily made baby talk. "Of course, we want to see our Auntie Kate, don't we, John Mac." Kate imagined Emily nuzzling John Mac under his chin, blowing raspberries on his belly. Reverting to adult language, she continued. "Jake and Ray are at the construction site. Won't be home for another two hours. Come over."

"On my way." Kate grabbed her purse, the flash drive, and headed over to Emily's. It was a warm afternoon. The walk was a delightful break in her day. Five minutes later, she was pushing through the front door.

"Knock, knock. I'm here looking for a chubby little guy to love on," Kate called, following the sounds of baby giggles at the back of the house. "There's my boy." She picked John Mac up from his playpen. "Now where is your mommy?"

"I'm here. Had to remember which box I packed this old thing in." Emily exchanged laptop for baby and followed Kate to the kitchen table. Kate quickly set up the laptop and she and Emily sat staring at the screen as Kate inserted the flash drive.

Slowly, a blurry video came into focus. What the women saw shocked and sickened them. What they were looking at couldn't be real. It was degrading. Kate and Emily watched as four young women, hardly over twenty, sat virtually naked, dressed only in sheer teddies. One lounged on a sofa, one sat on a single bed, listening to music, and two just paced, almost as if in some sort of trance. They all had the haunted look of someone under emotional distress or chemical influence. Kate slammed the laptop shut and turned wide eyes to Emily.

"Oh, my God. We have to tell Sam." Emily nodded in agreement. She rocked John Mac while Kate dialed Sam's number. It went straight to voice mail. She left a message for him to call back immediately.

"Emily, do you have a spare flash drive? I want to make a copy of this." Kate was thinking about sharing it with Janet Winburn, but something about their last conversation had her hesitating. A copy, though, she thought, was a good idea. She didn't know who sent it to her or who knew she had it. She needed to keep the information safe. Safe from what or whom, she didn't know, but safe. Once Kate burned the copy, she handed it to Emily. "Where can we hide this?"

Emily took the flash drive and, standing on tip-toes, dropped it into Marianne's soup tureen, sitting on the top shelf of her kitchen cabinet. Turning back with a smile, Emily confessed, "I never make soup." The two women stared up at the tureen, considering what they'd just seen. Emily blew out a breath, put John Mac back in his playpen, and opened the refrigerator. "This requires wine." Kate couldn't agree more and wished she could have some.

Kate sat, subdued, while Emily nursed her glass of wine, until Jake and Ray walked in. Jake made a beeline for Emily and Ray for the baby. Both men gave

Kate an absent greeting until they saw the expression on both women's faces. Jake rushed over to John Mac, fear clouding his eyes. Not finding any major injuries or missing limbs, he blew out a sigh of relief and turned back to Emily and Kate.

"What the hell's going on? You two look like there are incoming Scud missiles and we don't have time to take cover."

Both women simply pointed to the laptop, still holding the flash drive. "Kate received this in the mail today. You guys need to see it." Emily took the baby from Jake's arms and pushed him down into the chair at the table. Ray stood behind so he could watch the screen over Jake's shoulder. When the short video finished, Jake closed the laptop and looked at Kate, waiting for an answer.

"I called Sam and got his voice mail. He's down in south Texas, near Marfa. It's pretty remote. He might be out where there isn't a signal."

Jake rose and got a glass of water. He needed to rinse the smut from his mouth. "Kate, I know you have respected the confidentiality of Sam's work, but he shared some information with me. This looks like a sex trade to me. I don't know if it's part of the human trafficking Sam is working on. Where did you get it?"

"It came with the mail today, in a plain envelope. No stamps. So dropped, not mailed. They printed my name in block letters on it. Someone wanted me to see it. I've been thinking about the why of that. Whoever it is must know I have been investigating child exploitation. They must know I wrote the articles. They might also know I've stopped writing them."

Jake disagreed with a shake of his head. "No, Sam

has this case. They probably know that too. Why pull you in?"

"Perhaps they don't think Sam's sword is moving fast enough. They might want me to pick the pen back up." Kate laughed sardonically. "After all, the pen is mightier than the sword."

Ray had opened the laptop and watched the video a second time. "Did you tell anyone else about this?"

"No. I came straight over when I received the package. We made a copy. Emily hid it in Marianne's soup tureen." Kate stood, grabbing the drive and her purse. "I'm going to go home and see if I can pick anything up that will give us a clue where these girls are being held."

"Hold on," Ray cautioned. "Stick around long enough for me to throw some clothes into a duffle. I'll stay with you until Sam gets back."

Kate reluctantly agreed to wait. She felt the lifting of worry, knowing Ray would be with her in the empty house. It didn't take long for him to pack. He drove them home in silence.

"I'll fix dinner while you clean up, Ray. It won't be much. I usually eat light when Sam is out of town."

"Whatever you prepare will be just fine. Let me walk the perimeter and secure the place before I go shower." Ray made a circuit of the house, checking windows and doors, even going out to the back garden to check the gate by the garage. He returned from his task to find Kate standing at the kitchen sink, holding a head of lettuce, the water running and her mind thousands of miles away. He turned off the water and took the food from her hand. Then Ray led her to a stool at the island. "Kate, Sam is all right. He will call and Sam will know what to do. We'll find those girls. Get them out of there."

"But, Ray, we don't even know if it is a current situation or something that happened previously. We have nothing to go on. And why would someone send it to me? I have no legal authority. I can't do anything about it." Kate dropped her head into her hands. "I don't know what to think or do, and I hate that." She shuddered in revulsion and helplessness.

Ray patted her back. "Kate, Sam is good at his job. He'll find a way, figure it out."

Kate gave Ray a hopeful smile. "Yes, he will, but not soon enough. Whoever dropped that flash drive wanted me to keep writing, to expose the horror of these actions." She patted Ray's hand, and smiled. "I know, Ray. Sam should call soon. I'm sorry for going off into la-la land. I'll come back to earth and fix dinner. Go get cleaned up."

The two ate quietly, both sneaking looks at the silent cell phone, willing it to ring. When the dishes were done and put away, Sam still hadn't called. Kate checked her phone to make sure it was working. She tried Sam again. This time it disconnected before voice mail even picked up. Ray tried on his phone with the same results. Wherever Sam was, he was out of reach. Now Kate had two things to worry about.

Feigning fatigue, Kate said goodnight to Ray and went upstairs, ostensibly to bed. On the way, she ducked into the office and grabbed the flash drive and her laptop. Kate took time to wash her face and put on her pajamas before settling on the bed. Sitting cross-legged, she watched the video again and considered what she'd write. The disgust she felt would help to form the outrage she'd convey in her article. When the video finished, Kate opened her word document and composed an article describing the images she'd watched. She asked the readers to imagine the humiliation and fear the young women must feel. She damned the criminals that put them there as well as the corrupt individuals that use their positions and influence to protect the evil doers. The goal was to enrage every citizen with her words and enlist their aid in finding the house where these young women were being held against their will. Reviewing her work once more, she paused. It was hurried and lacking the polish of her usual efforts. Rereading it, she focused on the closing paragraph.

The images would sicken all but the most jaded individual. Yet, there are sick people who pander to these prurient appetites. They own sex clubs, topless bars, sell pornography, and produce X-rated movies. By their actions, they exploit and destroy our innocent and vulnerable children. The people who commit these crimes act with impunity, too often exonerated of their crimes because, as a society, we fear reprisal for taking a moral stand. And the blatant sexuality promoted, even encouraged by certain groups, has allowed us to become de-sensitized. The social pressure of political correctness has made us too frightened to take a stand for virtue and innocence. Someone placed a video depicting these horrors into the hands of this reporter. This reporter hopes to rouse your disgust and indignation. What will you do?

It wasn't her best work, but Kate felt the passion of her conviction. She wrote an email to the editor at the newspaper and producers of the local television news stations, attached the article, and taking a deep breath, hit send. Her only regret was that she couldn't attach the video.

She tried Sam one more time, told his voice mail she loved him, and turned out the light.

Early the next morning, Kate woke to her phone and laptop blowing up with messages.

Chapter 20

Sheriff Domingues briefed the team. "Thanks for coming, Ron. We appreciate the support of the El Paso Homeland Security office. Agents Slater, Shoemaker, I understand you are here from the Fort Worth office to observe. Welcome." Domingues scratched the back of his neck as he turned to the map on the wall. "I don't know if these are the smugglers that are connected to the dead girls, but I figure we need to start somewhere. They left those kids in the desert. They didn't deserve that." Domingues turned flint-colored eyes to the men. "I have a granddaughter at the age of those girls. I want them bad!"

Sam could understand the anger. Presidio County, hell, most of the rural parts of south Texas were under siege. It wasn't just the people crossing the border; it was the drugs and everything else the cartels and coyotes could make a profit from. Add to that the increase in crimes against the ranchers and farmers and it was unsustainable. Domingues had his work cut out for him, policing over 3800 square miles. Sam watched the Sheriff ice his anger and continue.

"We know they'll try the run tonight because the moon is at three-quarters. It would be easier with a full moon, but the coyotes think we are stupid. Even with a three-quarter moon, they can move their human contraband quickly and easily. I have cars driving along

189

FM 170 hoping to find the semi-trailers they use to transport their cargo to cities throughout the state. We'll have the drone with a thermal camera flying overhead, but the miles we have to cover makes it like looking for a needle in a haystack." Sheriff D blew out a frustrated breath. "I've done this more times than I care to count. Sometimes we succeed, sometimes we don't. Let's roll."

****

Sam checked his phone again. Still no bars. They were sitting out in BFE waiting for a group of illegal immigrants being guided across the desert. According to the intel the Presidio Sheriff and the El Paso Homeland Security office had uncovered this cell of coyotes helped the illegals cross the border at Candelaria. It was a small town with a demolished bridge over the Rio Grande. The coyotes required the immigrants to walk across the desert, burdened with their own personal luggage and the coyotes' delivery of drugs or crates of weapons. When the immigrants arrived at their destination, the weapons and drugs went to a separate vehicle to be transported elsewhere. The coyotes loaded the wretched immigrants into a semi-trailer parked somewhere along Farm to Market 170. From there, they would drive them to San Antonio, where they dropped them off to blend in with the local populace and go underground.

Sam blew on his hands to warm them, wishing he'd packed more than his windbreaker. The temp during the day was in the seventies but when the sun went down, it dropped like a rock, sometimes getting into the upper thirties. He hunched his shoulders into his light jacket, worried this was the time they wouldn't succeed. Sam stuffed his hands further into his pockets. Damn, he was cold. They'd been out here three hours with no sign or action. Tapping Shoemaker on the arm, Sam leaned over to whisper, "This is not getting us what we want or need. I hope we don't spend the entire night out here."

"I told you to bring a sweater," Shoemaker whispered back.

"Gee, thanks, Mom." Sam sneered in annoyance, crossing his arms to hold in his body heat.

Another hour and Domingues gave up. "They're not coming or we missed them. I'm calling it." Sam rolled his eyes heavenwards, thanking the gods and looking forward to a hot cup of coffee and a shower to thaw out.

Sheriff D relayed the instructions to call it a night and regroup in the morning at eight a.m. Sam and John pulled into their motel parking lot at 1:50 in the morning. Both wanted indoor plumbing, a hot shower, and sleep. Finally in a location where his cell phone had reception, he saw Kate's call. Sam punched in her number, only to realize the time. He didn't think she'd appreciate a call in the wee hours, plus he remembered she put her phone on Do not Disturb, from 11 p.m. to 7 a.m. Sam listened to her voicemail telling him she loved him. He went to bed with empty arms and a smile on his face. He'd call her in the morning.

Sam's phone rang at 5:15 a.m. It was Ron Hayward, the El Paso agent on site. "Sam, Domingues' guys found a tractor-trailer. It looks like it has been sitting there for a few days. We're going out with them. I'll pick you and John up in twenty minutes."

Sam roused John. The two were waiting for Ron

when he came to a screeching halt outside their motel room, leaving the car in drive while Sam and John got in. Sam gave a thankful nod of appreciation, relieved to see the to-go coffee sitting in the cup holders. "Hayward, thank God you're a caffeine junkie."

Ron shot Sam a grim smile. "Yeah, I grabbed it on the way, but Sheriff D and his men are ahead of us. We have to move it." Without waiting for the men to buckle in, he screamed out of the parking lot, cutting off an eighteen-wheeler at the turn to FM 170, earning him a one-fingered salute.

Domingues stationed a patrol car about a hundred yards from the tractor-trailer to intercept the Homeland Security agents. Ron pulled over and rolled down his window, looking for direction.

"Follow me, sir, I'll lead you to Sheriff D. We've been waiting for you to go in."

The patrol car led them to a siding where Domingues and another patrol officer waited. Sheriff D quickly outlined the plan. The six men approached the tractor-trailer with their weapons at the ready. It was deathly silent. One officer circled to the front, finding no one. Domingues cautiously walked toward the back of the trailer. A padlock secured the hasp on the door. He motioned, sending a man back to the patrol car for bolt cutters.

While five men formed a perimeter, Domingues pounded on the door. Muffled voices from inside cried out for help. He quickly cut the padlock and opened the door to their worst nightmare. A trailer full of people were crying, reaching for help. The two patrol officers knew what they were looking at. They ran back to their cars for supplies while the HSI agents helped the people climb down from the trailer.

Taking an elderly gentleman aside, Domingues asked, "Jesus, how long have you been in here?" Getting a blank stare in return, he repeated himself in Spanish. The gentleman dropped to his knees, kissing Domingues' hand and crying his response. Seconds later, the officers came with the water, blankets, and energy bars they usually carried for just such an emergency. The immigrants fell gratefully upon the food and water, grabbed a blanket, and went to sit at the side of the road. The haunted expression on their faces said it all.

Sheriff D called for a medic and vans. Seeing everyone situated, he walked over to the HSI agents. The three men were leaning against the front of their car, waiting for the status of the situation. Domingues removed his hat, working his fingers around the crown's creases.

"The old man is the patriarch. He organized his and another family unit. They pooled their money to make the crossing. The smugglers loaded them into the trailer, two gallons of water and a loaf of bread. The guide promised someone would transport them to San Antonio. That was about thirty-six hours ago, as best the old man could guess." Domingues ran his hand through his buzz cut, ending with the characteristic scratching of his neck. "There are twenty-two people ranging in age from two to sixty-two. They paid twenty thousand dollars. The gentleman claims they got a group discount because they were all one family and had healthy men to carry heavy crates. He also claims that the coyotes held back six kids. Told him the smaller ones couldn't walk the distance to the trailer.

They agreed to transport them in a separate van and meet them in San Antonio."

Sam felt the anger rush in and shook his head in disgust. "How old were the six kids?" He knew the answer.

"Five to nine, one boy, five girls." Domingues sent a look toward a candy wrapper trapped in the base of a Prickly Pear cactus. He raised hardened eyes to Sam. "It isn't what you need for your case, is it Agent Slater?"

"I'm afraid not. But you saved the lives of twenty-two people, one of those a toddler. You've done well here. Tell your men we appreciate their work." Sam clapped Sheriff D on the shoulder and nodded to Ron and John.

They drove back to the motel in silence. Sam called Kate while John changed their flight home. Getting her voice mail, Sam sighed. Too little sleep and nothing to show for it regarding Marchetti or the dead teenagers. "Sorry I missed you. I'll be home earlier than expected, around nine this evening. We'll try to make an earlier flight from El Paso. I'll call you later and let you know. Love you." Sam hung up, closed his eyes, and leaned his head back on the car seat.

Sam and John were sitting at El Paso International Airport waiting for their flight. They couldn't change to an earlier departure so were stuck cooling their heels. John had his chin resting on his chest, snoozing. Sam tried Kate again. He got her voice mail, again. He tried his dad with the same result. Finally, Sam called Jake and reached a live person.

"Jake, where the heck is everyone? All I keep getting is damn voice mail. Is everything all right?"

There was an edge of concern in Sam's voice he didn't bother to hide from Jake.

"Everything and everybody are okay. Where are you? We've been trying to reach you too." Jake's voice was calm and controlled.

Sam turned back toward his chair. "Hell, we're still stuck in El Paso, which, by the way, was a bust. Been out in the field so I didn't have any bars. Probably why you couldn't reach me, but now I have a signal and no one is answering. Are Kate and Emily out? Why isn't she picking up?"

"She probably had to turn her phone off. She is in a meeting. I'm waiting to drive her home. Dad is hanging out with Emily and John Mac, doing the grandpa thing. When will you be home?"

"Wait, what meeting? And why are you driving?" Sam asked.

Sam's puzzled expression caught the attention of a yawning John. He raised his brow in question, then glanced at the TV screen. Kate Slater was on TV being interviewed by an ABC news anchor. The caption at the bottom of the screen said it all. 'Sex House in Fort Worth.' Shoemaker reached out a hand for Sam's arm and pointed at the screen with the other.

Looking at Shoemaker's 'Holy shit!' expression and finger pointing to the TV, Sam's gaze followed. Kate was on the screen in living color speaking with David Morris, an ABC national news anchor. All Sam could get out before he hung up the phone was, "Never mind, Jake, I know the answer." Sam stalked to the TV, looking for the volume. When Sam saw the locked controls, he took out his phone to stream it. Sam stood in the middle of the terminal. Passengers rushed past him on their way to and from their flights. Sam was oblivious to everything but the small screen on his phone. The announcement of their flight prevented him from hearing all of the interview but he heard enough. Boarding the plane, Sam knew he'd be incommunicado for the next ninety minutes. There wasn't a thing he could do until he got home. He trusted Jake to watch over Kate, but it would be a long ninety minutes.

Chapter 21

Vincent read the spy book until it was dog-eared and the pages grungy. He successfully followed the bully, Donnie Little, and reported his activities to the school principal. Donnie got three days' suspension, and Vincent got a pat on the back. He didn't want public acknowledgement. Sam had told him a good spy was incognito. Vincent thought that word sounded so cool. Incognito. But having exhausted all the outlets of his curious mind, Vincent went back to watching his sister. Angela was doing weird things again. He caught up with her outside the coffee shop on Wednesday after her dance club practice.

"Hey, Angela. What ya doing?" Vincent skipped alongside her, bouncing on his toes. Angela tried to brush him off, ignoring his questions and his antics. Vincent danced in her path, blocking her progress.

Stopping, Angela stood with hands on her hips, impatient with her little brother. "I'm not doing anything. Go home, Vincent. Don't you have homework? You're always telling Grandma about how a spy has to get good grades." Angela shoved around him and continued on her way.

Not to be discouraged, Vincent resumed his slipping in and around her, talking. "Yep, a spy has to be smart. I got an 'A' on my history test. Sam says that's a really important subject. Bet you didn't get an

'A' on anything." He taunted her, successfully getting her goat.

Angela stopped short and turned angrily to him. "Go away, Vincent. I'm meeting a friend. I don't want my little brother tagging along. Go home! I'll see you there." She was seething with anger and frustration.

Vincent backed up a couple of steps, holding his hands up, palms out. "Okay, all right. Geez, I get it. Got a hot date? Meeting a boy?" he teased, dancing out of reach when she tried to hit him.

"Just go away, get out of here!" she screamed at him. Vincent backed up, shock on his face. He'd never heard Angela so angry.

"Wow," Vincent whispered. He watched her until she turned the corner, walking toward the park.

Vincent suspected Angela was probably doing something she wasn't supposed to, but he couldn't figure it out. When she got back to the house later, she claimed she wasn't hungry, had some stupid paper to write for school, and went straight to her bedroom.

She spent the next two days in her room with the door closed and locked. Vincent could hear music and figured she was practicing her dance moves. He thought it was for the dance club at school. All Vincent knew was that she kept muttering something about proving to their grandmother that watching dance videos was worth it. She'd be a dance star. *Aww, come on*, he thought, *in your dreams*.

****

Vincent looked up when Angela came into the house, slamming the door behind her. She barely contained her nervous energy. Running to her room, he heard her book bag being thrown on the bed. Angela closed the bedroom door. Her fumbling around the bedroom was clearly audible to Vincent. He could hear the wire hangers screeching on the metal closet pole as Angela pawed through the clothes stuffed haphazardly in her closet. There was muttering—*Where is it?*—with the sound of increasing anger. Angela yanked open her bedroom door and stormed down the hall to the living room, where Vincent lay sprawled on the floor, reading Sherlock Holmes.

"Where the hell is it, Vincent? What did you do with the dress?" She was flushed and panting. Her mouth formed an angry slash across her face. "I know you took it. Just like you did that blouse with the sparkles on the collar. You better not give it to Grandma. I know someone that will punch you in the nose if you don't give it back." Her face was red. She was spluttering with rage.

Isabell came running from the kitchen. "What is going on here? What is all this shouting?" She looked from Vincent's confused face to Angela's furious one. "Why are you yelling at your brother? Has he done something wrong?" She tried to put her arm around Angela, but Angela shrugged it off.

"Vincent is going through my clothes and taking them. He probably likes to dress up in them at night. That's it, isn't it, Vincent? Do you like to wear dresses? Do you want to be a girl?" Angela sneered, pushing forward toward Vincent, fists clenched at her sides. She was all but spitting in his face.

Isabell yanked her around and gave her a hard slap, snapping her head back and getting Angela's immediate and astonished attention. "Stop it this instance. You will keep a civil tongue in your head and not threaten your brother. Family is everything. If you are talking about the dress you tried to hide under your winter coat, I took it. That and the red one. They are dresses a slut would wear. You are not to wear clothes like that, *ever*. Do you hear me?"

Angela stepped back; her hand pressed to her flaming cheek. The shock and embarrassment quickly turned to fury. Her eyes narrowed. Angela turned without a word and went to her bedroom, closing the door, the click of the lock sounding loudly.

Vincent looked at Isabell, his mouth hanging open.

"I'm sorry, Vincent. I'm sorry you had to see that and I'm sorry I struck Angela. But she needed some sense knocked into her. She'll lick her wounds and come out for dinner, all apologetic." Isabell ran a hand over Vincent's hair, chucking his chin. "Don't worry. Go back to your reading."

Vincent swallowed and nodded. Isabell returned to the kitchen. He heard her switch on the TV to watch Judge Judy and prepare dinner.

Vincent couldn't believe his sister and grandmother had a major row. Man, it was the first time he'd ever seen his grandmother raise her hand. It must have royally pissed her off. When Isabell left the living room, Vincent stole down the hall to listen at Angela's door. He could hear her moving around, but she wasn't crying. When Vincent heard her window sliding up, he ran to the front door and peered out. He watched Angela come around the side of the house, keeping to the shadows and away from Ray's. She had her purse and a very full backpack. Vincent didn't hesitate. He quietly opened the door and snuck out to follow her.

Angela waited until she cleared the neighbor's

house. Stopping at the corner, Vincent watched as she pulled her cell phone from her back pocket and made a call. She spoke for a few minutes and nodded. His sister turned toward the park. She walked with confidence now.

Vincent stuck with Angela. She wasn't very observant, and he could easily trail her. Sam had taught him all about surveillance techniques. Keep your distance, don't crowd the subject, get a description of any contacts, car make, model and color. Getting the tag numbers was a bonus, Sam had explained. He remembered the times with Ray at the mall, practicing. It was fun. Little did Vincent know it would come in so handy.

Angela was standing near the picnic table where she danced for the driver guy. She kept looking at the corner, impatiently rocking from foot to foot. Occasionally, she glanced back in the direction of their house. Vincent was almost ready to give up and just call her out when a dark gray Chevy drove up and she climbed into the front seat. The driver leaned over and kissed her. Kissing! Yuck! It grossed Vincent out.

They sat in the car talking for a while. Angela was crying, and the guy was patting her back. She was talking, and the driver guy was nodding, then he started to shake his head. Angela grew agitated and slapped at him. Her voice grew louder, and Vincent could make out what she was saying.

"I don't care! My grandmother hit me. She doesn't want me to dance. I won't go back there. You have to take me away."

The driver guy was shaking his head, running his hands up and down Angela's arms. "You don't mean that, Angela. She is your grandmother. She loves you." Vincent didn't think the guy wanted to take Angela away.

"You're against me too. Against my dancing." Angela was boo-hooing, and the guy looked uncomfortable. Finally, in resignation, he shook his head and started the car.

Vincent watched in horror as they drove away. He ran into the street, following the car with squinted eyes until it disappeared around the corner. The last thing he remembered to do was to note the tag number. Vincent repeated it to himself over and over as he rushed to Ray's house.

****

Ray paced nervously, waiting for Jake to bring Kate back following the interview with ABC Nightly News. With Sam out of town, he was responsible. Everyone was waiting at Jake's house. Isabell was helping Emily with John Mac. The two women visited at the kitchen table.

"Kate is brave to take on something like this. You must be very proud of her," Isabell said, giving John Mac his pacifier. "The article she wrote will surely get the attention of the authorities and they will find this evil place, and put those men in jail."

Ray exchanged looks with Emily. The worried expression on her face matched his. They knew Kate had also put herself in the crosshairs of bad people by going public. When Jake and Kate walked in, Ray pulled Jake aside. After a brief conversation, Jake nodded and left the room. When he returned, Ray noticed the bulge under his shirt.

Everyone took seats at the kitchen table so Kate

could share the experience of meeting and being interviewed by a national newscaster. Suddenly, Vincent burst through the door, shouting. Jake was up, hand on his weapon. Seeing it was Vincent, Ray shot him a look. Jake relaxed his hold.

Not bothering to acknowledge the women, Vincent blurted out. "Ray, Jake, Angela's gone. She went with this guy. She ran away. We have to find her." Vincent was stumbling over his words in distress.

The adults exchanged looks of alarm. Jake stood to check out the windows and lock the door. Kate reached for Isabell's hand while Ray stood, grabbing Vincent by his shoulders, attempting to hold him still so he could get a handle on himself.

"Whoa, take a breath, son. Who's gone?" Ray forced Vincent to look at him and take a deep breath.

"Angela! I followed her, just like Sam taught me. She went to the park and this guy in a gray Chevy picked her up. It's the guy she's been meeting. He gives her stuff. I thought he was nice, but he's not. He's gross."

Vincent looked at his grandmother. He kept turning toward the door, pulling at Ray's hand. "Come on, man. She's gone. We have to find her. That guy, he's the driver guy."

None of this made sense to Ray, but he could tell Vincent was trying to hold back his tears. It was obvious it frightened him. Ray remained calm despite his intense worry and Isabell's cry of dismay. His first thought was to call Sam, but then remembered Sam was in Marfa, following up on the case he was working on. Ray sat Vincent at the kitchen table and gave him a glass of water. "Okay, Vincent, start over. Remember your training. Tell us exactly what happened."

Vincent calmed, swallowed his fear, and recalling the lessons he'd learned from Sam, recounted events that led up to Angela driving away with the man.

"That's good, Vincent. Now, what can you tell us about the car and the guy? Details, son, details."

Vincent described everything he could remember, ending with the license plate number. Walking to the phone, Ray picked it up and gave Vincent a nod. "That's good work. Let's call Sam. He'll know where to start."

Jake stepped in, placing a hand on Vincent's shoulder. He calmly stated, "Sam's in the air. We can't call him. Call the police and report Angela missing, possibly abducted. Be careful. Kate is probably already a target and if this has anything to do with what Sam is investigating, I don't want any of the rest of you involved. Vincent, you did very well with this, but now we need you to rein it in. Stay calm. Sit tight. I'll make a call to Sam's team."

****

The police came immediately in response to Ray's call. The detective took down the information and issued an Amber Alert. It was difficult for Isabell to go through the process. After they left, she paced the room, too full of anxiety to sit. Her words were a mixture of anger and worry.

"My baby. It's my fault. I never should have slapped her. She's just mad, she'll be home. I'll lock her in her room when she gets here. I'll ground her until she is eighteen." Her voice wavered from hurt to fear. "It's my fault. I failed her, just like I failed her mother." Isabell buried her face in her hands. Her shoulders shook with deep, gut-wrenching sobs.

Ray had heard enough. "Stop it! Just stop it! You did your best." Isabell turned a tear-streaked face to Ray. This kind man had selflessly helped her build a stable environment for her grandbabies. She reached out a hand to him, but his eyes stayed focused on a time long ago.

"There is evil in this world and you can't expect to know it all or see it all. Parents can't expect to be perfect, to prevent bad things from happening. To stop hurt or death." Ray was no longer talking about Isabell and Angela. He was seeing himself and a lost baby, himself and a second son that he'd almost lost with his pride and foolishness.

A knock brought his head up and his mind back from a past he could never change. Jake answered the door and escorted the agent into the small kitchen.

"Mr. Slater? I'm Agent Tom Seifert. I work with Sam. Jake called. How can I help?"

Ray had Vincent recount his story for a third time. The boy was maintaining admirable control. Ray was proud of him. When Vincent finished, Ray sent him to comfort his grandmother. He told Siefert about the steps taken by the police and their plans.

"The police think it is a case of a disgruntled teen running away. You need to know something else, Tom," Jake confided. "Kate uncovered a video of a sex house where someone has imprisoned teenagers. They are in a dormitory-type setting, being held without clothes. We don't think the girls are aware of the cameras. I'll show you the video. Kate wrote an article that has gone viral. Every national news outlet has contacted her. She did a live interview with the national news tonight. Sam is heading back from El Paso. Right now, we don't know where this all fits in with Angela running away."

Agent Seifert acknowledged Jake's input. He didn't know how much the family knew about their investigation into Marchetti. He couldn't mention the connection without tipping the investigation, not without Sam's orders. Agent Seifert asked if there was somewhere private he could use to make some calls. Vincent took him to Ray's garage apartment.

Jake paced between the kitchen where his wife and son were sitting, to the front windows, looking for any threats. Ray walked over, laying a calming hand on his arm. Jake stared at Ray with frustration.

"I hate this. Look, Ray, we both recognize the danger. I've weighed my options and responsibilities. Emily and Jon Mac have to come first. You've got to cover Kate."

Ray nodded. They'd all have to sit tight until Sam got home before anything could be done. Jake stepped into the backyard to confer with Agent Seifert. Emily went to put John Mac down for the night. Isabell sat at Jake's kitchen table, struggling to hold it together; an iron grip on Vincent's hand.

Ray felt disconnected from everything. He watched the emotional devastation Angela's disappearance was causing Isabell. He understood Jake's worry and vigilance. And Ray blamed himself for his failure.

Standing with his hands stuffed in his pockets, he leaned despairingly on the doorjamb, staring at nothing. Kate paced from one side of the living room to another. Ray watched her growing frustration. She was chewing her lip, deep in thought, pulling on the threads of information she knew, unraveling the mystery of Angela's running away.

Suddenly, Kate turned to Ray. Her hand went to her mouth, and her finger came up, shaking as if counting each step, leading her to the answer. She pulled Ray into the living room and whispered, "Ray, I've been trying to think this through. What was it Angela was upset with before she left?"

Ray rubbed his chin, recalling Vincent's narrative. "She accused Vincent of taking her dress, the one Isabell had taken. What has that to do with anything?"

Kate was doing the goalpost sign with her index fingers, focusing on her thoughts, and her memories. Kate gave herself a dope slap, berating herself out loud. "Think, Kate, think! How do all these pieces fit?"

Ray had been around long enough to understand Kate's thought process when writing. She would do the same thing solving puzzles and Angela running away was a puzzle. Kate would shift through all available information, review everything Isabell had told her. How Angela was obsessed with dance videos. Claimed she was going to be a dance star someday. Ray was watching in fascination when he saw Kate's face change with her sudden horrible epiphany.

"Ray, I think Angela is a victim of exploitation. She has always dreamed of dancing. I'm not sure how, but someone convinced her she could be a professional dancer. He must have given her the dress, feeding her fantasy. Now, he has taken her away to fulfill that dream."

Ray saw goose bumps rise on Kate's arms. She ran her hands up and down them. Her fear that what she suspected might be true, evident.

"I know this sounds crazy, but when I was working on the exploitation articles, my contact, Janet Winburn, said there were gentlemen clubs that use teenage dancers. She took me to one. The bust failed but, what if that is where Angela is? We have to go see. You have to go and see if she is there."

Kate grabbed Ray's arm. She squeezed it forcefully to make him see the danger, the horror.

Ray touched her shoulder. "Calm down. Let me think. What you are saying makes sense. The older men, the gifts, and from what Vincent described, the sexual favors the girls were giving them. These girls are young, impressionable, and lonely. I think you might be on to something." Ray grabbed his coat. "Where is this club?"

Kate was pulling on her jacket. "It's off Highway 99. I'm coming with you."

Standing in the backyard, Seifert paused in his conversation with Jake at the commotion from the front of the house. Kate was calling out something about her and Ray going to follow on a lead. They slammed out the door and drove off.

"Jake, your father-in-law and Sam's wife just drove off like the demons of hell were on their tail. Any idea why?"

Jake's head jerked around. "Jesus Christ. Follow them, Seifert. Kate's put two and two together. They're probably heading over to Fantasy Palace. Try to intercept them before they go in. I have to stay here with my family. Catch them before they do something rash." A string of cussing followed Seifert as he ran to his car. There was more fear than anger in the words.

****

Ray jerked to a stop in front of the door. Slamming out of the car, he marched into the building. It was loud. Music blasted out of four huge speakers. Ray stood, hands on hips, taking in the scene. The place was dark except for a brightly lit stage. Smoke filled the air from cigarettes and the special effects of fog machines. A lithe black girl gyrated to the heavy bass of some disco song. Ray thought he recognized Michael Jackson's "Thriller". Kate rushed in and stood behind him. It was the same layout from the CCTV footage on the failed bust.

"Over there, Ray," she said, pointing. "I think that's the dressing room. The dancers enter from there. If Angela is here and going to dance, she'll be back there."

Ray took Kate's hand, and they double-timed their walk toward the backstage. A bouncer tried to stop them. Ray simply straight-armed the man aside, pulling Kate behind him. Bursting through the door to the cramped dressing room, Ray stepped back, averting his eyes. Four young women stood in various stages of undress. None were Angela.

"Damn. No good. She's not here." Ray was turning to leave when the first bouncer came back, following in the wake of a larger, muscular man. Kate remembered him from her first visit to the club with Janet Winburn. He was the man Spencer had called a goon. Rushing Ray, the larger of the two pinned him against the wall with his forearm pressing against Ray's throat. The other one grabbed Kate from behind, lifting her off her feet.

Ray gazed into angry eyes. The man spoke clearly. "No need to cause a scene, old man. You want a private show, you can call and arrange it. For now, you need to leave. We'll show you out the back." He whipped Ray around, twisting his arm into a rear wrist lock, and marched him down a dark hall, past the restroom and out the door. The second guy grabbed Kate's arm in a vice-like grip and followed. Once outside, a third man came up. The guy grabbed Ray and held him as the goon punched him over and over in the face and stomach. Ray fell to his knees, nose bleeding, eye blackening, swollen lips and a cut on his brow. The muscle used his foot to push Ray over and gave him a couple of swift kicks to the kidneys. The second guy shoved Kate. She fell to the ground next to Ray. Kate curled defensively around her abdomen, fearing a similar kick, but the second guy pulled the first one back.

"No, wait." The second man put a restraining hand on the other guy. "It's better if we let her tell her story to Slater. She's caused enough trouble as it is. He needs to shut her up. If he is worried about her, this might make him think twice about her mouthing off." The two men laughed and went back inside.

Seifert pulled up as Kate was helping a badly beaten Ray limp to their car. "Jesus. What happened?"

Ray spit out blood and gave Seifert a look through his quickly closing eye. "I tripped." Kate helped him into the passenger seat and moved behind the wheel. "Seifert, we're going home."

Chapter 22

Sam called Kate when he landed. "Where are you and are you okay?" Sam listened intently for danger as he climbed into the car, slamming the door, the seat belt clicking into place.

"I'm at Jake and Emily's. Marchetti's men beat up your dad. At least I think they were Marchetti's. I recognized them from the failed bust. Spencer had referred to them as Marchetti's goons." Sam heard the concern in Kate's voice, but thankfully, no fear. "Emily has been nursing him as the best she can with an ice pack and a couple of butterfly bandages to the cut on his eyebrow. Jake doesn't think it needs stitches, but he is worried Ray might have some broken ribs. We are all safe. Hurry home, Sam."

Sam felt a rush of déjà vu. He remembered when he was investigating Carlos and how the man had threatened to harm Kate. Now Marchetti was doing it to his family. "Put Jake on, Kate."

Kate motioned for Jake to come over. "Sam wants to talk with you." She thrust the phone into his hand and walked over to Emily, who was placing a fresh towel on Ray's brow. Both women strained to listen to Jake's side of the conversation.

Jake, a man of few words, walked to the front windows, gazing out, looking for threats. "Yo."

"Seifert?" Sam wasn't much for small talk in these

circumstances, either. Jake snorted. It was the same as when they worked together in Afghanistan. Some things never changed.

"Watching your place." Jake flicked back the curtain, satisfied all was clear. "If anyone is coming for Kate, they aren't coming here."

"Everyone hunkered down and safe? Dad's okay? The Camarillos?"

"Yeah, we're all here. Your dad will have some colorful bruising for a while. Probably be sore as hell, but he's okay. Camarillos are here. Isabell and Vincent are sitting quietly in the living room. This is all new to them. Not like our women who have been there and done that and have the t-shirts to prove it. I think they are shell-shocked." Count on Jake to find the humor in any situation. "I also don't think your target is interested in them. What's your ETA?" Jake asked, glancing into the living room at his family. "They made an explicit threat to Kate. The sooner you hear it, the better we can make a plan."

"I'm twelve minutes out. See you soon." Sam disconnected and called Seifert. "Seifert, Sam here. Are you sitting on my place? See any activity?"

Tom was a seasoned agent. "Nothing so far. I think they believe you will reconsider your position once you see your dad and hear what they told Kate. Sorry, Sam. Your dad got there before I could intercept them. They beat the crap out of him, didn't hurt Kate. Scared her and threatened but, nothing physical. Could have been worse. So far, your house is clean. I have two other agents covering the back. Do you want me to be at Jake's when you arrive?"

Sam urged John to drive faster. "Yes. See you

soon." Sam hung up, then slammed his hand on the door panel. "God damn it!"

"Whoa, Sam," John replied laconically. "In the immortal words of Ricardo Montalbán, that's 'rich Corinthian leather'. We're four minutes out. Just hang on."

"You have got to stop watching Peacock, Shoemaker. No one gets your references to commercials and shows from the seventies."

"What do you mean? 'Da plane, da plane?'" Sam rolled his eyes at John's bad impersonation of Herve Villechaize. Little people fascinated Shoemaker.

Sam pinched the bridge of his nose and took a deep, cleansing breath. He felt a lightening of the pressure with John's attempt at humor, but knew he had to remain focused and unemotional. It was his wife and father in the crosshairs now.

John cut the four minutes down to three. Sam was jumping from the car and running to the door before John had it in park. Siefert pulled up behind him. Both men checked their guns and spare clips, then followed Sam into the house.

Sam was in a hurry. Jake opened the door to let Sam in before he could bust it down. His eyes scanned the room, looking for Kate, only Kate. Nothing else mattered. Sam saw her standing by his dad. He crossed the room in two strides and had her in his arms. Holding her, then pushing her away so he could look at her, top to bottom, and make sure she was unharmed, then pulled her back into his arms again. Sucking in a deep breath, Sam looked around as John and Seifert came in. Jake locked the door behind them.

Ray tried to get up, but Sam pressed him back

down. "We got this, Dad. You did well. Now focus on yourself." Getting a nod from Emily, Sam knew his dad was all right. Keeping a firm grip on Kate's hand, Sam led her and his agents into the kitchen, followed by Jake.

Kate, then Seifert, told Sam everything that had happened, from Kate's suspicion that Angela was a victim of exploitation to Seifert's arrival on the scene too late to stop Ray from going in.

"The last thing they said was that if you were worried about me, this might make you think twice about my mouthing off *and* pursuing an investigation. Sam, he could only have been referring to my interview tonight and your work. They were confident you'd stop pursuing it if you were worried about me." Kate gripped Sam's arm, digging her nails in to drive her point home. "I'm sure these men are evil and you need to stop them. I don't want to be the reason they get away with it."

Sam covered Kate's hand with his. It was so delicate, the fingers slender and long. When she moved them, there was an indefinable grace. He knew what Marchetti was capable of. Sam saw them bloody, broken, and mangled. "Trust me, Kate. You won't be the reason they get away with anything. Give me a moment, please." He stood, pulling her up with him, placed a kiss on her forehead, and sent her into the living room to sit with the Camarillos, Emily, and Ray.

Sam laid out his plans. His first and primary aim was to get Angela back before they could hurt her. It was simple. He'd go ask them to give her back.

****

The sign out front advertised AMATEUR NIGHT.

This was when all the wanna-bees showed off. Sometimes they got a few sorority girls during hell week that came in wasted and got up on stage. That always got the crowd going. During that time, the frat boys came in droves. This was a special night. A dance competition for new young talent was taking place at The Silver Slipper. Ricco had come up with the idea. It gave a nice boost to the business, and Marchetti liked the additional revenue from one of his less-than-fancy clubs. Ricco was in line to take over the business when the old man retired. Tonight, Angela would make her debut.

The colored lights were swirling, touching on the mirrored ball and shooting darts around the room. The music was pounding, sending vibrations through the floor of the stage. Tony handed Angela a glass of water and touched his lips to hers. She sighed and leaned into him.

"Tony, I am so nervous. Where are the talent agents seated? The lights are so bright and the audience so dark, I can't see beyond the stage. How will I know where to look, focus my dancing?" Angela was standing on tiptoe, bright eyes darting left and right.

"You'll be fine. I'll be in the sound booth with my friend. That's at the back of the room, remember? You dance for mc and thc talent agents will have a perfect view. We'll do it like we did last time. Remember? Dark, then spotlight, then when the song gets going, I'll flip on all the bright lights. You just let your natural instincts take over. Dance from your heart and you'll wow them." He ran his hand down her arms and kissed her sweetly on the cheek, placing a caramel in her palm. There was regret in his eyes and in his voice.

Chapter 23

Sam outlined his plan. Jake stood by quietly while John and Tom argued with him.

"Sam, this is insane. You can't just walk into the club. They could take you out in a heartbeat. Don't be reckless just because he threatened your family. Give us some time, we can make a plan, get a warrant, take them out legally."

Sam put his hand on John's shoulder and shook his head. "You know, that's what I like about you, Shoemaker. You don't want my job so badly that you want me to die." He smiled and gave the shoulder a squeeze. "I have no plans on dying. Not tonight, at any rate. Marchetti doesn't want me dead. He wants me to stop looking, chasing. Right now, he has Angela. Marchetti has the upper hand. Let me get the kid back. Then we'll talk about plans and warrants and doing things by the book." Sam included Seifert in this explanation, then circled his gaze to Jake.

"I need you to stay here with your family. No matter what goes down, they are your primary responsibility." When Jake objected, Sam gave him a stern look. It wasn't easy for either of them. Going into a fight without Jake having his back was foreign to Sam, but he knew that Emily and John Mac came first for Jake now. "That's an order, soldier." Jake nodded and stepped back, opening the way for Sam.

Sam had felt Kate's eyes on him during the entire exchange between him and his men. He knew she'd read their body language, the disconcerted looks on their faces; the frustrated buzz of their voices. Sam shook hands and walked over to her.

"Kate, I'm going to get Angela. Wait here. I'll be back." He reached out to hug her, but she would have none of it.

"What do you mean, going to get Angela? You can't just walk in there." He heard the hitch in her voice as it rose in panic. She tried to push him away, but Sam took her in his arms and held her as she pummeled her fists against his chest. Her angry sobs made her words hard to understand, but Sam knew her heart, her fears. "They'll kill you. I won't have it. I can't lose you."

Sam held her tighter until her blows grew weaker and her fists opened to lie flat and defeated on his chest. "And I can't lose you, Kate." He tilted her face up to him. "I have to do this. No one else can. Let me do my job. Let me save Angela. Then, let me save those girls you saw on the video. But let me do it my way. Now give me a smile to see me on my way."

Kate swallowed the lump in her throat, and mustered a tremulous smile for her life, the light in her darkness. He kissed her and walked out the door.

****

Sam climbed into his jeep. He checked his weapon but instead of putting the Glock in its holster on his belt, put it in the glove box. He knew carrying a weapon into the club only increased his chances of starting trouble. His showing up was enough. Dropping the vehicle into gear, Sam drove to the club where Kate and his dad had made their valiant attempt at rescuing

217

Angela. His plan took on greater clarity as the miles passed. When Sam arrived, he pulled into the porte-cochere where VIPs parked. Leaving his hands at 10 and 2, he waited for Marchetti's muscle to come out.

It took less than thirty seconds before a large man with fists the size of pork butts and a face to match walked up to his window. He gestured for Sam to keep his hands where they were and opened the car door.

"Welcome, Mr. Slater. We were hoping you would grace us with your presence and here you are."

The goon grabbed Sam by the collar and pulled him from the vehicle. A young man who could have played defensive tackle for the Cowboys pushed him up against his jeep, smashing Sam's face against the window.

"You know the drill. Spread them." Sam did as he was told while rough hands did a thorough pat down for weapons. Once satisfied, the goon grabbed the back of Sam's jacket, turned him around, and shoved him toward the door.

A second man waited inside to escort him to a private room where Marchetti offered close and personal viewing of, and if a client was willing to pay the right price, 'touch' the entertainers. A young, well-dressed man opened the door. Marchetti was waiting.

"Good evening, Mr. Slater. We have been circling around each other for so long. It is nice to finally meet you. I understand this has been a long day for you. I trust your flight from El Paso was pleasant. May I offer you some refreshment?" Marchetti snapped his fingers. The young man placed a bottle of 18-year-old Grangestone, single malt, and two cut crystal glasses on the table. Sam watched him pour two fingers into each glass, the stage lights glinting off a blue star sapphire pinkie ring. Capping the bottle, he stepped back to the door and stood at ease until his next order.

Marchetti leaned back in the leather club chair. Crossing his legs, he fastidiously flicked a piece of lint from his trousers. He studied the nicely manicured nails of his left hand and sipped his scotch. Raising his eyes to Sam and tilting his head just slightly to the side, he smiled mockingly. "So, Mr. Slater, to what do I owe this pleasure?"

Sam mirrored Marchetti's calm. Raising his glass, he sipped his scotch, enjoying the smoothness of the alcohol as it warmed his throat. Giving a nod of approval, he slid his eyes to the viewing window and watched the dancers on the stage. They had replaced the younger women Ray and Kate saw earlier with veteran performers.

Marchetti's brows rose. "I'm surprised, Mr. Slater. I have seen your wife. She is exquisite. I wouldn't think you'd find these distractions of interest. But then a man sometimes enjoys variety."

Sam's fingers tightened ever so slightly on his glass, but when his eyes turned to Marchetti, he shuttered the anger and disgust rising in his throat like bile. "Perhaps it would be best if we left my wife out of our conversation, Marchetti. I believe we have other business to discuss. I came to ask you to return the girl."

Marchetti tsked and leaned forward to place his glass on the table. "Ah, Mr. Slater. You see? I give you the respect by referring to you by 'mister' and yet you can't seem to return the courtesy. Why is that, I wonder, Mr. Slater?" Marchetti refilled his glass, motioning with the bottle to inquire if Sam wanted more. "I think we have many things to discuss. But, as you say, you want me to return a girl? I am confused."

Turning to the silent man at the door, Marchetti raised his hand, palm up. "Ricco, do you know anything about a young girl?"

Ricco smiled smugly, shrugging. "I can't say I do, Mr. Marchetti. Shall I ask if any of the guys have a new girlfriend?" Marchetti waved his offer away, turning back to Sam expectantly. It was time to deal, and Sam knew it.

"Look, *Mr.* Marchetti." Sam visibly swallowed the bitterness of having to grovel. "My apologies for any disrespect. I hope you will help me find a young woman who might have developed a crush on one of your young men, maybe gone on a date and stayed out past her curfew. Her name is Angela."

"Ah, of course. I have quite a few handsome young men working for me. Girls are always mooning over one. Let me think." Marchetti turned his gaze to the dancer on stage, his eyes brightening as she skimmed her dress down, revealing large, enhanced breasts. He tapped his index finger on his mouth. "Ricco, isn't Tony seeing a young woman named Angela? I believe he said she wants to be a dancer." Smiling brightly, like a little boy who just solved a riddle, Marchetti shrugged a shoulder. "Ricco, you have Tony's cell phone, don't you? Call him and ask him to take the young lady home."

Marchetti leaned back, smiling expansively, and waved a hand. "What can one do? Young people in love. I'll admonish him for keeping her out after her curfew."

Sam watched as Ricco exited the room, closing the door quietly behind him. He wouldn't return until Marchetti summoned him, leaving his boss to address the real meat of the issue.

"I'm glad we resolved this concern of yours, Mr. Slater. May I call you Sam?"

Sam held Marchetti's eyes and sipped his drink. Marchetti smirked.

"Apparently not. Oh, well." Marchetti gazed at the liquid gold in his glass thoughtfully. Minutes passed. Another dancer took the stage. This one no younger than the other but equally endowed.

Sam waited. His finely honed patience made his awareness so acute he could hear the ticking of the clock over the pounding bass of the music.

Marchetti shook his head, tsked, and sighed with resignation, like a worried father. "Young people. I know what it is to worry about those we love. One worries about so many things. I heard there was a story about young women being held in a sex house. Why, I believe your lovely wife uncovered the story. Some of what she said reflected poorly on my humble establishments. Exposing news like this could make someone very unhappy."

Sam watched Marchetti's manicured fingers caress the rim of his glass, like a lover. "There is always an inherent danger when one reveals such information. Your wife is very brave to take on someone who could hurt her. You must worry about her safety. I've heard people kill for less."

Sam listened to Marchetti's smooth voice spin the web that would trap Kate if she didn't back off. The veiled threat was crystal clear. Sam sat back in his chair, crossed his leg at the knee, and evaluated Marchetti, his meaning, and his resolve.

"Mr. Marchetti, I don't give a rat's ass about what you do here at your clubs. It's not in my jurisdiction. Just to be clear, I have no interest in your charming entertainment business. However, now that you say someone might be concerned about the information my wife uncovered? Well, that's something else. If someone were to threaten my wife, that would be an entirely different matter. I love my wife and I'll do whatever it takes to keep her safe."

Marchetti smiled. "That's good, Sam. That's very good. She is lovely and I am sure, well worth any sacrifice. Go home, kiss your wife."

Sam threw back the rest of his scotch and rose to his full height. Casting a steely gaze at Marchetti, he reiterated, "Whatever it takes," and walked out of the club.

****

Angela had her moment in the spotlight. She danced to Beyonce's "Dance for Me", receiving thunderous applause, wolf whistles, and shouts, asking her to take it off. When she stepped off the stage, Tony was waiting. Her face flushed with excitement, she ran up and hugged Tony's neck.

"Oh, Tony. It was wonderful. Do you think the talent agents liked it? I can do another one if they need to see more." She was dancing in place while a second girl skirted around her to get up on stage.

Tony placed his hands on her shoulders. "You were great, baby. I told you, didn't I?"

Angela guzzled some water. "You did, Tony, thank you. Did you hear the crowd? I couldn't understand everything they were shouting, but I think they loved it!"

Tony knew what the crowd of men had been shouting. Feeling the buzz of his cell phone, he checked the message. It was from Ricco.

—*Plans have changed. Take her home. Angela is not a candidate for advancement.*— Tony let out a breath of relief.

"You were great, baby. So sexy. But, the talent agents, they just texted. They are looking for a blond." Tony saw the sudden letdown on Angela's face. He hated to dash her dreams of dancing, but he also suspected what kind of dancing she would eventually have to do. Suddenly, Tony was glad plans had changed. He knew what needed to be done. "The agents promised to keep your resume on file but didn't have an opening for you at this time." Angela slumped down on the step, burying her face in her hands.

He placed his knuckle under her chin and raised her face so he could look into her eyes. They were swimming with tears of disappointment. "Hey, don't look so sad. You're good, really good. I loved watching you. Why don't you go get changed? I'll take you home."

Angela sucked in a panicked gasp, jumping to her feet. "Home? I can't go home. Oh my god, I left without permission. I walked out. My grandmother will ground me for the next month. Tony, what am I going to do?" She was wringing her hands.

Tony stood. He brought her into his embrace and rubbed her back. "Don't worry. I'll be with you. We'll talk to your grandmother." He stood back and looked at her. "Go change. I'll wait here." Angela sniffled and returned to the dressing room.

Tony texted Ricco. —*Taking her home. What is the next assignment? If nothing urgent, need a couple of days.*—

—*Take what you need. I'll be in touch.*—

****

Marchetti stood at the window, gazing at the stripper on stage. She was one of his veteran performers, danced well, and entertained customers in special ways for the right price. Unfortunately, she was thirty-two and beginning to show the usual decline the lifestyle caused. He stared down at his scotch. Letting Sam win this one and walk away might make others think Marchetti was weak, but he had a plan. One that would take finesse and time.

But did he want to take the time, make the effort? Hell, the lifestyle wasn't just getting to his dancers. It was getting to him. His wife had given him two sons. Thankfully, they had taken their mother's name and pursued honorable careers. One, a stockbroker in New York and the other a real estate broker in Kennebunkport. Perhaps it was time to retire. The young guns were interested in taking over, and he was happy to oblige.

But where would be the jazz? It wasn't just the clubs, the porn. It was the satisfaction of besting a worthy opponent. Marchetti inhaled deeply, then breathed out slowly, savoring the rush of power. He poured himself a celebratory drink and sat back, satisfied with the outcome.

Sam was a worthy adversary. It was invigorating to spar with such a man. In the old days, he'd have tried to turn him, use him to his advantage. Now, he was happy to run a few strip clubs, invest his profits, and lie low. No need to draw unnecessary attention. No, if Ricco, his nephew, was interested in taking over the business, Marchetti would let him try to turn Sam. The kid bragged he had others in authority under his thumb. Well, with Sam's precious wife in the mix, perhaps, just perhaps, Ricco would try it. But for himself, Marchetti found it quite distasteful to think about eliminating Sam or his lovely wife. Ricco though? Marchetti shrugged and downed the last of his scotch.

Turning at the knock on the door, he watched his nephew enter. This was the legacy. Ricco was ready to take over.

"I called Tony. He is taking the girl home. The kid let her get to him. He didn't want her to dance and move forward in the program. What would you like to do with him?"

Marchetti shook his head and took a seat, motioning to Ricco to sit, and poured him a scotch. "Isn't that what Michael did? Fell for one of the girls?"

Ricco watched the amber liquid fill his glass and looked at the old man when he mentioned Michael. "Yes, sir. We discouraged him, perhaps a little too aggressively. But he won't make the same mistake again. The hand will heal well enough. He's working in Phoenix now."

Marchetti swirled his drink, breathing in the bouquet. It was almost as powerful as the liquor. Taking a slow sip, he savored its heat as it flowed down his throat. "Good, good. The occasional example helps the troops stay focused. Tony, though, he is young. Do you think your cousin will learn from his errors? I recall his father wasn't the brightest bulb in the box."

Ricco sat back with a pensive look on his face. "He is young. Hasn't had a lot of experience with women. I'll get him laid and he won't be sniffing after the girl. At the same time, I'll finish the job. She is an excellent dancer. The crowd really liked her. Once she is turned, Tony can have her anytime he wants." Ricco downed the scotch in one gulp, the star sapphire ring catching the light as he set down his glass. "Leave it to me."

Ricco rose to leave, but before he could go, Marchetti reached out a hand, grasping his forearm. "Do what you need to, Ricco, but be careful. Slater has the girl on his radar."

****

Sam was climbing out of his jeep when a late model gray Chevy sedan pulled to the curb. A young man jumped out of the driver's door and went to the trunk to grab Angela's backpack. Angela got out and stood waiting at the passenger door. The young man took her hand and gave her an encouraging smile.

Sam melted into the shadows and watched as Angela stared at her home. He saw her shame, her hesitation. Sam imagined the dread she felt thinking about facing her grandmother. He wondered if she understood the fear and anxiety she had caused for those that loved her.

There was a tenderness between the young man and Angela. Was this one of Marchetti's goons? The kid hardly looked like he was out of high school.

Sam's heart broke when Angela's face crumpled, and she started crying. She rubbed the heels of her hands over her eyes, smearing the exotic eye makeup she wore. Angela looked at the young man, chewing her bottom lip.

"Tony, what will I do? My grandmother will ground me for life. I'll never see you again."

Tony handed Angela her backpack. "You'll be okay, Angela. You've talked about how your grandmother took you and your little brother in. How she has been there for you since your mom went away. She loves you. Everyone makes mistakes. She'll be mad, but she'll be happy you are safe and home. I can go in with you if you want me to. If not, I need to get back."

Sam recognized his cue and stepped from the shadows. "Angela, we're glad you're home."

Angela turned to Sam and ran into his arms. He hugged her to his chest and looked at the young man over her head. He extended his hand to shake.

"I'm Sam Slater, a friend of the family. Thank you for bringing Angela home."

Tony stood staring at Sam's hand, finally returning the shake. "It's Tony, sir. Tony Columbo. I don't want to cause any trouble."

"And I don't plan to give you any. It's clear you are a good friend of Angela's. We are grateful to you for keeping her best interests in mind."

"Yeah. She's okay." He smiled at Angela. "Hey, um, I might not be around for a while. I have some business to take care of."

Angela pulled back from Sam's embrace. "What business? Is it traveling with Ricco again? When will I see you?"

"I don't know. I'll call when I can, okay? Take care and, um, listen to your grandmother. She loves you. It was nice meeting you, sir."

Tony handed Angela a caramel, then walked

around to the driver's side of the car. "You are a good dancer, Angela. Better than those talent scouts deserve." He climbed in and drove away.

Sam watched the car turn the corner, thinking the young man had a lot of courage. Sam wondered how long he'd be alive if Marchetti learned of their meeting and Tony's genuine feelings for Angela.

"Come on, let's go in. I'm sure your grandmother will be relieved to see you." Sam was turning Angela toward the door, when Isabell's cry of joy rang out from Jake's front porch.

"Oh, Angela, my baby. We were so worried." Isabell, followed by Vincent and Ray, came running out to the sidewalk, smothering Angela with questions and hugs. They hustled her into the Camarillos' house. Kate stood waiting on the porch. Sam's eyes met hers, thankful she was safe.

Chapter 24

Sam cradled Kate in his arms after making love. He smiled into her hair and sighed in pure contentment. The moon was shining in the window, its beams gliding across the floor. They lit the painting of a woman, the most precious woman currently in his arms.

"Kate, we should discuss the video. Tell me again where it came from." Sam had pulled himself up, bringing Kate with him. He was leaning back against the headboard, idly running his hand up and down her smooth back. Kate signed with pleasure and explained about receiving the plain envelope in the mail. How its mysterious presentation and appearance made her suspicious.

"I mean, Sam, it didn't take Sherlock Holmes to surmise that the envelope might be evidence. I was very careful when I opened it and saved the envelope. Do you want to run it for prints?" she asked, intrigued by his questions.

"I would, however, it isn't my jurisdiction. You should turn it over to the police. I'm not real impressed with Spencer. I'm still pissed at him for putting you in danger. It was inexcusable." There was a hard edge to Sam's voice as he remembered the unidentified car that followed Spencer's Crown Vic back to the station with his wife in the back seat.

Kate smothered a laugh. "Yes, I remember. Let's

not go there again. But, seriously, other than Spencer, who else? Janet Winburn?"

"No. No, I'm getting some weird vibes from her and she might try to suck you back into the case. I don't want you involved with that anymore. I really don't want you involved with anything concerning exploitation or sex houses or Marchetti. Jesus, Kate. I was so scared all the way back from El Paso. You did something very dangerous. Sometimes, I can't keep up with your adventures."

"I know, Sam." He heard her regret.

Confident Kate would back off the whole damn issue and be safe, Sam pressed his lips together, breathing in deeply and blowing out a heavy breath. "So, as much as it pains me, let's give it to Spencer. Obscenity Crimes is the proper division and Spencer is the proper authority. We'll take it over first thing in the morning."

Sam turned Kate's face up to him, kissing her tenderly on the lips. Kate returned his kiss, adding several along his jawline. She nibbled on his earlobe, then whispered words of love, sending darts of pleasure throughout his body. Kate continued to nibble her way down Sam's neck to his chest and lower until he could stand no more. Flipping her on her back, he entered her slowly, but Kate was greedy. She took him in deeper and when the rhythm of their lovemaking brought them gently over, clung to him, tears wetting her cheeks.

Sam used his thumb to wipe away her tears. "What's this?"

"I'm so stupid, Sam. I put you in the middle all the time. It scared me when I learned you were going to confront Marchetti. He could have killed you. Why can't I be happy writing about flower shows and restaurant reviews? You shouldn't be at risk because of me."

"Risk is part of my job. It shouldn't be part of yours. Your courage takes my breath away, Kate. I am baffled. Why? Why do you do it?" Sam's hands stroked Kate's hair, weaving his fingers through it.

Kate sighed. "I guess because someone has to. I couldn't turn away. The girls in that house need saving."

Sam cuddled her closer. "Kate, you see with your heart and your head. I work with talented investigators and they don't see the detail you do. It's a gift and a curse sometimes, I think."

"It is, Sam. I see so many things. Things that to others may seem silly, clothes, lighting, knick-knacks. For example, one of the odd things I noticed on a girl in the video? She was wearing a tennis bracelet. Of all the odd things to lock in on. Jewelry. I guess it's a woman's thing."

Sam's hand paused. Then he tugged a lock of Kate's hair. "Wait. What did you just say?"

"Ow. Hey, I'm not hinting for a tennis bracelet for Christmas, though it might be nice. It's just a woman thing to notice jewelry."

Sam pushed up out of bed, bringing Kate with him. "Come with me." Kate looked at him with a puzzled expression. Pulling on her robe, she followed him down to his office. Sam was rapidly paging through his files when Kate walked in. "There it is." Turning to Kate, Sam held out the photo of the bracelet the Presidio Sheriff had found on one of the dead girls. "Does this look familiar?" he asked.

Kate took the photo and studied it. She nodded and looked at Sam with certainty. "Yes, Sam. That's just like the one the girl was wearing. I'm sure of it. Where did this come from?"

Sam tapped the photo on his fisted hand. "South Texas, and it might be what we need to nail Marchetti."

Chapter 25

Sam looked up as Kate kissed him on the top of the head. He was relieved she had turned the video over to the authorities and dropped all thoughts of exploitation. The news cycle had turned and Kate and the sex house weren't headlining anymore. The less she was involved with that, the better. They had intentionally bypassed Janet Winburn with the video. Sam still didn't trust her. The surveillance they'd put on her hadn't turned up anything concrete, but every time he considered her actions, the hairs on the back of his neck stood up. Now, if the woman would just leave Kate the hell alone, it would be perfect.

It was a rare warm late fall morning and Kate was going out to the garden to do her yoga. Sam smiled, thinking he'd join her for savasana and some other moves as soon as he finished the report he was reading when Sam heard her scream.

Sam's heart jumped into his throat as he ran to the backyard, ready to take on whatever threat there was to his woman. Kate was standing still as a statue. He could see her profile and her face had lost all color. She had one hand on her mouth and the other on her stomach. Sam reached for her just as she turned and retched into the flower bed. She turned into his arms, burying her face, and pointed toward the fountain. His gaze moved in that direction. Sam swallowed hard and kept Kate's face pressed to his shoulder. A pink froth spilled over the top and down into the pool where a black and white furry body floated. Someone had severed the neck with such ferocity that the head hung by a thread. Blood had splashed all over before they tossed her into the fountain.

Sam sat Kate down, where she lowered her face into her hands and wept. Getting a black trash bag, Sam went over to the fountain to dispose of Ophelia's body. Sam felt the sad irony of her death. She'd been rescued from a black plastic trash bag and left to die in a garbage can at the park and now, he was placing her lifeless body into another one. Sam closed his eyes, feeling a moment of déjà vu and failure.

The silence was shattered by Kate's sudden cry. "Ophelia! Oh my God, Ophelia!" He turned in shock to see his wife scoop up their black and white fur ball, hugging it to her chest. "Don't you ever do that again. You scared us so much."

Sam went to Kate, who continued to scold the cat. Feelie was grudgingly putting up with all the hugging and petting, while Sam thought about the wrong cat found floating in a bloody fountain. His eyes narrowed. Someone had just made a big mistake.

Chapter 26

Kate picked up the flat of pansies, placing them in her cart. Red would be lovely in the porch pots, and now that it was getting cooler, there would be color in the garden over the winter. When she turned, she came face to face with Janet Winburn.

"Janet, what a surprise. How are you?" she asked politely, hoping to avoid any lengthy conversation. She had been purposely ignoring Janet's attempts to reach her and felt a little guilty for the lack of courtesy.

"I'm fine, Kate. I'm sorry I've had to track you down this way, but I really need to speak with you." She looked around nervously. "It's about the video. I know where it came from."

Kate tried to hide her look of shock. "What are you saying, Janet? I sent it to the vice squad special task force for Spencer and you to follow-up. Of course you know where it came from."

"No, Kate. You don't understand. I sent it to you in the first place. I can't say where I got it, but I think I can help Sam find the location and take down Marchetti."

Kate sucked in a breath. She didn't know what Janet was talking about, but she believed Winburn knew something. Something Sam needed to hear. She checked for prying eyes and ears. "When and how can we meet? I'll call Sam."

Janet's head swiveled again, looking for who or what Kate didn't know. Threats, she assumed. "Not here, not today. The Yoga Center tomorrow. There is a class at seven-thirty a.m. I attend. Park in the rear. I'll walk through the building and out the back to meet you. No one will suspect." Janet turned, then looked back. "I heard about your cat. I'm sorry. It was horrible, and the threat was real. I know."

Kate left the pansies and called Sam. A maroon coupe followed Janet Winburn.

****

Sam and Kate arrived at the Yoga Center at 7:10. If Janet was like Kate, she arrived for yoga class early. They wanted to be waiting when she stepped out the back door. Sam carried his Glock and insisted Kate wear a vest. She thought it might be overkill, but didn't argue. Things were just too weird at this point.

The morning was cool, so Sam kept the engine going but rolled down the windows. Once Janet arrived, they'd take Sam's car and drive to a secluded place for their meeting. When Janet emerged from the building, she looked around. Spotting Kate's wave, she started toward their vehicle. A single shot rang out. It threw Janet back against the building, blood stained her yoga shirt. Sam shoved Kate to the floorboard. "Call 911," he told her, then drove his jeep to shield Janet. Looking around for the shooter, he took a breath and rushed to Janet. They'd hit her on the right side of her chest. Sam couldn't tell how bad it was. Kate crept up behind him. She had Sam's running towel in her hands. He motioned her forward. Taking the towel from Kate, he staunched the bleeding. Letting Kate take over, maintaining pressure on the wound, Sam pulled his weapon and kept watch. The ambulance and two squad cars arrived a few minutes later.

Sam and Kate waited outside the surgery room. Janet was in critical condition. If the shooter had intended to kill her, he'd missed his mark. The hospital notified her family. Her ex and her daughter were flying in from the east coast. Fort Worth PD had placed an officer outside her room. Janet would be safe for now. For how long, Sam couldn't say, because until they put away Marchetti, the threat loomed large.

Chapter 27

Angela put down her phone. Tony had called. He asked if she could meet him at the park. She thought he sounded nervous and agreed immediately. Opening her door as quietly as possible, Angela listened for Judge Judy playing on the TV in the kitchen. Grandma Isabell always watched Judge Judy while preparing dinner. Angela could be gone and back before anyone missed her. What she hadn't considered was Vincent seeing her.

She turned on her radio at a low level. If anyone walked by her room, they'd think she was hanging out, dancing or studying. Pulling on her jean jacket, Angela stole from her room and slipped out the front door.

Vincent was walking back from Ray's when he saw Angela glance over her shoulder at the house and walk away. Vincent wasn't a graduate of Spy School 101 for nothing. Angela was sneaking off. He needed to follow her.

Allowing her to get ahead by a block, Vincent walked, keeping to the shadows, dodging behind trees and shrubs. When Angela took a left at the corner, he knew where she was going and cut across the park, coming out at her usual meeting place just as she arrived. The driver guy from the Chevy was waiting for her.

Vincent watched them hug. The guy took her hand

and walked her to a picnic table. This was good, Vincent thought. He could sneak up behind them, crawling under the shrubs that backed the picnic area. Their voices were low but distinct.

"Angela, are you okay? Was your grandma very mad?" Tony put a caramel in her hand.

Angela gave Tony a sweet smile. "She was more worried than mad, just like you and Sam said she'd be. She gave me extra chores to do as punishment, but she didn't ground me, only gave me an early curfew. I can't be out past seven p.m."

"That's good. You shouldn't be out later than that, anyway. Not for a while." Tony hesitated and looked around as if checking for any threats. "Look, Angela. That Sam guy. Is he like a cop or something?"

Angela looked puzzled. "Not a cop, no, but he works for Homeland Security. He carries a badge and a gun. Why are you acting so weird? What's going on? Why are you asking about Sam?"

Tony's voice grew quiet, secretive. "I…I need to talk to him, help him. Do you think you can ask him to meet me?"

Vincent was confused. Tony sounded sincerely concerned about Angela getting into trouble. He was prepared to think this guy was a sleaze, but maybe he really cared about Angela, and the guy said he wanted to help Sam. Vincent was considering stepping out of his hiding place to offer help. After all, he and Sam worked together on spy stuff, but before he could, a gray panel van pulled up behind the Chevy and three very mean-looking men climbed out.

Wasting no time, they approached Tony and Angela.

"Ricco, what are you doing here?" Tony asked, stepping in front of Angela protectively.

Ricco laughed and grabbed Angela, pulling her away from Tony. He held her while the other two beat up Tony. One held Tony, pinning his arms behind his back. Tony took several hits to the face and stomach. Blood poured from his nose and mouth. When the two guys released him, Tony fell to his knees. Vincent froze in place.

With a tone that had Vincent cringing deeper into the shade of the shrubbery, Ricco spoke quietly. "Consider this a lesson, Tony. Marc will drive you back to the club. We'll take care of the girl."

When the guy, who must have been Marc, hauled Tony to his feet and pulled him to the car, Tony tried to tell Angela to run. Marc gave him another cuff to the head and shoved him into the Chevy. Ricco held Angela as they watched Marc and Tony drive away.

"Why did you hurt him, Ricco? I thought he was your cousin. What are you going to do?" Angela sounded scared.

"It's not what I'm going to do, baby. It's on you now." Ricco dragged Angela toward the van. She pulled against him but was no match for his strength. "Do you want your boyfriend to live? Keep that pretty face?"

Vincent watched in horror as Ricco tossed his sister, screaming for help, into the back of the van and it drove away. He made a beeline for Sam's, telling him everything he'd seen. Sam was pleased with the amount of details Vincent shared, down to and including vehicle identification and descriptions of the men that took Angela. Vincent even identified the star sapphire pinkie ring.

Sam took Vincent home, calling Emily on the way, filling her in on the details. "You should go over to Isabell's. She'll need your support. We'll be there in a minute."

Gathering at Isabell's house, Sam had Vincent recount the abduction while he called Detective Spencer.

"Best I can figure it, Spencer, some of Marchetti's goons beat up one of their own and then took Angela Camarillo. I think she has been on their radar for a while. Your initial investigation was spot on. They are using teenage girls to dance at the Fantasy Palace. I don't know if they coerced the girls or not. Look, I'm with the family right now, but I'd like to accompany you on the bust."

Sam paced impatiently, shaking his head at whatever was being said on the other end of the line. Time was flying, and it was the enemy. "I don't know for sure if she is there, but if a minor might be in danger, do you really need a warrant?" The reply he got didn't make him happy. If the club was open for business, anyone could walk in, but if it was closed, then a warrant would be better. Considering the situation, they would move on the club and hope for something that would give them probable cause to enter.

Motioning Emily and Jake aside, he gave them the jest of the information Spencer had shared. "You stay here with Isabell. She needs to be home, ready to welcome and comfort Angela when we find her." They nodded mutely, turning troubled eyes toward Isabell, who sat hunched on the couch, staring at nothing, a hankie clutched in her hand.

Isabell turned frightened eyes to Sam as he sat next to her. Taking her hand in his, Sam did his best to calm her fears. "Isabell, Vincent did an excellent job helping to identify the men that took Angela. We will find her and she will be all right. You must have faith."

Choking back a sob, Isabell scrubbed her face with her hands. Her strength shone through the tears in her eyes. Then Isabell Camarillo rose to her full height of five feet three inches. Sam stood with her. Isabell swallowed hard. With her fists clenched at her side, her chin came up in defiance. "You find my baby, Sam. You find her and then you make them pay!"

It astounded Sam to witness the fierceness of this small woman. The fight for her family. "You can count on it," he promised.

Sam arrived at Fantasy Palace right behind Spencer. He watched as the Fort Worth SWAT team surrounded the Gentleman's Club. Since it was open for business, he and Spencer, backed up by two other plain-clothes detectives, walked in the door. Spencer approached the man at the door, held his badge up, and told him the reason for the visit. They rousted a handful of customers, two bouncers, three bartenders, and a half-dozen twenty-something women who served as waitresses when not dancing. Spencer politely asked everyone to wait in the parking lot while the SWAT team cleared the building. No Angela. No Marchetti goons. No pinkie ring.

Sam felt the weight of failure. Spencer's ass was in a sling. Entering private premises without a warrant and, in this case, no probable cause because they hadn't found Angela, violated Marchetti's civil rights. His attorneys were going to have a field day with that one. And they were no closer to finding Angela. Sam dreaded having to give Isabell the news.

An anxious Isabell met him at the door. It was obvious from his expression he did not have good news. Emily took a devastated Isabell into the kitchen for a cup of tea while Sam spoke again with Vincent.

"Vincent, do you remember anything else? Did they mention any places they might go or people's names?"

Vincent sat with his hand clasped between his knees. He racked his brains, trying to remember every bit of the conversation he'd overheard. "That driver guy asked Angela about you. Wanted to know if you were a cop or something. He said he needed to talk to you, help you."

Sam leaned forward. "Did he mention what he wanted to talk to me about, help me with?"

"No." Vincent ran a hand through his hair in frustration. He jumped up in agitation. "No! The guy didn't say anything helpful and then those other guys came. They scared me. I should have helped him. I should have helped Angela. She tried to get away. I could have helped her, and I didn't. I didn't and now she is gone."

Sam watched as the horror of Vincent's inaction crushed him. Sam remembered how destructive self-doubt and recrimination could be.

"What if they hurt her? What if they kill her?" Vincent turned guilt-filled eyes to Sam, begging him to make it right, make it better.

Sam watched Vincent's sense of failure escalate and felt his pain all too acutely. "Stop it, Vincent." He grabbed the young boy and wrapped him in his arms. "God, Vincent! Stop it!" There was a shared anguish in Sam's voice.

Vincent pulled away and wiped his hand under a flowing nose, sniffling loudly. He threw himself down on the couch, crossing his arms stubbornly. Sam knew his words hadn't eased the guilt yet.

"Look, Vincent. You did everything you could and were supposed to. If you'd gotten physically involved, they might have hurt you. Then who would have been able to report the abduction to us, give us the detailed information you did?" Sam sat down on the coffee table in front of Vincent. He leaned his forearms on his knees and forced Vincent to look at him, to hear him. "I won't sugarcoat it for you, Vincent. A good spy, a leader, has to make hard decisions. Sometimes those decisions put others at risk for the short term; until you can muster your forces and save them. You did that. You called in the calvary. I'm here and we will find Angela and bring her safely home. And we can do that because you kept your head *and* your temper in check and gave us the information we need."

Vincent looked at Sam. There was hope in his eyes. Hope he'd made the right decision and hope that Sam would be true to his word and save his sister.

Sam laid a firm hand on the boy's shoulder. "You are the man of this house. You made the decision a man would have made. And because of your courage and level-headedness, I have some ideas."

Sam stepped away to run through all the possibilities. Spencer had done leg work and knew about Fantasy Palace, but what about other properties? Marchetti owned several Gentlemen's clubs. Spencer had only concentrated on the one where it was suspected they used underage dancers, but what if this was a traveling show? What if they had taken Angela to another club? Janet Winburn had provided the sex house video. She had reached out to Kate. How was she involved? What information did she have? Realizing Janet Winburn was the best lead to Marchetti's operation, he called the hospital to check on her, only to learn his wife had already visited with the patient and left.

Chapter 28

Marc dumped Tony unceremoniously on the ratty couch behind the stage at the Silver Slipper Gentleman's Club. "You're a dumb shit, Tony. Ricco could kill you for this. You're lucky you're his cousin. Blood is thicker than water, I guess."

Tony held his head with one hand and his ribs with the other. He was sure they had broken something. No one had ever beaten him like this before. God, it hurt. "Can I get some water, Marc?"

"Yeah. Just cause you're young and dumb doesn't mean you have to be treated like this. Ricco is crazy, though. The old man is looking to retire and Ricco means to take over. He won't put up with stupid shit. Don't push it. Let the girl go. There are plenty of others out there. Some with bigger tits." Marc shoved a glass into Tony's hand, laughing at his crude joke.

Tony drank his water and laid back, closing his eyes. Marc was wrong. There weren't plenty of others.

He slept. For how long, Tony wasn't sure, but Ricco came in, mad as a hornet. He walked straight to the couch and kicked it, jolting Tony awake.

"Look at what your little girlfriend did!" Ricco pointed to the scratches Angela had put on his cheek when he pushed her into the van. "The bitch sat there cringing and crying, then lunged at me. Oh, I gave her a what for. She'll think twice before doing something that stupid again."

Curling his lips in disgust, Ricco grabbed Tony by the collar, pulling him up. "God, what do you see in her? She's skinny and whiney."

"She is not!" Tony screamed, pushing Ricco's hand away. He threw a weak punch at Ricco, which only reopened the scratches Angela had inflicted.

"God-damn it! You're just as dumb as your little bitch." Ricco backhanded Tony, sending him flying against the back of the couch. Tony slumped and curled into a ball.

Ricco walked away, gingerly touching his cheek, and saw the fresh blood. "Fuck!" He rounded on Tony, shouting angrily. "You can forget about letting her take the easy way! She ain't going to just be dancing."

Tony rolled to his feet, staggering toward Ricco. "Please, she'll dance. She'll do it for me. Just don't let anyone hurt her, Ricco. Don't let anyone touch her. Please." Tony sank to his knees, begging. He was crying, clutching at Ricco's jacket.

"Shit. What a sniveling baby." Ricco placed his foot against Tony's shoulder, pushing him away. "I went to bat for you, asshole! I told the old man you could do it and you end up falling for the little twit. No more, do you hear me? No! More! Leo took her straight to the house. Your little girlfriend will be a nice addition. She'll learn what she needs to and then you can enjoy her. Lick your wounds. You're leaving tonight. I'm sending you to Phoenix."

Tony cowered as Ricco slapped him once again. The cut over his eye reopened and fresh blood oozed out. Tony might have been fuzzy before, but when Ricco mentioned the house, he knew he had to do something.

"I'm sorry, Ricco. You're right. I'm an idiot. I won't do it again. Please, don't hurt me anymore. I'll do whatever you tell me to do."

"Your damn right, you will! Get him out of here, Marc. Let him get cleaned up and help him pack." Marc nodded like the soldier he was.

Tony watched Ricco stalk out. His mind was buzzing with thoughts of what to do. He had to get to Sam. Angela said the guy was some spy or something with Homeland Security. He'd be able to help rescue Angela.

Tony looked over at Marc. He was involved in some stupid video game, not really paying a lot of attention. Marc wasn't the smartest of Ricco's enforcers. Tony rolled to his side and moaned, retching.

Marc jumped up, looking around for a trash can or anything else. "Whoa, dude. Are you going to be sick? Hey! Don't puke in here. Go use the john."

Tony secretly smiled and lurched to his feet. Marc followed as he staggered toward the bathroom, fell to his knees over the toilet, and made the most hideous sound. "Sorry, man. It hurts so bad. I'm sick. I think I'm going to shit myself, too." Tony fumbled for his belt.

Marc turned a sickly shade of green. "I don't need to watch you do this. Gross." He slammed the door and walked back to the TV and his video game.

Tony faked his sick sounds while working at the latch to the window. When the volume of the video game rose, Tony climbed out and ran to the parking lot. No one was around. There were three vehicles parked in the lot. The older model Ford pickup belonged to the janitor. It was unlocked. Tony climbed in. He didn't have a clue how to hot-wire a car. He frantically checked the visor and ashtray for keys. No luck. Tony slammed his hand on the steering wheel, trying to think. He remembered his dad keeping one of those magnetic boxes with a spare key tucked into the wheel well. Tony jumped out of the truck. He reached above the front tire, feeling the familiar metal box, and thanked his old man for being a forgetful drunk. Tony climbed back in the pickup and committed grand theft auto, hightailing it to Angela's house, intent on asking Mrs. Camarillo how to find Sam.

****

Once again, Isabell sat with Emily, Jake and Vincent, waiting to hear news about Angela. Sam had said he had another avenue to investigate. He promised to get back to them as soon as he had anything of note.

Emily had just put down a fussy John Mac for a nap. Jake played gin rummy with Vincent to keep his mind off things. Isabell stood staring out the front windows, a cup of tepid tea in her hands. The house was deathly quiet when a strange pickup truck screamed to a stop and broke the silence. It almost jumped the curb. Isabell stepped back as Jake moved swiftly to the door, hand on the butt of his gun. Vincent stood behind him, looking through the curtains as a young man, badly beaten, pulled himself out of the truck. He staggered to Isabell's door and banged loudly.

"Mrs. Camarillo, please. I know you don't know me, but they have Angela. I need to find Sam. He can save her! Please, Mrs. Camarillo. I'm Tony. I am…I want to help her." Tony sank to his knees. His ribs were burning with pain. The world was going in and out of focus.

Vincent grabbed Jake's arm. "That's the driver guy, Tony. Angela's boyfriend. He wanted to help Sam. Let him in, Jake. Let him in."

Jake pulled the door open and knelt, pretending to check Tony's injuries while he searched him for weapons. Satisfied the kid was unarmed, Jake helped him to stand and practically carried him into the house, setting him down on the couch.

Emily came in with water, handing the glass to the young man. "Who are you?" she asked gently.

Tony gulped down half the glass and looked thankfully at Emily. "Thank you. I'm Angela's friend. I need to talk to Sam. Is he here?"

Jake took over the conversation. "He isn't but we are family. What do you know about Angela? Where is she?"

Isabell interrupted. "Is she safe? My baby." She broke down and began sobbing again. Emily gathered her in her arms and led her to a chair.

Tony shook his head, frightened. "I don't know. Ricco was going to make her dance, but she fought back. She scratched his face. Got him good. It pissed Ricco off. He said she was going straight to the house. I don't know where the house is, but girls that make Ricco mad go there and they don't come back."

Everyone exchanged frightened and horrified expressions. Jake reached for his phone.

****

Kate wasted no time when she learned Janet Winburn regained consciousness. Knocking lightly on the door, she peered in.

"Janet, how are you?" Kate noted the dark circles

of pain surrounding eyes in a face too pale. They still listed her status as critical. The bullet had ricocheted off her ribs and fragmented. One small piece had nicked her liver. She'd suffered significant blood loss, but from the way Janet gripped Kate's hand, she wouldn't let it stop her from speaking.

Kate followed Janet's eyes as they moved to the ice water on her tray. "I don't think you can have anything but ice chips. Is that okay?" Janet nodded, opening her mouth like a baby bird, waiting for the spoonful of chips. "Can you tell me the information you have on the video?"

Janet took the tiny spoon of ice from Kate, and closed her eyes, savoring it like the finest wine. "It's old. Might be gone…McCart. Had my daughter. Marchetti let her go for my cooperation." Her grip tightened on Kate's hand. "He kills them when trouble. Must find it, stop him." Janet panted, exhausted from her efforts. "No, wait. Not Marchetti. Marchetti's man." Janet lay back on her pillow, exhausted.

The doctor stepped up, laying his hand on Kate's arm. "I'm sorry. She is too weak. That's all she can do for now."

"Thank you, doctor. Do your best for her." Kate stepped out of the room. McCart. *It's too long a street. How am I to find a house I've never seen from the outside?*

Kate sat and put her head in her hands, overwhelmed by the task. She felt the tide of hopelessness wash over her. But something clicked. Kate had never given up on a story because it took work to dig up the facts. Nodding her head determinedly, she reviewed what she knew and what she could surmise. McCart was a thread that she just needed to pull and see where it led. She would drive up and down that damn street and look for anything that appeared to be…What? Kate wondered what a sex house would look like. The girls had to be kept from escaping. Barred or boarded up windows, maybe?

****

Sam wasn't answering his phone. Knowing time was of the essence, Kate called Ray. He was at the job site, taking delivery of the light fixtures. She shared her suspicions and told him she'd swing by the job site and pick him up.

Kate did a quick search online and determined that north of I-20 was the best bet. Driving slowly on McCart, both Kate and Ray looked for any houses with boarded-up windows. The postage-size lots held tiny frame houses. Some needed repair, but others were clean and nicely maintained. Some looked like new builds replacing a teardown. But none looked like what Kate imagined a sex house would look like. When she reached an industrial part of McCart, she pulled over.

"Why are you pulling over? We're not at the end of the street yet." Ray was frustrated. It showed in his voice.

"Ray, this isn't getting us anywhere. What are we missing? South of I-20 was a mixture of retail and residential, but none of the houses faced the street. I got the impression from Janet that the house faced the street. We're beyond the houses. This area is industrial, factories. Janet referred to it as a sex *house*. What do we know? Think. What did you see in the video?"

Ray pulled off his cap and scratched his head. "Okay, let's see. Small room, low ceilings. Vinyl flooring, cheap lighting. Only the bathroom, no kitchen set up I could see, but the space was finished, livable. Rental space? Couldn't have been over eight hundred square feet, about the size of a three, maybe four-car garage."

Kate sat up straighter. "Yes, that's it. We were looking at the houses facing the street. What if the sex house is a separate building behind the house? We need to take another run." Kate did a Y-turn and headed back the way they came. Both she and Ray changed their focus. Now they were looking at structures behind the houses.

Kate slowed, then stopped. Turning the corner onto Gambrel, she pulled over. She looked at the gray craftsman with a multi-car garage in the back. It was on a corner with the house facing McCart. The driveway entrance was on the side street. Shrubs and a fence shielded the backyard from view. "This has to be it, Ray. The house out front is simple and well-kept. Look at the garage behind it. It's about the right size. Four-car like you said and in good repair. But look at the windows of the upper level. They are all boarded over. It's exactly like others I've researched."

Kate parked three houses down from the one they suspected of being the sex house. She and Ray got out of the car. They carefully walked toward it, looking at the layout. There was a sheltered walkway between the two buildings. From what they could see, Kate guessed they held the girls in the upper level above the garage and entertained the gentleman callers in the house. Returning to Kate's car, they got in and Ray tried to talk some sense into Kate.

"We just can't go busting in there," he said as he

tried to reach Sam again. That was when a gray van pulled into the driveway. Kate and Ray scrunched down in the car to avoid being seen. A man opened the side door and dragged a disheveled and crying Angela from the back, taking her to the garage. He banged twice on the door and an old woman opened it. She stood back to let them in. Fifteen minutes later, the same guy came out, leading another young woman to the frame house in front. The van drove off, leaving Kate and Ray looking at each other. Ray called Sam once more, leaving another voicemail with the status and location. Turning concerned eyes to Kate, he nodded.

"Okay. Now we have to go busting in there. I'd bet the only one in the garage is the old woman. You wait here, call 911. I'll go get Angela."

Kate watched Ray walk with purpose to the garage and bang twice on the door like he'd seen the other man do. When the old woman opened the door, he pushed his way in. Kate hung up with 911 and followed him. She was coming around the back of the house when the man who had arrived with Angela came out of the small frame house. Tucking his shirt into his pants, a satisfied smile on his face, he pushed a tearful young girl toward the garage. She wiped blood from a cut on her lip and stumbled when he gave her another shove. He was walking to the garage when Ray came out, leading Angela and three other young girls.

"Hey. What the hell?" The man charged Ray, hitting him like a fullback, taking him down. While Kate hustled the girls to safety, Ray grappled with the larger man, landing a couple of good punches. He was up and running toward the girls when the man rose and pulled out his weapon.

"Ray, look out. He has a gun!" Kate shouted, pushing the girls down behind the air conditioning unit and running back to Ray.

The man heard Kate's warning. Ray spun back around. The man had turned his gun toward Kate and pulled the trigger just as Ray threw himself in front of her.

****

The sound of sirens filled the air as Fort Worth's finest came screeching to a halt in front of the house, followed by Sam. Leaping from his jeep, Sam outran the police and Spencer, going straight toward the sound of the gunshot. A large man was standing over Kate as she held Sam's bleeding father.

Yelling in rage, Sam drew a bead on the man. "Freeze mother-fucker! Drop your weapon."

The guy didn't look like a Rhodes scholar, but he was smart enough to drop his weapon and raise his hands. Sam called for medical and ran to secure the man threatening his family.

Kate, knelt at Ray's side wearing only her camisole. She'd stripped off her shirt and was pressing it to his chest. Sam knelt next to his father. "Ah, shit, Dad. What were you thinking?"

Ray's eyes opened, and he gave Sam a lopsided grin. "Thought I had to keep her safe, son. Just like I taught you." He passed out.

Sam and Kate stood aside as several ambulances arrived to transport Ray and the girls to the hospital. Turning into Sam's arms, Kate lay her head on his chest, felt the strength and safety of his arms around her. When the hammering of his heart returned to its normal rhythm, she tipped her face up to his, kissing him lightly on the lips.

"I swear to God, woman, you're going to give me a heart attack." Sam kissed her forehead. "Come on. Spencer can deal with everything at the scene. Let's go to the hospital." He walked Kate to her car, ever vigilant for threats, then followed her to the hospital to be with Ray.

****

Ray was being wheeled into surgery. The ER doc had been confident it was a clean wound and Ray would be up and about in no time. The girls they'd rescued were in the hands of the police and social workers. They would receive medical care and their families contacted. Angela was safe. She had a few bruises, and one would have expected, emotional trauma but, instead, she was spitting mad. When Sam saw her, she was telling everyone that would listen about Ricco, the scumbag. In great detail, she told everyone what she was going to do the next time she saw him. It involved scissors and a nut cracker. Sam stifled a smile. He was pulling his phone out to call Isabell with the news when it buzzed. Jake's number showed on caller ID.

"Jake? What's up?" Sam answered, forgetting the good news to share, apprehension sounding in his voice.

Jake responded, easing Sam's concern, the epitome of calm and control. "We're all good. We got a visitor. Tony, Angela's friend. He says he has information to help us find Angela. Where are you?"

"Thank goodness. First off, good news. We found Angela. She is fine. Unfortunately, we didn't get Marchetti or Ricco. Spencer's crew is on that." Jake interrupted Sam long enough to tell Isabell. Sam heard the cries of relief in the background.

"That is great news. Everyone here is dancing in delight." Isabell's excited voice rang out in the background. Sam could picture her tugging at Jake's arm.

"Where is my baby? Is Sam bringing her home? When will he be here?"

Jake patiently replied to Isabell, "I don't know, let me ask." While everyone chattered excitedly, Jake stepped away from the noise to hear. "Okay, Sam. You heard the questions. What can you tell us?"

Sam paused. "Jake, Angela is fine, but Dad and Kate were instrumental in the rescue. They shot Dad. The doctors say it's not bad, but I'm sure you and Emily will want to be here when he gets out of surgery."

Sam heard the insistent voices of Isabell and Emily. Jake's unruffled tone carried through the phone lines. "You're probably right, Sam. Here, all the women want to know what's going on. Let me put you on speakerphone." Sam knew he and Jake would communicate details without alarming the women. "Angela's getting a once over at the hospital?"

Sam replied, equally calm, "Yes, the EMT's suggested she get checked out before I took her home. Just routine. Why don't you load everyone up and meet us here?" Sam heard the chorus of agreement and the bustle of preparation.

"Well now, that sounds like a good idea. While we're at it, the kid, Tony? He probably needs to see a doctor. Might have a broken nose, some cracked ribs. We'll pack up the gang and head to the hospital. You can meet us there and talk to him. Might take a little maneuvering. All our available babysitters will be with us. Good thing Emily insisted we buy that 'mom mobile'."

Sam heard Emily's voice calling out. "I'll run next door and pack the baby bag. Vincent, can you help me, please?"

"Yeah, good idea, babe," Jake called after Emily as he took Sam off speakerphone. "How fast do I need to get us there, Sam?"

"Jake, Dad will be in surgery for another hour at least. The doctor said it was minor. I don't think he'll die on the table. It might be better all the way around if Emily knows later rather than sooner."

"So says the man she doesn't live with. And if she finds out I knew about this and purposefully hid it from her as well as delayed her getting there? Shit, I might live in the doghouse for the next month. One I still haven't built."

"Well, make sure you build one with indoor plumbing and A/C." Sam laughed as they disconnected. He turned to see Kate smiling at him. "I love you, Sam Slater."

"Right back at you, Kate Slater," Sam said as he enfolded her in his arms.

Twenty minutes later, Sam met everyone at the entry to the ER. He handed a subdued Angela over to a grateful Isabell Camarillo. The family enjoyed a tearful reunion. The minor emergency department went to work patching up Tony. Vincent promised to call Sam when they finished so he and Tony could talk.

Jake held Emily's hand with a bouncing baby John Mac on her hip as Sam escorted them to the sixth-floor waiting room. Kate took John Mac from a puzzled Emily. Jake looked at Sam and stood firm, next to his wife as Sam explained Ray being shot and in surgery.

Emily sucked in a gasp and turned angry eyes toward Jake. Sam had expected the explosion of anger. He stepped back with Kate out of the line of fire.

"You knew. You didn't bother to tell me. Why? Why didn't you tell me? He's my dad, damn you!" She was crying, slapping at him until Jake took her in his arms, shushing her like he shushed John Mac. She struggled against his embrace, which only tightened more around her.

"Don't you dare try to calm me, you bastard. I'm mad at you!" Jake's arms around Emily softened as the resentment seeped from her. "You, you…Oh, damn it, Jake Edwards!" She stopped, going silent as suddenly as her anger and voice had risen.

"I'm sorry, babe. It wouldn't have made a difference if you knew twenty minutes sooner. Only upset you and John Mac in the process. Look at him. His little face is all scrunched up in confusion. He isn't used to hearing his mommy cry or yell." Jake's voice had taken on the child-like tone people use when talking to babies or animals. Hearing it come from a 230-pound grown man was incongruous as hell. He tipped her face to his and kissed her forehead, nose, and mouth. "I love you, Emily, and I didn't want you to worry any more than necessary. I'm sorry."

Emily's frustration was already lessening when the doctor came into the waiting room. All eyes turned to him expectantly. He directed his comments to Sam.

"Mr. Slater? I'm Dr. Meta. I take it, this is the family?" His eyes swept the group, noting the concern on their faces. Palms out, the doctor reassured them, "Everything is going to be all right. Your dad is in good shape for his age and the gunshot wound didn't damage any vital organs. We removed the bullet, and patched up the hole. We'll keep him overnight for observation. Unless something unexpected happens, we should release him in a couple of days. He'll probably need some physical therapy to help with shoulder mobility. He'll be swinging a hammer in a few weeks." Dr. Meta smiled widely. "Oh, yes. Before the anesthesia kicked in, your dad told the nurse he didn't have time for this nonsense. He had an apartment complex he was rehabbing. Asked if she was in the market for a nice place near the hospital. Is he part of the construction crew or marketing team?" Dr. Meta chuckled. "He's in recovery right now. We'll let you know when you can see him."

The group let out a collective sigh of relief and a laugh. Sam pulled his ear, thinking. "Sounds just like Dad. He'll have an entirely new advertising campaign in place by the end of the week. Jake, you should probably plan on redesigning the common areas and amenities. I can see it now." Sam waved his hand across an imaginary banner. "'Apartments designed for the Medical Professional'."

Jake quirked his brow, giving it serious consideration. "Actually, that's not a bad idea, especially this close to the hospital district." He put his arm around Emily's shoulder, hugging her to his side. "Honey, put on your thinking cap about the type of workout space and equipment we need to order."

Jake and Kate waited while Sam and Emily saw Ray in recovery. When they moved him to his room, everyone crowded in, hugging him and talking his ear off until Ray finally told them to get the heck out. He was tired and wanted to take a nap. Following more hugs and well wishes, the gang finally said goodbye. Sam lagged behind. Taking Ray's hand, he said the words Ray had always prayed for.

"Dad, I can't thank you enough for putting yourself in front of Kate. Your actions saved her and our child." Sam hesitated, then nodded to himself. "I get it now. I understand what you were doing when I was a kid and why it was so damn important. Mom once said we were more alike than either of us knew. She was spot on. Dad, and I'm sorry it's taken me too long to figure this out and finally say it. I'm proud to be your son and to call you dad."

Ray had to clear his throat to reply. "Thank you, son. You don't know what that means to me. I love you, Sam." The two men hugged until Ray winced. "Ooh, still a little tender." Ray lay back on the pillows and grinned. "Your mom is smiling down from heaven thinking '*Those two block*-heads. *They finally figured it out'*."

Sam grinned back, a perfectly mirrored reflection of his father. "Probably thinking we needed a couple of dope slaps before this." The two men shared a meditative moment, thinking of Marianne, missing her love and wisdom. "Take your nap, Dad. You need your beauty rest."

Ray scowled lovingly at Sam, punching him playfully on the shoulder. "Damn right, I do." Sam left him to it and went to speak with Tony.

Sam walked into the minor emergency waiting room. Tony sat in a molded plastic chair, eyes closed, looking worse for the wear. He had a cast on his left arm, a bandage over his broken nose, stitches on the cut over his eyebrow, and three fingers of his right hand in splints. The bruises had begun to purple up beautifully. He'd be a sight for a couple of weeks as the purple faded and green and yellow tinges settled in. Angela was sitting with him, petting his uninjured hand. Isabell and Vincent were sitting across from them, silently watching with a good dose of distrust. Who was this young man and wasn't he the one that put Angela in danger to begin with?

Tony looked up at Sam's arrival and pushed slowly to his feet. He extended his right hand to shake, wincing in pain. Sam took it, looking the young man in the eye. He gently pressed his shoulder, urging him to sit. Taking a seat across from him, Sam leaned forward, elbows on his knees.

"You wanted to speak with me, Tony?" Sam watched the clouds of fear build in Tony's eyes. After the beating he took, the kid was showing tremendous courage.

"Mr. Slater, sir. I did some bad stuff. I'm not making any excuses. But, my cousin, Ricco, he uses young girls, makes them do things. At first, I thought they wanted to, but then I saw things, heard things. Ricco, he told me to get Angela to dance. He'd have made her strip or pose for pictures. That's what he did with others." Tony had the good sense to look abashed at his actions. He looked at Angela out of the corner of his eye, then back at Sam. "I didn't want that for Angela. I like Angela. I like her a lot."

Tony stopped, embarrassed. He swallowed hard and inhaled deeply, digging deep for the courage Sam had seen before.

"Angela told me about the house. Some guys talked about it, but I heard no details. They bragged they could have any girl any time they wanted. It was a perk of the job, they said." Tony reached out and grabbed Sam's hand, squeezing it. "Thank you for saving her."

Sam shrugged. "Actually, I went to Fantasy Palace. It was my dad that found Angela. You'll have to thank him. But, Tony, you know Angela wasn't the first girl Ricco took. This will continue unless we stop him."

"That's why I wanted to speak with you. You see, Mr. Marchetti, he owns the clubs but Ricco, he runs them. Gets the girls. Ricco has been building a different business than Mr. Marchetti thinks. Mr. Marchetti doesn't go to the other clubs he owns. He prefers Fantasy Palace. It's more upscale. Whenever Mr. Marchetti is there, Ricco makes sure all the girls that dance are of legal age. But the other clubs? Mr. Marchetti leaves the running of them to Ricco. Ricco is good at convincing girls to do things. Sometimes Ricco pretends he is a photographer. He promises them modeling gigs. Others want to be movie stars. He makes movies and they do things, bad things. But most start out dancing. They dance at Silver Slipper. That's where you'll find him."

"Is this the young man that wears a star sapphire pinkie ring?" Sam asked, knowing the answer. Tony nodded. "You know you'll have to tell this to the police and they may charge you with abetting."

"Yes sir, I know. I was stupid, blind to what was really going on. I'll take whatever punishment they say. What's important is that Angela is safe." He'd put his arm around her protectively. The significance of the action wasn't wasted on the family.

Nodding a thank you to Tony, Sam texted Kate. He'd see her at home later. He had another stop to make.

Sam called Spencer and filled him in. Spencer needed to get a warrant. Putting the address for The Silver Slipper Gentleman's Club into GPS, Sam arrived before Spencer and the SWAT. He pulled next to the side of the building. The metal building was a dive just off the freeway behind a XXX-rated video shop. The place was shuttered and quiet as a tomb. There was a Lexus parked behind a maroon coupe near the front door. Sam exited his jeep and crept toward the building. Hearing shots ring out in rapid succession, he jumped behind the cars. He held his breath for five minutes of interminable silence. Holding his Glock along the side of his leg, Sam cautiously approached the door, surprised to find it propped open, as if inviting him to enter.

"Come in, Mr. Slater. I assure you, I am alone and unarmed." Marchetti called from inside.

Stepping through the door, Sam surveyed a room with comfy banquets and low-slung tables surrounding a stage. A man was lying face down, blood pooling around a hand with a star sapphire pinkie ring. Marchetti sat on the floor nearby, his hand over his stomach. Blood seeped through his fingers. Sam tucked his Glock into his back and checked Ricco, then went to Marchetti. He pulled out his phone and dialed 911.

"Hold on, Marchetti. Help is coming," Sam said, easing the man back against the banquet.

Marchetti used his free hand to grip Sam's arm.

"Mr. Slater. I expected you would come. Had hopes you'd get here in time. You're a good man. I need you to understand. Some people may think my business is vile and evil. But men have certain appetites. And some women enjoy satisfying those hungers. I provided an environment where it could be done legally and safely. My girls made a good living, and it was their choice."

Marchetti coughed, and a little blood dribbled from his mouth. "I wanted to retire, move to Florida. My wife always wanted a condo in Miami Beach. But this small-minded, overly ambitious young man thought he could take my simple operation and make it better." Marchetti's lip curled in disgust. "Ricco wasn't satisfied with owning gentlemen's clubs. He didn't appreciate the business, the long-term earnings if one only stayed within the law. No, Ricco wanted the fast buck. Had to have them young. He forced them and when they didn't want to play anymore, he disposed of them."

"Marchetti, save your energy. The ambulance is on the way."

"I'm sorry I let this young man sway me. I won't say I wasn't aware of everything he was doing. But I closed my eyes to it. I am a good businessman and even though some people may think this is an evil business, I ran it honestly."

Sam heard the approaching sirens. "Hold on, Marchetti, hold on."

Marchetti's gaze moved toward Ricco's body. "He was greedy and mean. Now he's dead and will burn in hell." Marchetti groaned and shifted his eyes back to Sam. "Some people will tell me I deserve to be right alongside him."

Sam heard the death rattle as Marchetti gave up his last breath. He reached over and closed the man's eyes as the ambulance pulled up, followed by Spencer and SWAT.

Chapter 29

Sam stood, hands in his pockets, staring out the windows of his home office. Kate was fixing dinner. He listened to her singing along to the radio. "Dancing Queen"? He laughed, reveling in the normalcy of it all, feeling blessed. His wife was tenacious and courageous. Kate would never let evil go unpunished, would fight for the oppressed and help lift those less fortunate than herself. Smiling ruefully to himself, Sam realized that meant he would always have to watch out for her, keep her safe. And he could because she had healed him. She loved him.

Sam straightened the papers on his desk, inserting them into a case file. He had just come from his meeting with Detective Spencer, shared information to close out both their investigations. It all made sense to him now. Janet Winburn had confessed everything. Ricco had cat-fished her daughter. He had made several pornographic videos, then threatened to release them on social media unless Winburn did his bidding. She tipped him off on any raids and misdirected Spencer and the vice squad. Janet fought back the only way she could, feeding Kate the information on exploitation, leading her to uncover the crimes. And using her to get Sam to add the weight of Homeland Security to the mix.

Sam had been wrong. Marchetti wasn't the

connection to the human trafficking. Ricco Corelli was the key player. He was a master at finding and exploiting young women. Ricco chose his targets well. He'd convince them they had talent, either as models or dancers, and using artistic deception, slowly pull them deeper and deeper into his evil, twisted darkness. He didn't use the coyotes to import the girls from Mexico, as Sam originally suspected. Ricco recruited his own. Corelli and the coyotes had a symbiotic relationship. The coyotes used Ricco for the distribution of their pornographic materials. Ricco kept a percentage of the profits from the pictures and videos of the children the coyotes produced. Ricco used them to dispose of the girls that outlived their usefulness or caused problems. During the search warrant of Ricco's apartment, they had discovered a zip lock baggie containing a dozen cheap tennis bracelets. They matched the one found on the dead girl.

Tony cooperated when Spencer interviewed him. He helped to identify the bodies of Melanie and Sandi, two naïve young women who fell victim to the promises of a ruthless and talented abuser. Tony was only seventeen, so the prosecutor agreed to a plea bargain, giving the kid probation until he turned eighteen. Since he had no family, Ray and Jake took him under their wing. They gave him a job cleaning up the construction sites. He could afford a tiny studio apartment. As long as Tony stayed out of trouble, worked part-time, and continued with his studies at junior college, keeping his grades above a B average, Ray would continue to employ him.

Ray was back swinging his hammer and the apartment complex he and Jake were rehabbing already had pre-rental agreements from several medical professionals. Sam figured his dad was a genius. He and Jake were looking at another property on the north side of the hospital complex.

Emily forgave Jake for keeping the news of Ray being shot from her. She proudly watched her husband and dad expand the construction business. Sensing it would be a family business, she purchased a set of overalls for John Mac and gave him his own plastic hammer and saw. Never too early to learn the trade, Jake had said.

Angela was on a short leash, at least for now. Isabell was too worried about the whole exploitation episode to give her too much freedom. Soft-hearted to a fault, though, she invited Tony for Sunday dinner every week. He and Angela watched TV together until 9 p.m., holding hands. Then Isabell would shoo Tony out the door. He'd give Angela a chaste kiss on the cheek and hand her a caramel.

Vincent grew two more inches in height and two feet in pride at the results his spy training had accomplished. Sam expected there would be a dedicated recruit to Homeland Security, or maybe the FBI. Vincent was obsessed. In a good way.

Sam heard Kate calling to him. "Honey, would you …Eeww! Feelie! Another trophy? Sam, you need to have a conversation with your cat. Right after you take her present out to the trash. Yuck!"

Sam smiled at Kate's expression of 'girlie' disgust. "Good job Feelie! Mighty huntress." He patted her on the head, giving her a quick ear rub, and wrapped his arms around the love of his life. "I love you, Kate Slater," Sam whispered into her ear as he kissed her.

Kate smiled, returning the kiss. "Right back at you, Sam Slater!"

A word about the author…

Musician, actor, and retired sales & marketing rep, CA Humer, Cheryl to her friends, grew up in small town Wisconsin. She was born into a family that valued the arts but had a firm foundation in practicality. As a child, they encouraged her to express herself in a variety of ways. Music, dance, and performing were passions growing up, but she always felt a tug toward writing. Tamping down her creative side, Cheryl chose business and sales–relegating her artistic inclinations to a side-line. When her creative hunger bubbled to the surface, she satisfied the urge to write by creating marketing campaigns, scripts, and newsletter articles. Now retired, the book that percolated in her imagination for decades, *Art from Darkness*, became the first in a series of Sam & Kate adventures, along with several others waiting to break free. Before, music and acting were her all-consuming passions. Now, Cheryl can't stop imagining or writing.

Cheryl and her husband live in the Fort Worth metroplex with their two cats. She enjoys travel, reading, and a good glass of wine.